THE GHOST
AND THE FEMME FATALE

CLEO COYLE
WRITING AS ALICE KIMBERLY

WHEELER
CHIVERS

This Large Print edition is published by Wheeler Publishing, Waterville, Maine, USA and by BBC Audiobooks Ltd, Bath, England.
Wheeler Publishing, a part of Gale, Cengage Learning.
Copyright © 2008 by The Berkley Publishing Group.
A Haunted Bookshop Mystery.
The moral right of the author has been asserted.

The text of this Large Print edition is unabridged.
Other aspects of the book may vary from the original edition.
Set in 16 pt. Plantin.
Printed on permanent paper.

LIBRARY OF CONGRESS CATALOGING-IN-PUBLICATION DATA

Kimberly, Alice.
  The ghost and the femme fatale / by Cleo Coyle writing as Alice Kimberly.
    p. cm. — (A haunted bookshop mystery) (Wheeler Publishing large print cozy mystery)
    ISBN-13: 978-1-59722-833-6 (softcover : alk. paper)
    ISBN-10: 1-59722-833-8 (softcover : alk. paper)
    1. Women booksellers—Fiction. 2. Film festivals—Fiction. 3. Actresses—Crimes against—Fiction. 4. Rhode Island—Fiction. 5. Large type books. I. Title.
  PS3611.I458G476 2008
  813'.6—dc22   2008028057

BRITISH LIBRARY CATALOGUING-IN-PUBLICATION DATA AVAILABLE

Published in 2008 in the U.S. by arrangement with The Berkley Publishing Group, a member of Penguin Group (USA) Inc.
Published in 2009 in the U.K. by arrangement with The Berkley Publishing Group, a member of Penguin Group (USA) Inc.

U.K. Hardcover: 978 1 408 42123 9 (Chivers Large Print)
U.K. Softcover: 978 1 408 42124 6 (Camden Large Print)

Printed in the United States of America
1 2 3 4 5 6 7 12 11 10 09 08

*To the noir filmmakers of
the '40s and '50s
for the remarkable art they left behind.*

ACKNOWLEDGMENTS

Sincerest thanks to
Wendy McCurdy, executive editor,
and John Talbot, literary agent.

Like Jack, they are entities unseen,
yet absolutely vital to the existence
of this book.

AUTHOR'S NOTE

Although real places and institutions are mentioned in this book, they are used in the service of fiction. No character in this book is based on any person, living or dead, and the world presented is completely fictitious.

CONTENTS

But that was life . . . light and shade . . . a coming in of the tide and a going out . . .

— *The Ghost and Mrs. Muir* by R. A. Dick (a.k.a. Josephine Aimée Campbell Leslie)

PROLOGUE

I don't mind a reasonable amount of trouble.
— Sam Spade, *The Maltese Falcon,* 1941

The Empire Theater
42nd Street, Manhattan
April 16, 1948

The spring evening was cool, the 950-seat movie house was packed, and Jack Shepard was on the job, watching a too-young chippy enjoy a night at the pictures with her paramour.

The doll was no raving beauty, more like the girl next door, with a pert face and dimpled chin, mustard yellow dress with a cutesy lace collar, curls the color of Cracker Jack, and young — seventeen, eighteen, if that.

Planted next to her was the sugar daddy: thinning brown hair, Errol Flynn mustache, face like a flushed baseball. Not fat, but a

15

torso plump enough to annoy the buttons of his three-piece suit. Hired cars and steak dinners every night would do that to an Alvin, not to mention downing case after case of prime tonsil paint.

It was the sugar daddy's wife who'd hired Jack for this tail. Just a few days earlier she'd invited him up to her East Side penthouse . . .

"I've suspected Nathan of stepping out on me before," the wife said, "but he always denies it . . ."

"And now?" Jack asked.

"And now I've finally made the decision. I want out of this marriage, and I need help proving his infidelity."

Jack had taken dozens of cases like this, with one exception: None of the cheating Charlies had been anywhere near as powerful as Nathan Burwell. Building a case against the District Attorney for the City of New York wouldn't be any private investigator's first choice of assignments. Jack would have preferred taking drags off a lit stick of dynamite.

"I wonder, Mrs. Burwell, how many private dicks did you try hiring before me?"

"Twelve," said the DA's wife. She lifted her porcelain cigarette holder — a favorite relic of an aging flapper — inhaled deeply, and blew a smoke ring. "You're lucky thirteen."

Jack already knew he was pretty far down the food chain, not that his office didn't have a charming view of the Third Avenue El. Maybe he was crazy for even considering taking the case, but his current list of clients had more than its share of deadbeats, his rent was coming due, and Mrs. Nathan Burwell was offering three times his usual rate. For that kind of lettuce, Jack figured even a turtle would consider sticking his neck out.

Besides, reasoned Jack, he'd never had any great affection for the DA. The man's greasy thumbprints were all over the dismissal of charges against a Fifth Avenue brat accused of sexually assaulting a young waitress in an alley during a night of carousing. "Not enough evidence," old Burwell had claimed. 'Course the young man's daddy also happened to be one of the state's biggest contributors to the DA's political party.

Yeah, thought Jack, *putting the screws to ol' Burwell wouldn't exactly be torture.*

"All right, Mrs. Burwell. Guess thirteen's your lucky number."

"Good." She blew another gray, hazy ring. "Nathan doesn't want a divorce, you see."

17

"Because . . . ?"

"When I met him, he was a struggling lawyer. It was my inheritance that kept us living high, got him where he is now, and I intend to take it with me — the fortune, I mean. He knows it, and he's in a powerful position to oppose me."

"So you need evidence to get out. I see."

"Not that I want any of it to be made public, you understand? I just want Nathan to be made to see that it's in his best interest to let me, and my twin daughters, and my money go. And —"

"And that's where I come in. I get you, Mrs. Burwell."

Less than a week later, Jack was tailing Nathan Burwell and his chippy to Forty-second Street and taking a seat behind them in the packed Empire Theater. With nothing much to spy on but two heads watching a movie, Jack glanced up to do the same.

Black-and-white B pictures like *Wrong Turn* were a dime a dozen, made on the cheap and frustrating to watch. There was always a rube taken in and destroyed by some too-slick dame. Jack expected no less from this lengthy roll of lamplit celluloid. In fact, he was set to be bored stiff — but then something interesting happened.

As the treacly music pulsed and swelled, a real knockout entered the picture. Hedda Geist, the female lead, raced forward onto a deserted road, waving at a passing car.

"Stop, please!" she called.

The actress was young and beautiful, with waves of gold flowing over shoulders as creamy smooth as a marble statuette. She looked scared and vulnerable running along in bare feet, wearing a silver gown that cut like moonlight through the evening mist. The garment was ripped at the shoulder and she held it up with one hand while waving at the car with the other.

Behind the wheel was some regular Joe, on his way home from a long day of lousy sales calls. One look at Hedda and his tires were squealing.

Don't do it, buddy. Jack thought. *I've seen enough of these pictures to know where she's going to take you . . .*

In the next row, the DA's young paramour began bouncing up and down in her seat, obviously excited about the appearance of Hedda Geist on screen. She pointed and whispered to Burwell, pantomimed a clapping of her white-gloved hands.

The picture played out much as Jack expected, and he watched the two couples — the one on the screen; the other in the audience. Eventually, the credits rolled and then the A picture played: a sappy romance with songs, no less, a real snoozola. Then Jack's payday got up with the crowd and vacated their chairs. Jack tailed the two, careful to keep his distance.

The DA and his date strolled down Forty-second Street's crowded carnival of noisy marquees and greasy eateries, legit theaters, and burlesque houses — exactly the direction Jack figured on — toward Hotel Chester, the quiet inn near Bryant Park where Burwell had seen the girl a few nights before.

Just before crossing the intersection of Broadway and Seventh Avenue, with its railed streetcars and blinding billboards, they approached a concession booth. PHOTOS WHILE U WAIT! TAKE A PICTURE WITH YOUR DATE!

Jack moved carefully ahead of the DA and his mistress, signaled the photographer that he'd paid earlier in the evening. The photographer nodded and pulled out his assistant, made like he was taking her picture on the Times Square sidewalk, but as the flash lit up the DA and his chippy, the focus was on them. Now Jack would have a picture for the Mrs. B. file.

More evidence.

Jack trailed the couple to the Chester. Burwell followed Miss Innocent inside, and Jack loitered outside. As the minutes ticked by, Jack surveyed his surroundings, noticed a gull gray Lincoln Cabriolet idling in the shadows across from the hotel. He couldn't see much inside the car, just a male driver and a woman in a wide-brimmed hat. He waited for someone to exit the vehicle, but no one did. No one entered, either. They just sat there, burning gasoline.

After another five minutes, Jack became suspicious. There were a few other sedans parked, all empty. At this time of night, there were plenty of people having a gay old time two long blocks away in Times Square, but this part of Midtown was deserted. The office buildings were emptied out. Corner newsstands were closed up. And you'd have to hoof it at least ten blocks to find an open diner.

Jack began to cross the street; approach the idling car. Just as he did, the driver peeled away, sped toward the corner, didn't even stop for the red light. Jack glommed the license, jotted down the numbers in his notebook, noted the wheels were spode green, and went back to waiting.

Twenty minutes later, the district attorney emerged from the hotel again; hair mussed, tie askew.

"Not exactly a sixty-minute man," Jack muttered.

He wasn't surprised at the brevity of the encounter. For some of these slobs, their marriages had grown so cold that just being in a hotel room with a chippy was enough. A blouse was unbuttoned, a lacy brassiere peeked through, then it was wham-bam, Act Three, and curtain.

Burwell walked to the corner, hailed a cab on Sixth Avenue. Jack flagged down another and followed Burwell east to Park then north to the Upper East Side, land of cliff dwellers.

One of the grandest avenues in Manhattan, Park was bisected by an island of lush topiary, its sidewalks cleaner than a hospital ward. The hack coasted to a stop in front of one of the endless rows of majestic stone high-rises. The place wasn't as big as Buckingham Palace, but it probably held more servants. A doorman in a uniform stepped forward, opened the cab's door. The DA greeted the gold-trimmed attendant, moved out of the shadowy street, into the light of the building's lobby.

Jack made a note of the time. He was about to give the signal to his own cabbie to beat it when he noticed a familiar lady turning the corner. It was Mrs. Burwell, strolling alone down the avenue, a white stole glowing like a fur lifesaver around her neck. She smiled and nodded at a passing couple, approached her doorman, had a few quiet words with him, then ventured inside.

Jack recalled Mrs. B. telling him about her weekly Junior League dinner meetings. The DA obviously made interesting use of his evenings when his wife was occupied. Like clockwork, he'd had it all timed perfectly, making it home just before the little woman.

But Jack was on the job now. And once he got that flash picture in his hands, Mrs. Burwell would no longer be in the dark.

"Dust out, buddy," he called, then told the hack to take him back where he belonged. "Downtown."

CHAPTER 1
OPENING-NIGHT
JITTERS

When it concerns a woman, does anybody ever really want the facts?
— Philip Marlowe, *Lady in the Lake,* 1947

Quindicott, Rhode Island
Present Day
Listen, baby, you can't solve a puzzle when half the pieces are missing . . .

That's what Jack Shepard advised me after I'd found the corpse that bright, spring morning, even though I pointed out his declaration had a few holes in it. People guessed at half-solved puzzles all the time.

"What about *Wheel of Fortune?*" I argued. "You can buy a vowel and sound out the words. You don't need all the pieces."

Jack wasn't impressed with my TV game-show analogy, partly because the show hadn't been invented until decades after he'd been shot to death in my bookstore, but mainly because he'd had more experience with homicide than yours truly, and not just because he was a victim of it.

Jack Shepard had been a cop in New York City before heading off to Europe to fight the Nazis. After he returned from the war, he opened his own private investigation business — until 1949, when he was gunned down while pursuing a lead in a case.

Unlike Jack, I, Penelope Thornton-McClure, single mom, widow, and independent bookshop owner, was far from a professional sleuth. Sure, I was a longtime fan of the *Black Mask* school of detective fiction; but a few years back, when the Rhode Island Staties were eyeing me as a person of interest in a murder investigation, I'd needed more than a fictional detective, and I got one.

Not that I rely on the ghost exclusively. After I discovered the corpse that sunny May morning, I notified the authorities, like any sane citizen. But while our local police chief was still deciding whether or not the death was accidental, the PI in my head was pronouncing it murder. Not only that, Jack believed the first effort to end the victim's life had been attempted the previous evening, during the opening night screening of Quindicott's first-ever Film Noir Festival.

At the time, I hadn't realized the "accident" I'd witnessed was attempted murder. Nobody had. Most of us had been too distracted by the preparations for the long weekend of events, myself included.

The festival was going to feature book signings as well as movie screenings, lectures, and parties. At least a dozen of the invited speakers and panelists had front- or backlist titles to hock, and my bookshop was stepping up to handle the transactions.

The primary reason for the film festival, however, wasn't to hand me book sales, but to draw crowds to the Movie Town Theater.

For decades the old single-screen movie house had been a boarded-up wreck. Then a group of investors bought the property and worked for years to resurrect its spirit. I couldn't wait to see the renovated film palace, and on opening night, I was one of the first in line . . .

"So, Penelope, what do you think?" Brainert asked, rushing up as I stepped out of the sparkling new lobby and into the theater proper. "How do you like our restoration?"

J. Brainert Parker was a respected professor of English at nearby St. Francis college, a loyal Buy the Book customer, and one of my oldest friends. He was also a leading member of the group who'd bought and restored Quindicott's old movie house.

As the chattering crowd flowed around us, I stood gaping in shock at the theater's interior. When a few impatient patrons jostled my stupefied form, Brainert grabbed my elbow.

"Come on," he said, "we're in the reserved section."

As we walked, I continued to gawk. Every last chair in the 700-seat theater had been reupholstered in red velvet. The aisles were lined with a plush carpet of sapphire blue that matched the lush curtains, now parted to reveal a huge movie screen beneath a proscenium arch carved in art deco lines. The lines were reechoed in the theater's columns, where sleek, angular birds appeared to be flying up the posts toward a sky mural of sunset pink clouds painted across the ceiling, which supported three shimmering chandeliers of chrome and cut glass.

"Oh, my goodness, Brainert . . ."

"She speaks!"

"It's . . . it's *amazing!*"

Brainert straightened his bow tie and grinned. He had a right to preen. Few people thought restoring our little town's only theater was worth the effort.

"Looks a lot different from all those

Saturday afternoons we spent here, doesn't it?" he asked.

I pushed up my black rectangular glasses and shook my head in ongoing astonishment. "Do you even remember the last movie we saw here?"

Brainert pursed his lips with slight disdain. "*The Empire Strikes Back.* Don't you recall? It was your brother's idea to take us."

"Oh, my god . . . that's right . . ."

I'd almost forgotten my older brother's obsession with Luke Skywalker, lightsabers, and space travel. Shortly thereafter, Pete's passion had fallen from the fantastical heavens to more earthly pursuits: hot rods and a hot girl, to be exact, both of which had led him to showing off on a dark road, where a tragic accident had taken him to an early grave.

The Movie Town Theater had died around the same time: A brand-new multiplex had opened up on the highway. Eight screens meant eight different choices versus the Movie Town's solitary offering. Like a lot of businesses on Cranberry Street, it appeared to have outlived its era.

But Brainert disagreed vehemently with that mind-set. Retro was in. The nearby seaside resort town of Newport had been restoring like crazy, and he became obsessed

29

with returning Quindicott's own dark theater to its art deco glory.

"It's remarkable, isn't it?" Brainert said as we took our seats within a roped-off section. "Everything old is new again."

"Yeah, for a *price*," piped up the voice of Seymour Tarnish.

The fortysomething bachelor and avid pulp collector was sitting one row behind us. For tonight's big event, he'd exchanged his mailman's federal blues for khaki slacks, a loose cotton button-down, and an untucked avocado green shirt — the perfect camouflage for his daily indulgences at the Cooper Family Bakery.

"Oh, it's you." Brainert sniffed. "Haven't gone postal yet, I see."

"I'm waiting for you to go first, Parker. Everyone knows academics are highstrung."

Seymour was as famous in Quindicott for his lack of tact as his big win on *Jeopardy!* a few years back, but I'd learned to live with it. He was not only a reliable book-buying customer, he'd been surprisingly helpful to me in my nascent sleuthing.

"So Seymour," I said, half turning in my seat, "what do you think of the restoration?"

"Not bad." He tossed a fistful of popcorn into his mouth and began crunching away.

"I remember seeing *Jaws* here in the seventies. What a wreck! You couldn't find two seats together that weren't broken. The floor was sticky — and I'm not talking SweeTarts sticky; I'm talking toxically gross upchuck sticky. And the columns were brown, weren't they?"

"They were absolutely disgusting is what they were," Brainert said. "There was some sort of a . . . a *crust* on them."

"Whatever," said Seymour, stuffing more popcorn into his mouth. "They look pretty good now."

"*Pretty* good?" Brainert spun and glared. "I'll have you know we're going to get landmark status from the local historical society! And be careful with that popcorn. You're spilling it."

"It's the movies, Parker. Haven't you heard the term *popcorn flick?*"

"Theater *should be* where literature goes at night." Brainert snapped his fingers. *"Comprende?"*

Seymour squinted. "English, please."

"There are *enough* movie screens in this state devoted to comic-book heroes and computer-animated kiddy schlock," Brainert replied. "Quindicott's Movie Town Theater has a higher purpose: to uphold the light of the modern cinema. We are a

31

regional art house! We do not show popcorn flicks!" He lowered his voice. "Frankly, I'm perturbed that my partners outvoted me on even selling popcorn."

"You shouldn't be. When it comes to the movie theater business, concessions are where the cash cow moos." With a loud slurp, Seymour sucked on the straw of his extra-large soda. "And correct me if I'm wrong, but your little redecorating job here" — he waved his giant, plastic cup toward the restored art deco columns and shimmering chandeliers — "I'm guessing it all cost a *tad* more than an associate English professor carries around in mad money."

With a huff, Brainert turned to face front again.

"What's wrong?" I asked.

"I hate it when he's right," Brainert muttered. "And I wish that hot buttered popcorn didn't smell so good. I was so nervous about a crowd showing, I didn't eat a thing at dinner."

"Well, you shouldn't be nervous anymore." I patted the arm of his blue blazer. "This place is jammed."

"Ladies and gentlemen, good evening! If you'll all take your seats and quiet down, we'll get started . . ."

"Who's that?" I whispered, gesturing to

the man who'd just climbed the stairs to the stage.

"That's Wendell," Brainert informed me. "Dr. Wendell Pepper, dean of St. Francis's School of Communications."

"Oh, right," I said. "You've mentioned him before. He's one of your fellow investors in the theater, isn't he?"

"He was also instrumental in getting Hedda Geist to become a partner."

"Hedda Geist? You mean the famous film noir actress? The one who stars in tonight's movie?"

"The same. One of the woman's grandchildren was in Pepper's Media Matters class, and he used that connection to meet Hedda and secure her investment." Brainert lowered his voice again. "That's the reason we selected film noir as the theme for our very first festival. The woman *insisted* we showcase her movies this weekend."

I raised an eyebrow at that. "Once a diva, always a diva, huh?"

"Indeed."

"Well . . ." I shrugged. "It's a small price to pay for her contribution. Besides, her movies are good."

"Yes, I know." Brainert shook his head. "I only wish her funds had been enough to complete the project. Dean Pepper and I had to go to the college to pony up the final bit of cash. And Pepper didn't much like the idea, I can tell you. It took some real teeth pulling to get him to go out on a limb with me, but look at him tonight! The man's as jolly as the proverbial green giant!"

Brainert was right. The dean was an attractive, broad-shouldered man in his early sixties with a sturdy profile and salt-and-pepper hair. His attire, pressed chocolate brown slacks and a tweed jacket, was as somber as Brainert's, but his ruddy face was displaying the grin of a grade-school boy on a carnival ride. He looked practically giddy.

Brainert shook his head. "I still can't get over Dean Pepper's transformation! That man's been an anxiety-ridden wreck for the past year, convinced the restoration would never end. Until a few weeks ago, he was skeptical we could get ten seats sold for the opening-night screening. Just one mention of this theater and he'd give me a look like he was ready to kill."

"So what changed his mind?"

"Not what," Brainert told me with a roll of his eyes. "Who."

Seymour suddenly leaned forward to interrupt. "Did you say that guy's name is Dr. Wendell Pepper?"

"Yes," said Brainert.

"You're kidding," said Seymour. *"Dr. Pepper?* Like the soft drink with that old dopey song-and-dance-man commercial?"

"Don't even go there," Brainert warned.

"You mean he's not" — Seymour cleared his throat and sang, *"the most original teacher in the whole wide world?"*

Brainert rolled his eyes. "Real mature, Tarnish."

As Dean Pepper waited for the crowd to settle down, he checked his watch and directed a little wave toward a seat in the reserved section, two rows in front of us.

An attractive woman waved back. From her youthful hairstyle of bouncy, shoulder-length cocoa-brown curls with scarlet highlights, and trendy red-framed glasses, I would have put her age at around forty, but when she turned, the wrinkles betrayed her. She was obviously much older — in her late fifties, maybe, or even a well-preserved sixty. Between plastic surgery, laser treatments, and Botox, who knew what age people were anymore?

"Is that the dean's wife?" I asked Brainert, pointing to the woman.

"No," he said flatly. "The dean just got divorced." Then he turned toward the aisle to speak with an usher who'd approached him.

"Welcome! Welcome, one and all, to the new Movie Town Theater!" Dr. Pepper was now speaking into a standing microphone, which projected his voice through a large, black amplifier, hanging high above him. "What a turnout for the very first film of what I'm sure will be an *annual* Film Noir Festival! Give yourselves a hand!"

The crowd did, the college students adding high-pitched whistles and loud woofs.

"We have quite a lineup of movies and guests this weekend," Dr. Pepper continued. "And this evening we're all in for a real treat. The Poverty Row gem you're about to see was released in 1948, and in the decades following became a recognized classic of the film noir genre. After we've screened the picture, you'll hear much more about it from film historian Dr. Irene Lilly, just one of this weekend's many very special guests —"

He gave a private little wink toward the rows in front of us, and I noticed that same attractive older woman waving at him again. That must be Dr. Lilly, I decided, and asked Brainert if I was right.

"No," he said. "That's not Dr. Lilly. That's Maggie Kline."

"The screen and television writer?" I asked excitedly.

Brainert nodded.

I'd never met Ms. Kline, but I knew her by reputation. Years ago, she'd written two screenplays in a row for Paramount Pictures that were nominated for Oscars, and she'd penned dozens of teleplays for some of my favorite crime and mystery shows. She'd even published a few suspense novels, too. Her latest book was nonfiction — an encyclopedia of female sleuths. It was a wonderful title, and we'd ordered quite a few copies, hoping to snag her for a signing over the weekend.

I eyed the way she was looking at Dr. Pepper on stage. "So . . ." I elbowed Brainert, "is Maggie Kline the mysterious 'who' that's turned Dr. Pepper into a giddy schoolboy?"

"Isn't it obvious?" Once again, Brainert rolled his eyes. "They've been phoning and e-mailing for months — ever since Dr. Lilly suggested that Maggie Kline be contacted for a guest speaker slot. According to Pepper, they hit it off from the first phone call. Maggie even came out here a week early, just so they could spend time together. He's besotted with her, although I can't imagine why."

"What do you mean by that?" I asked, automatically feeling defensive. After all, I myself wasn't getting any younger. "She's obviously accomplished — attractive, too, for that matter. Sure, she's no spring chicken, but it's not like Dr. Pepper up there isn't eligible for an AARP card."

"No, no, Pen. You misunderstand me," said Brainert. "My objection has nothing to do with her age or looks. She lives in Arizona. End of story."

"Excuse me?"

"What's he going to do after she goes back there? Take a six-hour plane ride for a dinner date?"

"Love isn't a function of convenience, Brainert. The heart doesn't work like that."

"Well, it should. Otherwise, what's he in for? Heartache. Longing. Either that or jet lag."

"What does it matter to you, anyway?"

"It matters to me because the second that woman leaves, the dean's going to be in an even fouler mood than he was before, and he always takes his temper out on me! '*Parker,* I hope you fully appreciate what I've done, going out on a limb with the college, helping you secure that much-needed funding.' '*Parker,* what's your plan for the financial viability of the theater?' " Brainert massaged his temples. "I tell you, Pen, I can't take it anymore."

Before I could suggest reasonable alternatives to Dr. Pepper and Maggie Kline splitting up, Pepper's voice boomed. "Now, without further ado, I'm delighted to give you *Wrong Turn . . .*"

The crowd applauded loudly and Bud Napp, the lanky, silver-haired widower and owner of Napp Hardware, hustled to move Dr. Pepper's standing microphone back into the wings.

"What's Bud doing on stage?" I whispered.

"Oh, Bud's been a big help," said Brainert, "along with his part-time construction crew."

"I didn't know he handled the restoration."

"He didn't. He just came in for some last-minute stuff — painting and wiring, hanging that public address speaker . . ."

Brainert's voice trailed off as the house lights dimmed and the movie started. On the big screen, the Gotham Features logo appeared — white clouds parting to show the dark silhouette of the Empire State Building — and then came the view of a road at night, shrouded in shadowy fog.

Bright white headlights cut through the mist. A large black sedan rumbled by — the only vehicle on the empty road. Inside the sedan, the driver looked like an average Joe, coming home from a day of sales calls. He wore a cheap suit and battered fedora. His tie was pulled loose and his five o'clock shadow made him look haggard and beaten.

Then the sedan's headlights lit up a stunning sight. Hedda Geist, the female lead, raced forward, onto the deserted Long Island road.

The crowd began to applaud. "Hedda, we love you!" cried a young man's voice from the audience.

She was young and beautiful, with waves of gold flowing over shoulders as creamy smooth as a marble statuette. She looked scared and vulnerable running along in bare feet, wearing a form-fitting gown of shimmering satin, with a plunging neckline and a bow on the bodice.

"Stop, please!" she called. Her gown was torn off one shoulder. She held it up with one hand while waving at the oncoming car with the other.

The Joe in the sedan gasped, his leather shoe slammed on the brake, and his car squealed to a halt.

What's the pitch, sister? Last time I saw this flick, it was 1948. Did somebody dial back the cuckoo or what?

The gruff voice I'd heard hadn't come

40

from the screen. And it hadn't come from the audience. The voice had come from inside my own head. After a long day of slumber, the ghost of Jack Shepard had finally woken up.

CHAPTER 2
THE BIG DROP

NICK BENKO: You wait around long enough and sooner or later everything falls right in your lap.
EDDIE WILLIS: Like rotten apples.
— *The Harder They Fall,* 1956

"Keep it down, Jack," I silently warned. "I'm watching a movie."

I can see that, doll. I'm just surprised Hollywood took a turn for the worse. I thought by now they'd be making new pictures, not recycling the same old lamplit celluloid.

"Hollywood's made plenty of new pictures since you . . . since you . . . you know . . ."

Since I got lead poisoning? Got my ticket punched? My lights put out? What is it with you square Janes? Always tiptoeing around the bare truth. You're completely bughouse about prettying things up —

"Jack, please! Why don't you just settle back and watch the movie?"

Because I've seen it before, doll. And it's a B picture — not that the A pictures were that much better. At least New York was filming on the cheap. In my day, Tinsel Town was spending like drunken sailors — $600,000 for one movie. What a scam job. Leaking that kind of scratch for what? Costume and cardboard? A couple of chippies reciting lines off a pile of papers?

"Jack, we're not in your day anymore. And I'm sorry to tell you that budgets have only gone up. Six hundred thousand won't even cover a Hollywood production's catering bill, which is beside the point anyway. This film isn't being recycled for lack of product. It's part of a retrospective on the film noir genre."

The film what genre?

"Film noir. Don't tell me you've never heard of it. I know you were alive when it first emerged." I named some of the genre's titles to jog his memory.

Yeah, Okay . . . Jack admitted. *I remember seeing some of those movies, but I can't believe twenty-first-century eggheads are getting hot and bothered about a bunch of B pictures that couldn't afford color. Fancying them up with a French name's about on the level with your generation's buying water in a bottle.*

"Film noir simply means that these films all shared the same dark style and sensibility, especially the black-and-white palette, the morally ambiguous narrative viewpoint, and the realistic locations. All of that was new, revolutionary."

Realistic locations revolutionary? Listen, I knew some of those Poverty Row guys, working out in Queens. They set up in the streets instead of sound stages for one reason — because they were shooting on the cheap.

"Okay, but what about the films that featured anti-hero detectives like *The Maltese Falcon* or *The Big Sleep?*"

What about 'em?

"Weren't you a fan of them?"

Sweetheart, I didn't need to see 1,001 frames of Humphrey Bogart to tell me how the world turned. Sure, I watched those pictures — when I was tailing cheating spouses or sniffing out blackmailers and scumbag suspects. The balcony always was a nice, dark place for dirty deeds. And the only thing that made those movies worth my dime were the broads. I can't deny those long-legged starlet types were serious whistle bait.

"You mean like Hedda Geist up there?"

I waited for Jack to answer. He didn't.

"Jack?"

But there was no reply. The ghost had

44

abruptly withdrawn — an annoying habit of Jack's. Shrugging off his sudden departure, I turned my full attention back to the movie screen, where Hedda was playing one of her most famous parts, the femme fatale Sybil Sand.

With her shimmering, torn silver gown, Hedda flagged down the car driven by the haggard salesman "Joe." He pulled his car over and she pulled him into a web of lies about her "abusive" husband. By the time she was done with him, Joe had murdered Sybil's spouse for her, so Sybil could inherit the man's fortune. Unfortunately, the husband's older sister became suspicious, and Sybil once again called on Joe to kill for her.

In the last act, Sybil and Joe were on the run, staying one step ahead of the law until Sybil herself fingered the gullible salesman for the two murders, setting him up for the gas chamber, while she (nearly) walked away — except for that bullet in her back, when Joe finally got wise that he'd been played like a piano then tossed like a used toothpick.

As *Wrong Turn*'s score swelled to a climax and the end credits rolled, I noticed a man moving down the far aisle, then up the side staircase to the theater's stage.

The man wasn't very old, maybe late twenties, with a bulky body and round, baby face. He wore his blond hair in a ponytail and a Hawaiian shirt over baggy jeans.

From the wings, hardware store owner Bud Napp loped back out onto the stage. He nodded at the twentysomething man, set up the standing mike, and returned to the wings.

"Testing, one, two . . ." murmured Ponytail Man, tapping the mike. The noise came out of the speaker high above his head. The man greeted the audience, and a spotlight shined down from the projectionist's booth, making his gold loop earring sparkle.

"Who's the clown with the earring?" Seymour asked, leaning forward to stick his head between me and Brainert.

"That's no clown," Brainert replied. "That's Barry Yello, and he's been a big help organizing this weekend's events — he and Dr. Lilly."

"Oh, right," I murmured, "Barry Yello. I should have recognized him from his book cover photo."

After dropping out of film school, Yello had founded the influential Internet site FylmGeek.com, now read by film students and professionals in Hollywood who routinely left insider comments and opinions in the highly trafficked forum.

He'd recently published his first book, which — he announced to the crowd — he'd be signing at Buy the Book over the weekend.

"Good plug," Seymour whispered in my ear.

I gave a thumbs-up, even though his book — *Bad Barry: My Love Affair with B, C, and D Movies* — was only trade paper. Unit for unit, the store made better profit on the hardcovers.

"Yello's got a loyal following," Brainert assured me. "You'll be moving a lot of them."

"And now," Barry concluded, "to discuss *Wrong Turn* better than I ever could, I'd like to introduce a first-rate film historian, Dr. Irene Lilly."

I glanced through my program to refresh myself on Dr. Lilly's bio. A San Fernando University professor, she was best known as the author of *Cities in Shadow,* an award-winning study of film noir (in hardcover). But in our e-mail exchanges over the past few weeks, she was quite adamant that her appearance at the festival would be devoted entirely to promoting her brand-new hardcover, *Murdered in Plain Sight.*

There was nothing unusual about Dr.

Lilly's wanting to promote her front-list title. Traditional author tours and appearances were geared toward exactly that. But I did find it strangely dismissive of Dr. Lilly not to care about her backlist sales, too.

"Please, Mrs. McClure," she had written, "do not bother stocking my backlist. The new title is the one I wish to promote and sell — and I'll *personally* handle the order and delivery. Leave everything to me. . . ."

When she took the stage, the slender, fortyish Dr. Lilly appeared relaxed and confident — and very Californian with straight, dark blonde hair tied back into a ponytail. Even Dr. Lilly's attire was California relaxed: Her sundress was a loose shift of pale flowers, her necklace was hemp and natural beads, and her flat leather footwear had more in common with beach flip-flops than evening shoes.

With Dr. Lilly's laid-back style, however, came no lack of energy. Her voice was strong, and her spirits obviously high as she addressed the crowd.

"What a treat it is to see *Wrong Turn* on a big screen, the way it was first shown in 1948! Don't you all agree?"

The crowd applauded.

"*Wrong Turn* is a classic example of film noir . . . but what is film noir? And why is this American cinematic style described with the French words meaning *black film?* To explain, I'll have to take you back to the summer of 1946. For years, the French had been cut off from American cinema. Now that the war was over, ten American films were brought over to Paris and released in one six-week period: *The Maltese Falcon; Laura; Murder, My Sweet; Double Indemnity; The Woman in the Window; This Gun for Hire; The Killers; Lady in the Lake; Gilda;* and *The Big Sleep.*"

Dr. Lilly gestured to the screen behind her where a slide show of old movie posters was being projected. "The release of these movies in a concentrated time period caused a sensation. The French critics immediately recognized that a new style of film had begun to be made before and during the war. These were darker-themed pictures that dealt with crime, detectives, and middle-class murder. The films were sometimes based on, or similar to, the novels of Dashiell Hammett, Raymond Chandler, and James M. Cain — novels that the French already had labeled *serie noire* or 'black series.' "

I knew all of this already, but I listened patiently.

"As part of that movement," Dr. Lilly

continued, "*Wrong Turn* was produced in the late 1940s by Irving Vreen's Gotham Features — a Poverty Row studio, operating out of Queens, New York. The film's leading lady, Sybil Sand, played by Hedda Geist, shows us one of the genre's most powerful archetypes, the femme fatale. Tonight, in Sybil, you've seen the same kind of 'sexy but dangerous woman' that you'll also be seeing in other films scheduled this weekend."

"Hear that Jack?" I silently whispered, still wondering if the ghost was with me. "You're not the only one who remembers your film-making friends in Queens." I waited for Jack to reply. "Jack?"

The ghost still wasn't answering me, and I wondered if maybe he couldn't. I grabbed my purse off the seat's armrest, shoved my hand inside, and searched the tiny soft pocket sewn into the lining. The moment I felt the hard, smooth coin, I breathed a sigh of relief. Jack's nickel was there. I hadn't lost it.

What's the matter, baby? Miss me that much?

When the ghost first started haunting me, he couldn't seem to travel beyond the four walls of my bookshop. Then I got hold of his case files and found an old buffalo nickel inside one of the dusty folders. Jack had carried that nickel around with him in life. And, now, whenever I carried it with me, he seemed to be able to travel in death.

"Jack." I swallowed my nerves. "I thought I'd lost the nickel. Why didn't you answer me?"

Dames, he said in a disgusted tone. *Didn't you tell me to button my gabber?*

"Yes, but . . . I changed my mind. I mean, the movie's over. So it's okay if you want to talk."

The broad on stage is that boring, huh?

"It's not that she's boring. It's just that I already know what she's telling me. There are dozens of books in my store that say as much."

Okay, baby, I've got an idea. Let's blow this joint.

"What?"

I keep telling you, sweetheart, I can take you out on the town, if you let me. How about it? Dinner at the Copa? A room at the Plaza, just you and me . . .

I felt a thin, cool column of air swirl around me, tickle the back of my neck, brush past my cheek.

"Stop it, Jack," I whispered. "You're being silly now."

Am I? When you thought I'd beat it, you

51

couldn't reach for that nickel fast enough.

"I was simply worried about purse snatchers." I folded my arms and rubbed them, trying to ward off Jack's little chill. "I hear it happens in movie theaters, you know? And there's a lot of people here tonight from out of town."

The exasperating sound of decidedly smug male laughter rolled through my head as Dr. Lilly continued her lecture. Now she was explaining exactly why those noirs shot by Gotham Features studio were such a hit.

"While there were many films being produced at that time on the East and West coasts, the cluster produced by Gotham had made a small fortune because they had something the others didn't: the blonde bombshell Hedda Geist."

Dr. Lilly lifted her arm and gave a little wave toward the projectionist's booth. Suddenly, a new slide appeared on the screen, the 1948 movie poster for *Wrong Turn,* which featured the arresting image of Hedda Geist's beautiful face and form. Her hourglass figure was draped in the same shimmering, silver gown that she'd worn in the first scene of the picture, only it wasn't yet torn. And her big green eyes appeared wide, startled, and a little bit desperate.

Dr. Lilly fixed a smile on a section of college kids in the audience — the group was mostly young and mostly male, many of them wearing fraternity jackets.

"So what was it about this type of story and theme that appealed to audiences back in the 1940s and '50s, and continues to appeal to twenty-first-century film enthusiasts today?"

"Sex appeal," one of the young men shouted.

"Hedda's killer body," yelled another.

"Sadomasochism!" someone else called out, and the audience fell apart.

"Maybe a bit of that," Dr. Lilly said with a raised eyebrow. "But the truth is much simpler. The most subversive noir films — *Touch of Evil, Pickup on South Street, This Gun for Hire* — depict a world that is so morally bankrupt that it's lost its way. Good languishes and evil dominates, the bad guy has money and power and status and the good guys are lowlifes, social pariahs who live on the raw edge of society."

If that's what this broad thinks, she hasn't lived on the "raw edge of society" much. Someone should inform her there's not a helluva lot of "good guys" there.

"She's speaking relatively, Jack," I told the ghost. "You lived on the edge, and you weren't a bad guy. . . . Were you?"

No comment.

"Although the film movement began in the forties, filmmakers who came after, in the sixties and seventies, embraced its tenets. Movies like *Taxi Driver* and *China-town* may not have used the same stark, black-and-white palette of the early noir entries, but their cynical narratives were most definitely steeped in the same kettle. By the way, you'll also find the poster of *Wrong Turn* on the cover of my brand-new book, *Murdered in Plain Sight.*"

Dr. Lilly paused a moment. "While I've given overviews of noir in my past publications, this new book of mine is much more specific — and I believe it will be of great interest to all of you, as well as your local media. It's the first book ever to delve into the details of Hedda Geist's personal life and career."

Dr. Lilly frowned. "I must apologize for the mistake that prevented the publisher from getting my hardcover copies here in time for me to sign for you tonight in the lobby, as the festival's event planners wished — an unfortunate postal delay, I'm told."

In the next seat, Brainert turned to me and whispered, "You're kidding. That's very disappointing. We were all expecting a signing to take place in the lobby."

"I know," I said with a sigh. "Dr. Lilly made it very clear that she was handling the delivery of her new release, but Buy the Book never received a thing. We've already rescheduled her signing."

Brainert spun around to glare at Seymour in the row behind us. "What do you know about a *postal* delay?"

Seymour raised his hands. "Don't look at me, Parker. I only lose deliveries when somebody pisses me off, and I never even *met* that woman!"

"Shhh!" someone hissed.

On stage, Dr. Lilly continued: "I spoke to the people at San Fernando University Press, and they promised me that another shipment of my new book will arrive by private service tomorrow morning. The stock will be available at the Buy the Book store, where I'll be signing at twelve noon sharp!"

Applause greeted the news. Dr. Lilly smiled, and then she glanced over her shoulder at the poster featuring Hedda Geist.

"Ms. Geist, now Mrs. Geist-Middleton, has lived such a quiet life for the last two decades, few people were even aware that she was still alive. But she is! And she's here this weekend, as you all know, if you've reviewed your program schedule. She'll be on this very stage tomorrow, doing a Q&A session with Barry Yello. She might even be here in the audience tonight. Ms. Geist-Middleton, are you here? If you are, I'd love you to stand up and take a brief bow. . . ."

Like everyone else, I twisted around in my theater seat, scanning the crowd, dying with curiosity to see what the famous femme fatale looked like sixty years after *Wrong Turn.*

In the very back row of the house, an attractive young blonde rose from her velvet-lined seat. She stood and began to clap. Then people around her began to clap. The clapping grew louder, moving down the theater, row after row, until finally I saw what they were clapping about.

Hedda Geist-Middleton had stood up — but she did much more than simply take a "brief bow" as Dr. Lilly suggested. The elderly woman moved into the center aisle and began to stroll down the deep blue carpet. She walked with sure footing, her head regally high, on a slender but sturdy frame. She wore a gorgeously tailored white pantsuit dripping with silver embroidery. Large diamond earrings sparkled beneath white hair, which was pulled into a smooth French twist and held in place by a diamond-studded comb.

Applause followed the woman, thundering down from the back of the theater. The woman blew kisses at members of the audience, who began to rise from their seats for a standing ovation.

Once a diva, always a diva, Jack quipped.

"Is that really her?" I silently wondered.

Time's a witch, ain't she? Jack replied.

"You're not giving her much credit, Jack. For an eighty-five-year-old woman, she looks pretty darn good to me."

Though sixty years had passed since her stardom, I still recognized the same radiant beauty that lit up the screen in a half-dozen dark-crime dramas. Despite the wrinkles and age spots, Hedda Geist still possessed those incredibly high cheekbones and famous catlike eyes that had made her a star.

I'll give the old broad this: She managed to stay out of the skull orchard a whole lot longer than yours truly.

On stage, Dr. Lilly squinted against the spotlight, shading her eyes as she peered into the theater's aisle. "Is that her? Oh, yes. There she is, ladies and gentleman, Mrs. Hedda Geist-Middleton!"

Next to me, Brainert was having a fit. "She came! Oh, my goodness!" He sprang from his seat and rushed up the aisle to greet the woman. "Ms. Geist-Middleton! I'm honored. We all are! Please, won't you come on stage and say a few words?"

"That was my intention, Mr. Parker," the former actress imperially replied.

"Why didn't you sit in our reserved section?" Brainert asked.

She waved her hand. "I didn't need to sit through *Wrong Turn* again. My goodness, I've seen it enough times, you know. I just popped in at the end."

"Allow me." Brainert offered his arm. She took it, and they moved down the aisle toward the stage.

The young woman who began the applause followed them. When she moved past my row, I froze in surprise. The woman's hair was styled differently than the Hedda of the 1940s — it was shorter and cut in layers — but otherwise she was the spitting image of the young Hedda Geist, with a stunning, hourglass figure, big green, catlike eyes and finely sculptured features. Even Jack was affected, and given his state, understandably confused.

Wait a second, he said in my head. *Which one's Hedda?*

"You're in the twenty-first-century now," I silently reminded the ghost. "Hedda was in her twenties when she made *Wrong Turn.*

Now she's well over eighty. This young woman is obviously a relative, probably a granddaughter."

To sustained applause, Brainert led the elegant woman up the short flight of stairs and onto the stage. The young blonde followed, eliciting some whistles of her own from the male contingent.

Brainert and the blonde moved to the side of the stage as Hedda stepped up to the standing microphone. A smiling Dr. Lilly greeted the living legend, and the pair shook hands. Camera phones were held aloft to capture the moment.

Dr. Lilly stepped back and Hedda began to speak.

"Thank you all for such a warm welcome! I am ever so grateful for this opportunity to come forward again and greet my fans. You know, my screen career ended long ago. But this festival is truly a gift to me, showing my films, making me a star again." She smiled. "Or at least *feel* like a star again . . ."

The crowd laughed and applauded.

"Indeed, tonight truly is like yesteryear. You've made it all come back to me —"

An intense flash suddenly illuminated the stage. The silent burst of light was followed by a shower of sparks that rained down around the standing mike, where Hedda was speaking.

Another flash came from above, and the startled elderly woman looked up.

"Oh, my god!" someone cried from the first row.

"The speaker!"

"Look out!"

Screams came from all over the theater as the massive black audio speaker dropped from above, trailing sparking wires.

Brainert lunged for Hedda and pulled her away. The object struck the heavy microphone stand, smashing the metal flat. More screams filled the theater as the speaker bounced across the stage, then came apart. People in the front row leaped up as the debris scattered.

"Oh, my God, Jack," I silently cried. "That speaker could have hurt Hedda!"

You mean killed, don't you? Look at that steel microphone stand, baby. It's smashed beyond recognition.

Now I was on my feet along with everyone else, and another figure dashed onto the stage — Bud Napp. As sparks continued to flutter down like sizzling snow, Bud raised his arms and signaled for calm. "All right, people, settle down now," he declared in the same tone he used when presiding over our Quindicott Business Owners Association

60

meetings. "No one was hurt, and there's no cause for alarm!"

"What happened?" someone cried.

"Looks like our public address speaker fell, that's all," Bud continued. "There's no danger to anyone, so don't panic. But as you can tell from my *shouting,* we lost our audio system . . ."

Behind Bud, the young, blonde Hedda lookalike darted across the stage to put an arm around the elder Hedda. Appearing shaken, the actress quickly recovered, and the young woman led her off stage.

Brainert stepped forward, careful to avoid the sparking wires, as he loudly addressed the crowd. "I'm sure Dr. Lilly will be happy to finish her lecture tomorrow morning, at the Buy the Book store on Cranberry Street."

Dr. Lilly nodded. "I'm sure to have my new book delivered by then!" she shouted. "I hope to see you all there!"

"And we'll hear from the great Hedda Geist-Middleton later this weekend, too!" Brainert added, forcing a stiff grin across his still chalk-white face. "Meanwhile, I have an idea. Let's forget about this little mishap and proceed to the lawn party at the Finch Inn!"

Spotty applause followed, and then the

61

crowd began to buzz with excitement as it moved up the aisles. The electric reaction didn't surprise me. Witnessing a shocking accident was a gossip gold mine in this little town. Not only had these folks scored a story to tell for weeks to come, they could start rehashing it right now at a party with food and drink.

I remained in my seat, waiting for the mob to disperse. Then I approached the stage, one eye on the shattered speaker and the hot, sparking wires still flashing overhead.

That Hedda Geist . . . Jack remarked.

"What about her?"

She's one accident-prone dame.

"What do you mean by that?" I demanded.

But the ghost didn't answer.

"Jack? Are you there?"

He wasn't. For whatever his reason this time, the ghost of Jack Shepard had once again faded to black.

CHAPTER 3
NIGHT TRIPS

The work of the police, like that of a woman, is never done.

— *He Walked by Night,* 1948

I didn't go to the party on the Finch Inn lawn. Even though it was a Friday night, Spencer's sixteen-year-old babysitter had a midnight curfew. Normally, my aunt Sadie would have stayed home with Spence, but being in her seventies hadn't precluded accepting a hot date for the party with widower Bud Napp. I, on the other hand, was young, dateless, and had to get home.

After letting Spencer's sitter out the bookstore's front door, I relocked the shop, climbed the stairs to our three-bedroom apartment, and checked on my sleeping son.

Spencer was in dreamland on his narrow bed, his breathing deep and even; his orange-striped cat, Bookmark, curled up at his feet. He was eleven now, and, not for the first time, I noticed his growing resemblance to my late older brother: the thick, auburn hair with the stubborn cowlick, the long-lashed eyes, and light dusting of freckles. I had those features, too, but unlike my brother, who'd been a real lady's man, I'd never been anything close to a magnet for the opposite sex.

Thank goodness Spencer's too young for all that, I thought. But I knew it wouldn't be much longer before he started calling girls, or they started calling him. That was the sort of "problem" I'd be happy to deal with compared to what we'd already gone through.

A few years ago, after his father's suicide, Spencer had become increasingly withdrawn — not unlike Calvin's own behavior before he'd stepped out the bedroom window of our high-rise apartment.

After Calvin's funeral, my son seemed convinced that I was going to leave him next, so he didn't want to leave me — didn't want to go to school or summer camp, was reluctant even to step out of the apartment. Then nightmares plagued him; his fears increased, his grades fell, and the therapist my wealthy in-laws had hired for him was unable to help.

That's when the McClures began to pressure me. Spencer needed to "get away," they said. Their solution was boarding school. Mine was a whole lot different. I moved us up to my little hometown of Quindicott, Rhode Island.

It had been difficult at first. Calvin's mother and sister had hit the roof — fashionable, upscale *Newport* was the place to live in Rhode Island, not my dinky little hometown. They hadn't understood my decision, and Spencer had been angry that I'd forced him to leave New York, abandon everything familiar.

Instead of his exclusive private academy, Spencer was now attending public school. His new bedroom was half the size of his old one, the posh view of skyscrapers exchanged for a single old tree. His sleekly modern private bath was now a shared restroom with a claw-footed tub and a chipped sink.

Eventually, however, he came around; and now he was a completely different child. It was hard for me to admit, but even before Calvin's death, Spencer had been moody and taciturn; sometimes so shy he had trouble making friends. Maybe he'd been reflecting Calvin's own depression and aloofness. Or maybe being in the shadow of a spoiled, lousy, self-absorbed father was just as bad as dealing with the loss of one. (Not that I want to speak ill of the dead.) But my boy was so much happier these days; so much more *alive,* with blossoming interests and solid grades in school. He even enjoyed helping out at the store; and those terrible nightmares? *Gone.*

I smiled with that thought as I half-closed my son's door and moved to my own bedroom. Stifling a yawn, I kicked off my low-heeled shoes, changed out of my slacks and blazer, and slipped into my nightshirt. Then I settled under the covers, set my black-framed glasses on the nightstand, and clicked off the light.

Inside my head, however, the light remained on.

Looking at my sleeping son had raised my spirits, filled me with joy and certainty. But in the darkness, something else took over: a vision of what had happened less than an hour earlier, an image of danger and near death.

That huge, black audio speaker had fallen onto the theater stage like the grim reaper looking for a soul. The calm of the audience, followed by the shock, the screams, the chaos . . . it reminded me of my late husband all over again: of his being right there in our quiet bedroom one moment, and down on the sidewalk the next. I could still hear the shrieks on the street, the squealing of brakes, the sirens.

"There was a flash," I mumbled beneath my bedcovers. "And sparks. Why were there so many sparks? And then that awful smashing noise. Why? Why did it fall?"

My bedroom felt warm, but the temperature rapidly changed. An icy breeze began swirling around me. I opened my eyes. My flowered curtains weren't moving. There was no breeze. No wind; not outside, anyway. Beyond the open window, the black branches of the hundred-year oak appeared still as the grave.

"Jack?" I whispered into the chilly darkness. "Is that you?"

Miss me, baby?

"Where were you?"

Where do you think? I was back here, waiting for you. I'm going to take you out on the town . . .

"I don't know what you mean . . ."

Yeah, you do, baby. We've done it before.

"But I want to discuss what happened earlier at the theater. What did you mean by Hedda being 'one accident-prone dame'?"

I'm going to show you. It's something I witnessed years ago, and I want you to see it, too. But you have to close your eyes.

Once more, I tried to argue, but a giant yawn stifled my words. I began to feel incredibly groggy. My eyelids drifted lower, and then everything went black . . .

"Everything's so bright!"

Hearing the giggly voice of a teenaged girl, I opened my eyes. People surrounded me, raucous noise, honking car horns, and lights — thousands of lights.

"Where am I?" I whispered.

"Lady, you've got to be kidding!" exclaimed that giggly teenaged girl. "You're in Times Square! Sheesh!"

The girl scampered off with a group of her friends. I blinked and rubbed my eyes, but the bright mirage failed to fade. I was standing in New York's Times Square — only this wasn't the Times Square I remembered. The surrounding buildings were much lower than during my time, the billboards more primitive, with flashing lightbulbs instead of digital images, and most of them were advertising products I'd never heard of . . . Kinsey Blended Whiskey? Rupert Beer?

The marquees and landmarks were all wrong, too, I realized. Automat? Hotel Astor Dining? Capitol Theater? Where was the Virgin Records Store? The Bertelsmann

Building? The Toys 'R' Us, McDonald's, and towering Marriott?

Streetcars ran on tracks up and down Broadway. Cars the size of small army tanks spewed leaded gasoline fumes; and the men and women jostling me on the sidewalk were attired so formally — suits and fedoras, Sunday-best dresses, and white gloves. Not a pair of shorts, baggy jeans, or sneakers in sight. Not one miniskirt or belly-baring top.

I looked down at my own clothing and gasped. The evening gown I was wearing resembled nothing in my closet. The dress was a strapless, slinky number, a form-fitting golden yellow with black embroidery along the top edge of a shockingly low bodice. Opera gloves, dyed to match the gown, covered three-quarters of my arms, and black, peep-toe pumps with four-inch heels were on my feet.

"What in the name of Sam Hill am I wearing?!"

As a few passersby turned their heads, I felt a sharp tap on my bare shoulder.

"What's the matter, baby? Don't you like it?"

The deep, gravelly voice was one I knew well. It was the voice of Jack Shepard, now attached to the body he'd had in life. A gray fedora sat on his sandy hair; a double-breasted suit was attractively tailored to his broad shoulders and narrow waist; and despite his menacing iron jaw and the ominous dagger-shaped scar on his square, flat chin, he wore an openly bemused expression.

"Ava wore that little number in *Singapore*. I saw it last year at the Mayfair — or half of it anyway, before my mark took a powder."

"Ava *Gardner?*" I looked down at my gown again and frowned. "Did she have an acre of cleavage showing, too?"

"Yeah," said Jack. Then his granite-colored eyes took me in from my painted toenails to my upswept hair. With a single finger, he pushed back the front brim of his fedora and gave me a little smile. "But I prefer redheads."

I touched the back of my own shoulder-length auburn hair, now gathered into some kind of twist. I felt old-fashioned bobby pins holding it in place. I also realized that I wasn't wearing my black-framed glasses. I blinked, trying to discern whether my contacts were in. I didn't feel those, either, yet I could see just fine.

"What's this all about? I was trying to talk to you about Hedda Geist and what you implied about —"

"I know. Come on," he said, taking my

elbow, none too gently, and hustling me along the sidewalk.

"Easy! Not so fast! I can hardly walk in these torture devices!"

Jack barely slowed. "They're part of the cover, doll. So suck it up and march. You're on a case with me, now, and I'm not putting up with bellyaching."

"Case? What case?!"

Jack didn't answer, just kept hustling me up the block then around the corner. He slowed as we approached a dark green awning. There was no writing on the fabric, no sign on the heavy door.

Jack stopped and glanced down at me. "Got your breath, baby?" Before I could answer he pulled open the door and stood aside. "After you."

"After me? Where am I going?" I peered into the darkness beyond the door. "What is this place?"

"You'll get all the answers you want if you just move your skirt *inside*."

I tentatively stepped forward, teetering on my ridiculously high pumps.

"Good evening, miss," a voice called from the abyss.

My eyes adjusted to the dim lighting, and I realized I'd stepped into some sort of reception area.

"Do you have a reservation?" A middle-aged man in a tuxedo was addressing me from behind a wooden podium. "Are you meeting someone?"

"I . . . uh . . ."

"She's with me," said Jack, stepping up to the maître d'.

"And do *you* have a reservation?" The tuxedo-clad man glanced at the large open ledger on his podium.

"We don't have a reservation," Jack replied smoothly, "because, you see, the lady didn't like the Broadway show. So we left early. We've had dinner already, so we'll just be wetting our whistles at the bar until our friends leave the theater across the street. That okay by you?"

Jack palmed the man a bill.

"Of course, sir," said the maître d'. "Enjoy yourself."

Jack stepped up to me, and I expected him to grab me by the elbow again and hustle me inside. But he didn't. This time, he leaned toward me and offered his arm.

"Oh," I said with an undisguised smirk, "*now* you're going to act like a gentleman?"

"It's not a proposal of marriage, baby. I'm just trying to make it look good."

"Well, the way you manhandled me on the street, I'd rather not."

I tried taking a few bold strides all by myself, but I had zero practice carrying off four-inch heels beneath a slit-skirted gown, and I nearly fell on my face.

In a flash, Jack was there, propping me back up. "Take a break from Miss Prissland," he rasped in my ear, "and take my arm already."

I knew when I was licked. With a sigh, I wrapped my gloved arm around the gray fabric of his double-breasted jacket and let him escort me into the large dining room.

Two "M" words hit me the second I walked into that place: *money* and *masculinity*. The wainscoting and tables were dark, heavy wood. The walls and tablecloths were the forest green of a gentleman's club pool table. And the chandeliers and crystal decanters looked heavy, leaded, and very expensive.

Middle-aged waiters in bow ties, white shirts, and long white aprons moved silently around the buzzing room, serving craggy-faced men in three-piece suits, most of whom were smoking cigars and cutting up thick slabs of red meat with huge steak knives.

The leather booths around the edges of the room were occupied by couples. Almost every woman was young and beautiful;

almost every man paunchy, graying, and clearly much older.

One particularly creepy May–December couple caught my eye. Not because of the man, but because of the woman — or, more precisely, the *girl.* She was very young: seventeen, maybe even sixteen. With the heavy makeup on, I doubted very much she was the man's daughter or niece. And when her fingers began stroking the back of her dinner companion's hand, I threw that theory right out the window — while simultaneously trying very hard not to throw up.

The teen was no raving beauty, more like the girl next door with caramel-colored curls and a dimple in her chin. Her face also looked familiar for some reason, but I just couldn't place it. I could place the silver gown, though: It was the exact satin dress that Hedda Geist had worn in the opening scene of her famous noir picture *Wrong Turn.*

"What is this place?" I whispered to Jack as we moved across the bare oak floor.

"The Porterhouse."

"A steakhouse?"

"For our purposes, it's a *stakeout* house."

"Excuse me?"

"Take a seat," ordered Jack, gesturing to the bar stool.

I sat and Jack sat next to me. There was

only one other couple, at the far end of the polished oak bar, and the young bartender came over to us right away. "What can I get you both tonight?"

"I'll have scotch, straight up, and —" Jack turned to me. "Tell the man what you're drinking, baby."

I tapped my chin in thought. I wasn't a drinker per se, but we did ask to sit at the bar so a soft drink would look conspicuous. "I know," I finally said, "the perfect drink for this occasion would be a Vesper."

The bartender's brow wrinkled. "A *whatsper*?"

"A Vesper," I said, incredulous the bartender at such an upscale restaurant wasn't familiar with the most famous cocktail recipe in the English-speaking world.

"What's in it?" he asked.

"It's a martini," I told him, "made with three parts gin, one part vodka, and one-half part Lillet."

"Lillet?" The bartender frowned. "Not vermouth?"

"The Lillet adds more sweetness and tropical aromas than dry vermouth," I informed the man. "Or at least that's what I remember from *Casino Royale*. And, of course, it should be shaken, not stirred, served in a wineglass, and garnished with a lemon twist."

"We *stir* martinis here, ma'am. Nobody shakes them."

I threw up my hands. "James Bond does!"

The bartender glanced at Jack. "Is that you?"

"Of course he's not James Bond. Bond's the most famous Cold War spy in the world." I glanced around. "What year is this anyway?"

Jack visibly stiffened.

"It's 1948, ma'am," the bartender replied, eyeing me a little closer. "You that blotto?"

"Uh-oh," I said, realizing I'd been off by a few years. The first Ian Fleming Bond novel wouldn't appear until 1953. "I believe I've made a mistake —"

"Listen, buddy," Jack quickly told the bartender, "just give the doll a martini. A *gin* martini, *stirred,* and put the damn thing in a *martini glass.* Thanks."

The bartender walked away, shaking his head, and Jack glared at me.

"What?" I asked.

"Don't you know the meaning of *cover?* You're supposed to blend in, keep a low profile, be a fly on the wall — not order a drink from another century!"

"Cut me a break, okay? James Bond *was* invented in the twentieth century. I was only

76

off by a few years."

The bartender returned with Jack's Scotch and my *stirred, gin* martini in a *martini glass.* He dropped two napkins and placed the drinks on top, shaking his head as he set mine down.

"So, ma'am, I'm curious," said the bartender. "What's a 'Cold War,' anyway? Another type of cocktail?"

Jack tossed the man a large bill. "Keep it," he said. "We won't be needing refills anytime soon. We'd just like our *privacy.* Got it?"

"Of course, sir." The bartender nodded. "Privacy is what the Porterhouse is all about."

Jack knocked back some scotch and closed his eyes. I sipped my martini and waited. When the PI opened his eyes again, he began casually scanning the room.

"Are you going to enlighten me anytime soon?" I whispered.

"There's a booth at your three o'clock," Jack said, holding the scotch glass up to his mouth. "Now do exactly what I say. Cross your legs and as you cross them, slowly turn your bar stool halfway around. Keep taking sips of your cocktail as you take a casual look around the room."

I did what Jack told me. As I crossed my

legs, the slit in my gown showed a flash of stocking-clad thigh. Jack's eyes found it, and he stopped speaking for a full minute.

"Jack?"

"See the painting of Seabiscuit?" he whispered, his eyes still on my legs.

"Seabiscuit? Excuse me? Why am I looking at a picture of a racehorse?"

"Not the horse, doll, the booth underneath it. See the paunchy man sitting there, the one with the thinning brown hair and pale face. Seated across from him is —"

"A very young woman in a silver gown," I whispered back. "Yes, I see them both."

"They're it, doll. They were my meal ticket back here in '48."

"What's the name of the case? I still have your files in my stockroom. They're a total mess, all out of order, but I can try to find the file."

"Don't bother, baby. You won't find it."

"Why not?"

"Let's stick to the business at hand."

"Fine," I said. "I was going to tell you anyway. I noticed that young woman on our way in. She looks familiar to me for some reason. I'm sure I've seen her before, but I can't place her face."

"She looks *familiar* to you?" Jack finally moved his gaze off my gams. He sipped at his Scotch a moment, obviously considering my words. "But you weren't even born yet, doll. So how could you have seen her *before?*"

"I don't know . . . who's the creep she's with?"

"That's Nathan Burwell, the district attorney," Jack said. "His wife's the one who hired me. That's why I was here tonight. I was tailing Burwell, documenting his little trysts with Miss Innocent over there. In case you haven't noticed, this place is full of cheating Charlies. That maître d' is as good as an army sentry. If you'd showed up without me, a dame alone, you would have been turned away."

"But that's discriminatory!"

"That maître d' wouldn't have taken the chance that you were a wife, snooping up on the old hubby. Anyway, Mrs. Burwell wants a divorce and she wants her money, which means the DA's got to go away quietly — so she hired me to gather the dirt."

"And how exactly are you gathering it?"

"Detailed notes on where, when, and how long. Witnesses when I can get them. Photographs when I can set the pair up without their noticing."

"But I still don't understand, Jack. What

does Burwell and his disturbingly young mistress have to do with Hedda Geist? Other than the girl's gown."

Jack frowned. "What do you mean the girl's gown? What's with the girl's gown?"

"It's the same outfit Hedda wore in *Wrong Turn*. Don't you see it? The plunging neckline, the bow at the bodice, the way the shimmering silver satin is cut? It's the exact gown Hedda wore when she ran onto the dark road. Remember? The shoulder of the gown was torn in the picture. She was holding it up with one hand. But in the original movie poster for *Wrong Turn* it looks exactly like that."

"I don't believe it," Jack muttered.

"Believe what?"

"Believe you caught something I missed . . . but you did. You're right on the money. She's wearing the same gown, all right."

I smiled, proud of myself. "Thanks."

"Don't let it go to your head. We're not nearly finished here."

"What else is there to do?"

"You remember what I said back in your hayseed town —"

"Quindicott is not a hayseed town, Jack. It's a quaint New England hamlet —"

"Drive me buggy later, okay? I'm trying

to tell you something here. After that accident with the falling speaker at your egghead friend's movie theater, do you remember what I said?"

"Yes, of course. You implied that Hedda had been involved with another accident. But I don't see Hedda in the room."

"You will," Jack promised before another sip of Scotch.

Within minutes, Hedda Geist did show, just as Jack promised. The actress was young again and gorgeous, gliding into the exclusive steakhouse looking like the starlet she was, her stunning figure hugged by a seductively sheer gown of pale pink. The halter top showed off her creamy shoulders, the tight bodice flattered her hourglass curves, and a pearl choker complimented her long neck.

Jack's eyes — along with every other red-blooded male's in the restaurant — were drawn to the dazzling blonde, following her across the dining room on the arm of an incongruous escort.

Like every other couple in this restaurant, Hedda's date was twice her age. He was bald, had a slight build, and a rather short stature. With her heels on, Hedda was at least two inches taller.

"That's Irving Vreen," Jack whispered.

"He's the head of Gotham Features, the studio in Queens that made her the star of their B pictures."

"Knowing how well those pictures did for the studio, I'd say it was the other way around. It was Hedda who made Gotham Features."

"Can't argue there," Jack said.

I studied Vreen, trying to see whether or not he was wearing a gold band on his left hand, but he was too far away. "So what's up with Vreen?" I finally asked, turning back to Jack. "If this is a place for cheating Charles, am I to assume Vreen's a married man?"

"Bingo. Married to Dolores Vreen. They have one young daughter. Live on Long Island."

"How do you know that?" I asked. "Did you know Vreen personally?"

"No," said Jack. "But a little over a year before this night, I did some PI work for his movie studio's property master. The case of the disappearing props, some of them pretty expensive. It was an easy stakeout and an even easier bust — some poor slob of a production assistant swiping it after hours and stashing it in his mother's basement. Nothing to write home about, as far as my case files."

"Well, if you don't know Vreen personally, or *didn't* — gee, it's tough to know how to make tenses work when you're actually back in the past —"

"Get on with it."

"How do you know Vreen's really cheating with Hedda? They could just be colleagues sharing a business dinner."

Jack's head tilted ever so slightly. "Is that how 'colleagues' act during a 'business' dinner?"

I slowly turned on my stool again, lifted my martini for a sip as I casually glanced in the direction Jack had gestured.

"Goodness . . ." I whispered.

Hedda Geist and Irving Vreen had elected to cram themselves into the same side of a leather-cushioned booth. While Vreen was studying the menu, Hedda was practically in his lap, nibbling his weak chin with little kisses.

"Well?" Jack said.

"Well, I guess Vreen's cheating."

"The papers will say so, too. They'll be all over the story in a matter of hours."

"What story, Jack? What did you witness here?"

Just then, I heard loud voices coming from the reception area. Someone was arguing with the maître d'. Seconds later, a man came barreling into the dining room. He was quite handsome with a jutting, Kirk Douglas jaw, jet-black hair, and bright blue eyes. He was also tall and well-built, his physique closely outlined by a fitted tuxedo.

"Jack? Who is that? He looks familiar, but I can't place —"

"That's Pierce Armstrong," Jack informed me, "another actor at Vreen's studio."

Armstrong charged right up to the booth where Hedda was still cooing over Irving Vreen.

"I knew I'd find you with him!" Armstrong shouted.

The entire restaurant suddenly fell silent. Every face — including mine and Jack's — turned in the direction of Hedda's booth.

"How could you, Hedda?" Armstrong asked. "How could you break up with me and then throw yourself at Irving?! And after all we've been to each other? Why, I ought to slap you silly for this!"

"Don't you come near me, Pierce!" Hedda cried. She grabbed one of the Porterhouse's large steak knives off the table. "Stay back! I'm warning you!"

"Calm down, Pierce," said Irving Vreen. "Let's talk this over."

"Step aside, Vreen," Armstrong loudly warned. "My problem's not with you! It's with Hedda! She's the little tramp who threw me over for you!"

By now, the maître d' was rushing toward the kitchen doors, where the restaurant's uneasy waiters had gathered. The maître d' motioned to two of the larger men and began to lead them toward Hedda's table. But it was too late. Armstrong was already lunging toward Hedda.

"Stop!" Irving Vreen demanded, putting himself between the two.

But Pierce Armstrong didn't stop. He tripped instead, knocking Vreen's slight form backward, right into the steak knife that Hedda had been waving.

The scene was a horror show. Vreen's body slumped to the floor, Hedda's steak knife sticking out of its back. Blood gushed from the wound, spraying like a garden hose. Hedda's hands and gown were quickly saturated, and she screamed hysterically. Pierce Armstrong stepped back in complete shock, letting the maître d' and waiters hustle him away from the booth.

Stunned myself, I turned to Jack. "My God, that's some accident."

"Yeah, baby, if that's what it was . . ."

"What are you saying? That Hedda planned to kill Vreen? Why?"

"I don't know, and I'm sorry to tell you

that I was dead myself within a year of this little party. C'mon." Jack's strong grip closed on my upper arm and he pulled me off the bar stool.

"Slow down, Jack! Where are we going now?"

"Didn't you notice? My meal ticket's taking a powder."

Jack was right. As he guided me across the dining room, I saw Nathan Burwell and his barely legal date heading for the exit. So were the other May–December couples. It was practically a stampede!

"What's going on?" I asked.

"What do you think? These cheating Charlies aren't too keen to be interviewed as witnesses. Not with their chippies in tow."

I shook my head. "I can't believe even the DA isn't willing to stick around and give a statement to the police. But I guess the detectives on the case can always use the restaurant's reservations list to track down witnesses."

In response, Jack pointed to the maître d'. He was now rushing by us with the reservation book under his arm.

"Where's he going with that?" I asked as the man headed for the double doors leading to the kitchen.

Jack shrugged. "Dollars to donuts he's

about to add it to the flame-broiled menu."

"What do you mean?"

"I mean, doll, that there aren't going to be many on-the-record witnesses to tonight's little 'accident,' because the Porterhouse's book of reservations is about to go up in flames."

Ring-ring! Ring-ring!

"Jack, what's that?" We were moving with the crowd out of the dining room and into the dimly lit reception area. "Did somebody hit the fire alarm?"

Ring-ring!

"There's no alarm, baby. What are you talking about?"

"The ringing, Jack! Don't you hear it?"

Ring-ring!

We were in the small reception area now, shoulder to shoulder with the other patrons. There was so little light I could hardly see a thing. Then I couldn't feel Jack anymore. His hand had let go of my arm!

"Jack?"

Ring-ring!

"Jack! Where are you? Don't leave me!"

I peered into the darkness, but I couldn't see him. I couldn't stop, either; the crowd just kept carrying me forward. But I didn't know where I was going. I had to let Jack know where I was. I couldn't do this without

him! Squeezing my eyes shut, I cried as loudly as I could —
  "Jaack!"

I opened my eyes. Light was streaming in from my bedroom window. It was morning.
  Ring-ring!
  Ring-ring!
  Ring-ring!
  Ring-ring!
  I sat up, breathing hard, and slapped off my alarm clock.

CHAPTER 4
DEATH IN THE
PAST TENSE

I'm in the movie business, darling. I can't afford your acute attacks of integrity.
— *The Big Knife,* 1955

"Hey, Mom, any hopheads or grape cats in that movie you saw last night?"

Okay, there *was* a time when I would've dropped the buttermilk pancakes on the kitchen floor after hearing those phrases coming out of my son's eleven-year-old mouth. But given my disturbing dream of the night before, it would've taken a lot more than that for Spencer to rattle me.

I calmly set the warm plate in front of him. "So you learned some new vocabulary on the Intrigue Channel."

Spencer snatched the bottle of Vermont maple syrup and began to pour. "How about whistle bait?" he asked brightly. "Any saucy tomatoes?"

"You're a little too young to know about

'whistle bait' — and hopheads for that matter." I tightened the belt of my terrycloth robe. "What were you watching, anyway? An old *Mike Hammer* episode?"

"Actually, it was a *Naked City* marathon," said Spencer around his first gooey mouthful of pancakes.

"That old show from the sixties? I didn't know they were running those things."

Spencer nodded. "It was way wicked, Mom. One episode was about a dancing girl who fell down a flight of stairs during a party. Only she didn't 'fall,' you see what I'm getting at?"

"Yes, but you know what I think —"

"Somebody pushed her!"

I adjusted my black rectangular glasses. "You know what I think, Spencer?"

"What?"

"There are eight million stories in the Naked City, but you're not *old enough* to watch any of them yet." Reaching over with a napkin, I wiped a dribble of syrup from his chin. He waved my hand away — a big boy now.

"I got it, Mom."

"I can't believe Bonnie let you stay up to watch that show."

"Bonnie" was Bonnie Franzetti, my son's babysitter, and sister of my late brother's best friend, Eddie Franzetti. The Franzettis owned a successful pizza restaurant on Cranberry Street, but Eddie hadn't followed the family tradition. Instead, he'd become an officer on the Quindicott police force.

"The marathon started at seven," said Spencer. "Anyway, it was no big deal. I usually stay up until ten anyway."

I had the sneaking suspicion Spencer had stayed up later than ten, mostly because it was harder than usual to wake him up this morning — after my own alarm clock had nearly given me a heart attack, that is.

"Enough talk. Finish your pancakes. The coach will be here any minute to pick you up."

"Okey-dokey," Spencer replied, attempting an impression of Edward G. Robinson.

Minutes later, I was shoving my bare feet into penny loafers and we were heading downstairs. I grabbed the store keys from behind the counter and let Spencer out to meet Coach Farmer's minivan. Today was Saturday, no school, but there was an all-day baseball clinic for the regional Little League teams, and Spencer was eager to get tips on fielding and batting.

"See you, Mom!"

I waved to the coach and locked the door again. That's when Jack finally made an appearance.

Was that kid trying to sound like Little Caesar? 'Cause he sounded more like Spanky from Our Gang.

"Edward G. Robinson has become one of Spencer's favorite Intrigue Channel tough guys — second only to Jack Shield. I haven't the heart to tell him his imitation is a little off."

Maybe Spence should wait until he gets a little hair on his lip, or at least until his voice changes —

"Okay! End of conversation."

I glanced at my wristwatch. It was not yet eight, but with two hours remaining before we opened our doors, there was still plenty to do. I went back upstairs to shower and dress. After blowing out my shoulder-length auburn hair, I buttoned on a simple cream-colored blouse, stepped into pressed black slacks, and returned to the shop to open the register and boot up our computer system.

For years, my aunt Sadie had run the Quindicott shop just as her late father had — that is to say, she received book deliveries and placed them on the shelves for loyal customers to wander in and purchase at their leisure. But as the store's loyal customer base gradually died off and the town fell on hard times, Sadie prepared to pack it in, too. That's when I offered an alternative, along with much of the check from my late husband's life insurance policy.

With the ready cash, we remodeled the dusty old shop, overhauled the inventory, opened the Community Events space in the adjoining storefront, and launched a marketing campaign and Internet site. Sadie had always been New England practical, so she'd been tense about spending the money, especially when it came to mortgaging her original store to expand our space for special events. But now our business was going gangbusters. And this weekend was shaping up to be an especially profitable one for us.

I was just starting to tidy up the front display tables when Aunt Sadie finally made an appearance. She looked lovely this morning in tweedy brown slacks and a forest-green boatneck sweater, which nicely set off her short, newly colored auburn hair.

Dyeing her hair was about the only vanity Sadie allowed herself. She had a few pieces of jewelry, but seldom wore them. Necklaces were "plain useless" and "a waste of money," whereas a chain to hold reading glasses, now that had a functional purpose — which is why she had a serious variety of chains in her collection (today's consisted of small pink seashells). But that was Sadie Thornton: as averse to unnecessary ornamentations as a Shaker chair.

I noticed she was limping as she came down the stairs, which was unusual for my usually spry auntie.

"Backache?" I asked, pushing up my black glasses.

Sadie shrugged. "I woke up in the middle of the night with a sharp pain in my side. I thought it came from sitting so long in that movie theater seat, until I found my remote control underneath me on the mattress." She shook her head. "I don't know how the thing got there."

"I'm pretty sure I do," I said with a sigh. "There was a Naked City marathon on TV last night —"

"Spencer?"

"I'm betting Bonnie sent him off to bed, not realizing there was another television in the apartment." My suspicions vindicated, I shrugged. "That's *one* mystery solved, at least . . ."

"What do you mean one mystery?" Sadie's eyes met mine. "Is there another?"

"Maybe," I said, thinking about my dream. "But if I'm going to solve it, I'll need your help."

Sadie raised her eyebrows, obviously

intrigued. "What do you need, dear?"

"I'd like you to check your old contacts in the out-of-print book market. I'm looking for any books published about the history of Gotham Features studio."

"Gotham Features?" Sadie said. "Just what are you looking for?"

"A lot of things . . ."

Yeah, said Jack in my head, *like whether Hedda actually had a motive to set up Irving Vreen for the big knife. Or was it Pierce Armstrong setting Hedda up?*

"Or was the whole thing simply a tragic accident," I silently reminded the ghost. "Just like last night's falling speaker. Maybe Hedda really is just accident-prone."

Brrring!

The store's front doorbell interrupted us. I glanced at the locked glass door and saw Dr. Irene Lilly waving at me from the other side.

"What's she doing here so early?" Aunt Sadie asked. "Her book signing isn't scheduled until noon."

"She's probably worried about that overnight shipment of her new book arriving from the publisher. Remember? The first shipment never got here." I grabbed the key from behind the counter and hurried to open the door.

"Good morning, Mrs. McClure. Ready for another big day?"

Once again, Dr. Lilly looked very West Coast in a sunshine yellow ankle-length cotton dress and leather sandals. Her tanned complexion contrasted attractively with her straight, dark blonde hair. Despite the early hour, she was brimming with energy as she entered the store. Laugh lines deepened around her eyes when she greeted my aunt.

"Sadie and I were just about to set up while we waited for the delivery of your books," I told her, closing and locking the door again.

"Good," said Dr. Lilly. "I just know your shop's going to get a big crowd today. I wanted to bring you both coffee and pastry, but the line at your town's wonderful bakery is running halfway down the block!"

"Uh-oh," I murmured, glancing at my aunt. "I hope Linda Cooper remembers the order I placed." I'd requested four dozen of their lighter-than-air doughnuts and two giant thermal containers of coffee to be ready by nine this morning. "I'd better get over there and pick them up."

Dr. Lilly slipped the suede purse off her shoulder and set it down on the counter. "Go," she commanded. "Your aunt Sadie and I can get the event room set up."

"Thank you so much, Dr. Lilly —"

"Please, it's Irene."

"I'll be back with coffee and donuts in no time," I promised, snatching up my keys and purse.

I should have known this day would be a disaster when I turned the ignition key on my battered Saturn and nothing happened.

"Not now," I groaned. "How am I ever going to get everything back to the store without a car?"

I can't help you solve every *mystery, doll,* Jack replied.

"It was a rhetorical question," I pointed out. "Beside which, you don't have a body, so how could you help?"

Low blow, baby.

"Sorry. I'm not mad at you, it's just —"

It's just that sometimes a dame needs a real *man around the house, not just some spook. Well, open your peepers or you'll miss your pal, Charlie Big Suds —*

"Huh?"

Jack the Biscuit. The pie-eater who feather-beds for the mail service —

"Seymour!" I cried out the window.

Seymour turned on the sidewalk and waved. Then he slung his mailbag over one shoulder and sauntered up to my window.

"Car trouble, Pen?" he asked.

I nodded.

"It's probably a lost cause, but if you unlock the hood, I'll be glad to take a look."

I popped the hood and Seymour lifted it. He tinkered around for about a minute and told me to turn the key again. I did, and we both heard the sound of silence.

Seymour closed the hood. "It's your battery."

"What's wrong with it?"

"You're kidding, right? The thing's deader than a Kennedy. When I roll out my ice cream truck later, I'll give you a jump and you should be good to go."

When Seymour wasn't delivering mail, he was moonlighting as an ice-cream truck vendor. That was all well and good: "But I need a car *now* — this minute!" I told him. "I have to bring a bunch of goodies from Cooper's back to the store."

Seymour eyes brightened. "You're heading to the home of the melt-in-your-mouth bear claw? Treat me and I'll help you out."

"It's a deal!"

I opened the trunk so Seymour could stash his mail. Then we set off down Cranberry Street toward the busy bakery. All along the main street, the faux antique Victorian streetlamps were festooned with posters advertising the movie festival's films. Many featured the voluptuous form of the young Hedda Geist, star of *Wrong Turn, Man Trap, Bad to the Bone, Cruel and Unusual,* and *Tight Spot.*

"Did you go to the lawn party at the Finch Inn last night?" I asked Seymour.

"You bet," he replied. "I never miss a chance to goad Fiona Finch. Did you see the way she and Barney renovated that miniature storm tower she calls a light-house? I told her I liked it better when it was painted Day-Glo orange and covered with graffiti —"

"Oh, come on. I haven't seen it yet, but it can't be that bad. And who needs graffiti? It's just an eyesore."

"Hey, you can learn a lot from reading that stuff. Archaeologists search for Roman graffiti just to get a feel for what the common people were thinking."

"But that's history —"

"Yeah, and I learned the *romantic* history of Quindicott High School from that old tower, before Fiona defaced it. By the way, do you happen to know anything about a girl named Brenda? She'd probably be in her midtwenties by now, and —" Seymour stopped in his tracks. His slightly bulging eyes bulged a little wider.

I followed his gaze to the front of Mr. Koh's grocery store, where a beautiful young blonde was selecting fresh fruit from the store's wooden bins. I recognized her immediately.

"That girl," I whispered, "she was with Hedda Geist last night. Do you know who she is?"

"Her name's Harmony Middleton," Seymour informed me. "She's Hedda's granddaughter."

The girl wore a hot pink tank top over white, very short shorts, and a young man in jeans and a rock band T-shirt was obviously flirting with her. I recognized the shaggy dark hair and the shamrock forearm tattoo. It was Dixon Gallagher, one of Bud Napp's part-time employees at the hardware store, and I wondered if Bud had used him on the final fix-it work he'd done for Brainert's theater.

A roaring engine suddenly shattered the quiet on Cranberry. I turned to see a black-and-chrome motorcycle pulling up to the Koh's fruit stand. The rider was a big guy, wearing blue jeans and a black leather jacket. Without pulling off his ebony helmet, or lifting its tinted visor, he grabbed a drink from the outdoor refrigerator. Then he turned to observe Harmony and sauntered over to her. He finally pulled off his helmet. but I couldn't see the blond man's face. I could tell he was making some kind of joke, purposefully finding a way to join the conversation. Harmony laughed and smiled at him, pushing his beefy arm playfully while Dixon smirked and folded his own tattooed arms tightly.

Seymour shook his head. "Like moths to flame."

"Excuse me?"

"That same little scene got played at least ten times at last night's lawn party — except with different players."

"What do you mean exactly?"

I'll tell you what the postman's saying, Jack piped up in my head. *Harmony just might be a chippy off the old block.*

"Excuse me?"

She wears skirts that defy gravity. She buys underwear with loose elastic. In other words, she's a real —

"Okay, okay!" I told the ghost. "I get it!"

"That girl not only resembles her granny," Seymour said, "she attracts male admirers the way Hedda did back in the day. And let me tell you, the wolf pack was circling Harmony for hours — much to Hedda's chagrin."

"Oh, really? Hedda didn't like it?"

"As soon as Harmony started flirting with the young men at the party, Hedda had some trivial reason to call the girl over and order her around. It seemed pretty obvious she didn't like sharing the spotlight."

Seymour struck a diva pose and assumed a falsetto. "Get me another punch, dear! I don't care for this ballpoint they gave me; find me the one I brought to sign autographs! I need my wrap from the car!"

Seymour lowered his voice. "I'll give the girl this: She never back-talked her grandmother. Just scampered around and did the woman's bidding. Me? I would have told the old bag to go jump in the duck pond."

"Maybe Harmony simply respects and admires her grandmother. And Hedda's probably used to speaking to Harmony like a child —"

"More like an employee," Seymour said. "Which would be more accurate, because Brainert told me that Harmony isn't just a relative, she works full-time as Hedda's assistant. And, boy, does Hedda work it!"

Now the mail carrier's got me wondering . . .

"What Jack?"

When Grandma Hedda's finally six feet under, what sort of inheritance will Little Miss Harmony get?

"You're saying you suspect her of something?"

I suspect everyone of something, baby. The little miss I suspect of having a motive to off her grandmother. Last night's "accident" with the falling speaker almost flattened Hedda Geist — a dame who treats this girl like a servant, which must chafe, even if the girl doesn't let on. And didn't you just notice Harmony talking to one of Bud's employees?

"Yes, but there's no way Bud Napp could be involved with a murder plot. Not Bud."

Maybe not your auntie's boyfriend, but how well do you know the kid working for him?

"I don't know Dixon at all, except to see him behind the counter at Bud's store."

Well, Harmony seems pretty chummy with him.

"Or it's simply an innocent flirtation — like the big, blond guy who drove up on the black motorcycle."

Either way, I'd say the girl had a motive, and her little friend had the opportunity.

"To do what, Jack?"

To rig that speaker to fall smack on the old diva's noggin, that's what! Pay attention, doll!

"I *am* paying attention, but nobody's saying that speaker was rigged to fall. We'd need evidence for that."

So go get it. Talk to your aunt Sadie's Buddy

boy about it, if you trust him that much. Napp will give you the scoop whether something was hinky.

"Hey, look at that!" Seymour interrupted (not that he *knew* he was interrupting). He was pointing out a poster on the next block. "C'mon, Pen, let's get a move on. I want a look at that poster."

We strode quickly up the block and Seymour rushed toward a poster that someone had just put up. It advertised the screening of an old Gotham Features movie, *Mike O'Bannon of the Sea Witch.*

"Sweet!" Seymour said. "I'm a big fan of the Fisherman Detective! What about you, Pen?"

My brow wrinkled. "The *what* detective?"

"It's a series of movies from the forties, starring stunt-man-turned-actor Pierce Armstrong. He plays a private detective who's also a fisherman."

Fisherman detective? Jack snorted. *The gumshoes I knew only had one thing in common with fish — they drank like them.*

"Rumor has it Pierce Armstrong's going to be one of the surprise special guests this weekend," Seymour said excitedly. "At least, according to Barry Yello's Web site this morning —"

"Armstrong?!" I couldn't believe it.

"Pierce Armstrong is still alive? And he's coming *here* . . . to Quindicott?"

Quick, baby, ask Dizzy Dean what he remembers about Act Two of the guy's life.

"Yes, of course!" I turned to Seymour. "Wasn't Pierce Armstrong mixed up in the death of Irving Vreen, the owner of Gotham Studios?"

"Brother, is *that* an understatement!" Seymour declared.

"Tell me what you know."

"He stood trial for manslaughter, and they sent him to prison for five years."

Lucky he didn't get a dime, Jack said. *Judges and the public liked red meat back in the day . . .*

"I'm sure the district attorney would have stuck him for murder instead of manslaughter," Seymour went on, "but there was a glitch. Vreen died from a stab wound, but Armstrong didn't actually stab him. I don't know a lot of the specifics —"

"It was Hedda," I blurted out. "Armstrong tripped and fell in a restaurant. He knocked Vreen onto a large steak knife, which Hedda was holding."

Seymour looked at me, puzzled. "How do you know that? I mean, it isn't exactly in the mainstream. The only reason I know about Pierce Armstrong going to prison is

105

because of a bio attached to his filmography in *Films of the Forties.* That's the only thing in print about the man, as far as I know, and it's been *out* of print for thirty years."

"Oh . . . er . . . someone told me last night — at the theater."

"Well, Armstrong did hard time in Ossining — you might know it better as Sing Sing. And by the time he got out, his star turn was over."

Tell your mailman pal to keep wagging his tongue, Jack urged. *He's giving us good gravy.*

"So what did Armstrong do?" I asked Seymour. "After he got sprung from Sing Sing."

"Well, people on the East Coast wouldn't hire him, since they still remembered the Vreen murder and held it against him. So Armstrong went back to Hollywood, where he still had friends in the stunt profession. They helped him get back his old career as a stuntman in cowboy pictures. If you know what to look for, you'll see him taking punches or bullets in just about every classic Western, from John Ford's *The Searchers* to *The Gene Autrey Show.*"

"What about Hedda?" I asked.

Seymour shrugged. "She was never charged with anything, as far as I know. In fact, I'm pretty sure she testified against Armstrong at his trial."

I frowned. That didn't seem right at all. "But she was holding the knife."

Seymour shrugged. "If you're implying that Armstrong was railroaded, I won't argue. He's always been one of my favorite B-movie guys, so I'd be the first one to give him the benefit of the doubt. And Hedda paid another way. With Vreen dead, Gotham Features collapsed and her career was over."

"Did you hear that, Jack?" I silently asked.

I heard, baby. If Hedda set up Vreen for murder, then she simultaneously set up her own career for sudden death.

"Then what possible motive could she have had to kill Vreen?" I quietly wondered. "It must have been a tragic accident . . ."

"Yeah," Seymour went on, "today's Tramp Pack of starlets and pop divas may thrive on bad-girl publicity, but back then, scandal was heavy baggage. Hedda's ex-boyfriend had been sent to prison for the death of her married lover. It was obviously too much for the public to accept because no studio would touch Hedda after that. But I guess she made out okay, anyway."

"How do you mean?"

"I chatted with Brainert's soda pop academic pal last night — you remember, Dr. Pepper? He told me Hedda lived the life of Riley after her movie career was over. She married Lincoln Middleton, a television executive. When he died, she inherited a ton of money, along with his family's horse farm in Newport." Seymour snorted. "Nice life, if you can steal it . . ."

CHAPTER 5
AN EXPLOSIVE
NOTION

Thanks for the ride, the three cigarettes,
and for not laughing at my theories on life.
— *The Postman Always Rings Twice,* 1946

The mailman and I arrived at the Cooper
Family Bakery to find it mobbed. Dr. Lilly
hadn't been exaggerating — the line of
customers ran down the block. Some were
locals, but most appeared to be festival attendees.

"Look, Pen!" Seymour elbowed me. "A
friend of ours is almost up to the counter.
C'mon!"

Seymour was fine with cutting the line.
Me? I wasn't so comfortable with the dirty
looks we were getting until I saw who the
"friend of ours" was: Bud Napp.

*This is your chance, baby. Wait till Buddy
boy's all sweetened up with pastries, then grill
him!*

"Check!" I told Jack. But Seymour beat

me to the lanky hardware store owner.

"Hey, Thor, where's your mighty hammer?"

It was Seymour's favorite joke with Bud, who used a ball peen hammer to maintain control over the Quindicott Business Owners Association meetings. Bud used to have a real judge's gavel, until someone lifted it. Now he carried his "good-as-a gavel" to and from our meetings on his tool belt.

"Hi, Bud!" I said brightly, hoping to make up for Seymour's jibe.

"Hello, Pen," Bud said, touching the brim of his Napp Hardware baseball cap. Then he frowned at Seymour. "Cut the crap, Tarnish. I'm not in the mood."

Seymour's eyes bulged. "My, we're testy today. What's eating you?"

Bud was silent as he eyed the people around us. "Nothing I care to talk about."

Noting Bud's surly mood, I quickly changed the subject by explaining my plight. Bud immediately offered to help me transport the coffee and pastries back to the bookshop in his hardware store van.

Ten minutes later, he'd downed two doughnuts and a large coffee, then rolled the truck up to the front of the bakery and unlocked the rear double doors. The crowd parted as Seymour and I loaded up the goodies. The three of us wedged ourselves into the front seat of the van. With my elbow jammed into Bud's overalls, we were off.

During the short drive down Cranberry Street, Jack reminded me to get going with the grilling, and I cleared my throat.

"So, Bud, what did you think about that accident last night at the theater?"

Bud cursed and shook his head. "I won't take the fall for that one. No way," he declared.

"Who's blaming you?" I asked.

"Who isn't? Your pal the Brainiac for starters." Bud's calloused fingers squeezed the steering wheel. "That's the thanks I get for stepping in at the last second when that fancy restoration firm in Newport couldn't be bothered with final fixes."

A bicyclist swerved into Bud's path. He hit the van's brakes and horn. The van lurched, throwing me and Seymour forward and back.

"Woah, Speed Racer, chill!" Seymour cried.

"I've got a good crew. The best!" Bud continued, ignoring Seymour. "Not a bunch of bums hired off the street. My guys know what they're doing!"

"Including Dixon Gallagher?" I asked.

Bud frowned. "I know Dixon looks too

young to be skilled, but believe me, he is. He's been working for me part-time for more than ten years. I taught him some, but he already knew plenty because his dad's a master electrician. When that boy finally gets over his rock-star fantasies and quits his garage band, you can bet he'll quit me, too, and start earning serious money in the union."

"So Dixon hung the speaker?"

"No, Pen. I hung that speaker *myself,* and I know the job was done right."

I watched that cyclist in front of us pedal casually off to the side of the street, as if he hadn't almost been run over. Festival attendees took advantage of Bud's situation and jaywalked in front of his van. Bud cursed and honked again.

"What did Chief Ciders say?" I asked.

"That moron with a badge? He claims crossed electrical wires sparked a fire, which damaged the support rack and caused the speaker to drop onto the stage." Bud slammed the steering wheel. "That dog don't hunt, I tell you! I've been saying we need a real fire marshal in this town, not a bunch of know-nothing volunteers who see two wires within fifty feet of one another and immediately cry 'electrical fire.' "

The street cleared and Bud pushed the

pedal to the metal. I was forced back into my seat again as we raced the final few blocks. Then the van screeched to a halt in front of Buy the Book. Seymour immediately popped the door and hopped out.

I stayed. "Tell me more."

"There was no fire and no fire damage, Pen," Bud asserted. "The ceiling wasn't even scorched, and the fire alarm and sprinkler system never went off."

"What do you think happened?"

"The speaker was hung from the ceiling on a metal brace. One of the struts actually broke. Truth is, Penelope, I think a small explosive was used."

"What?!"

"I know it sounds crazy. But I also know construction materials. A short, electrical fire could not have generated enough heat to snap steel. A long fire might, but a fire of any duration would have left evidence. Smoke, scorching — and we'd have heard the fire alarms go off." A shadow crossed Bud's face. "I'm positive there was an explosion."

"How could someone plant a bomb up there? On the ceiling?"

"Easy. There's a ladder in the wings. It goes right up to a catwalk, which runs along the ceiling above the stage. The speaker mount was within easy reach of anyone standing on that catwalk."

"But if it's vandalism, who did it? And why?"

Bud couldn't answer that one, but I was sure someone else had some theories.

"Jack? Are you hearing this?" I quietly asked the ghost.

Yeah, baby. If someone blew the speaker to kill Hedda, they almost succeeded. It could have been little Harmony who'd arranged it. She was probably the only one who knew her granny was going to make a last-minute appearance.

"You're right, Jack, but if the explosion had a remote device, it could have been triggered by anyone in the audience that night. You heard Seymour — he said Pierce Armstrong might be showing up at the festival. What if he's here already? Hedda testified against him at his trial. What if he was in the audience last night and rigged the speaker to kill Hedda in some kind of long-overdue revenge scheme?"

Good call, baby. After all, old Hedda's been out of the spotlight for decades. Your pal Dr. Lilly said few people even knew she was still alive. It's darn coincidental that the first night she steps into the public light again, bam!

"Hey!" Seymour cried from the sidewalk.

"Are we gonna unload here or what?"

I climbed down out of the van, then turned and leaned through the open window. "We'll talk about this later, Bud."

Bud nodded, then left the cab and unlocked the rear doors. Despite the bumpy ride, everything looked fine. Seymour carried the thermal containers to the front door of the bookshop and set them down on the sidewalk. Rather than fumbling in my purse for the keys, I rang the bell. Sadie would show Seymour where to put the coffee when she came to the door. Meanwhile, I went back to retrieve the neat stack of boxed donuts from the back of Bud's van.

Before I could grab the goodies, Bud jerked his head in the direction of the street. "Here comes trouble," he warned.

I peered around the van's rear door — and my heart sunk.

It was Councilwoman Marjorie Binder-Smith. She'd recently abandoned her wannabe-Hillary hairstyle for a "Nancy Pelosi look" (according to Colleen at the beauty shop). Her formerly short, blonde hair had been dyed chestnut brown and grown to her shoulders; her ubiquitous pantsuits were gone, replaced with calf-length skirts and sweater sets.

A uniform of dark blue followed the

woman as she charged across Cranberry Street, her hair rigid in the spring breeze. The Quindicott police officer had his hat pulled low, his gait was much slower than Marjorie's, his broad shoulders slumped.

Abandoning the donuts, I moved to defuse what looked like a ticking bomb. "Good morning, Councilwoman," I said brightly. "You're looking senatorial today or should I say Madame Speaker-ish?"

The councilwoman ignored my greeting, swung around to face the cop. Only then did I realize the policeman was my friend Eddie Franzetti.

"Look at the condition of this sidewalk," the councilwoman told Officer Eddie with theatrical outrage. "There's garbage everywhere. It's just a disgrace, and a clear violation of the town's sanitation ordinances. I want you to issue a littering ticket to this business, right now."

I looked down at the pavement around my feet. Okay, there were a few gum wrappers, paper cups, and napkins blowing around, but there was still more than an hour before we opened our doors — plenty of time for me to sweep the sidewalk.

"Excuse me!" I interrupted. "We have an entire hour to deal with this little bit of rubbish, and we will."

116

I was proud of taking a stand, but Marjorie Binder-Smith didn't appear impressed with my little protest. In fact, she was wearing the same smirk she'd worn the day she'd temporarily halted the restoration of the Movie Town Theater over some minor ordinance violation. It had taken an entire month for Brainert to straighten out the red tape — and it had cost him and his investors quite a bit of cash, too.

"The ticket stands," the councilwoman declared with a note of finality. But her eyes were still boring into mine, as if waiting for me to challenge her. I was about to open my mouth when Bud Napp stepped between us.

"Now wait just a doggone minute, Councilwoman," Bud said. "Everyone knows that storefront businesses have until opening hours to clean their sidewalks. It's standard practice around here."

"What you people collectively do for your own convenience has nothing to do with the *official* rules on the town's books, Mr. Napp," the woman shot back. "And if it's not on the books, it doesn't exist. Not where I come from."

Where's that? Down in the bunker with Eva and Adolph?

"Shut it!" I told Jack.

The councilwoman wheeled. "What did you say to me, Mrs. McClure?"

Uh-oh. "Did I say that out loud?"

Don't fold now, baby. Show some backbone!

I knew Jack meant well, but I suspected arguing would only make things worse.

"Write that ticket, Officer Franzetti," Marjorie commanded.

Eddie frowned as he opened his ticket book. He began to scribble, his eyes avoiding mine.

"Come on, Marjorie," Bud said, stepping up to the woman. "Cut Pen a break. A warning is all she should get. She doesn't know about the town's ordinance."

"Ignorance of the law is no excuse!" Marjorie asserted.

Bud turned crimson. "Having an ignoramus like you write our laws is no excuse, either!"

Now we're getting somewhere! Jack boomed in my head.

I ignored Jack and jumped between the two. "Look, it's no big deal. Take it easy."

An elbow dug into my ribs and I was thrust aside. "What did you call me?" the councilwoman cried.

"I called you an *ignoramus*," Bud said. "I'd also like to add that you are a petty bureaucrat on some kind of twisted power trip!"

I tried to step between them again, but Seymour pulled me back. "Let Bud go, Pen. Someone should have put a stake in that woman's heart and filled her mouth with garlic a long time ago."

"I heard that!" Marjorie cried, wheeling on Seymour. "You'll be very sorry you said that, Mailman. And that goes double for you, Mr. Napp."

I heard paper tear. Eddie Franzetti slipped the ticket into my hand.

"What's going on here?" Aunt Sadie finally made an appearance, but not from inside the store. She was hurrying up to our group from down the street, carrying a Bogg's Office Supply and Stationery bag. "What's this?" she asked, snatching the ticket from my fingers.

"It's a littering citation," Officer Franzetti informed her.

"A two-hundred-dollar fine!" Sadie cried.

Eddie shrugged. "I don't make the rules."

Marjorie Binder-Smith was still sputtering. Finally she managed a coherent sentence. "I am going to sue you for slander, Bud Napp. You wait and see!" Then she faced Seymour. "And let's just see where you can park that ice cream truck of yours

119

after the *next* town council meeting!"

"You leave my ice cream truck out of this!" Seymour shot back.

Bud stepped up to the councilwoman again. "You have more to worry about that an ice cream truck, Marjorie. I've decided. Right here and now — I'm going to run against you in the fall election. *You* wait and see —"

The woman blinked. "What?"

"I'm going to run against you and I'm going to beat you, too," Bud declared. "And when I take charge, I'm going to teach that band of parasites called a town council that you don't have to stick it to the small-business owners to raise town revenues. Got it?!"

For a moment, it was so quiet you could have heard a gum wrapper drop (which probably would have earned me a second ticket). Marjorie glared at Bud for a good ten seconds but said nothing more to him. Instead, she whirled to face Eddie. "You come with me now. The sidewalk in front of that baker up the street is a mess, and so is the area around your family's pizza kitchen —"

Eddie stopped in his tracks. The council-woman placed her hands on her hips. "Or you can forget writing tickets, and I'll have a conversation with Chief Ciders about how one of his officers shows favoritism in how he applies the law."

Marjorie spun around and headed for Cooper Family Bakery. Eddie hesitated for a moment — no doubt thinking about his wife and children, and pondering what they'd do if he lost his job.

With an air of defeat, he followed the councilwoman across the street.

"That witch," Sadie hissed, narrowing her eyes at the departing sweater set.

"I prefer *vampire,*" Seymour noted.

I turned to Bud. "Did you mean what you said, Bud? Are you really going to run against Marjorie?"

Bud watched the councilwoman's back, squinting like a sniper taking aim. "You bet I am!"

Sadie exchanged glances with me. "Good!" we both said.

I retrieved the donuts and as Bud locked up his truck, I thanked him again.

"No trouble, Pen. Sure you don't need help getting those things inside?" he asked.

I shook my head. "Seymour will help me."

"Then I'm heading over to the theater." Bud climbed into his truck. "I want to check out the place before Brainert opens for the matinee."

"What are you looking for?" I asked.

Bud's face darkened. "I don't know."

Seconds later, the van's engine roared, and Bud was speeding away. When I returned to the front door, Sadie was fumbling in her pocket for the keys.

"Where were you?" I asked.

"That banner behind the podium kept on falling," Sadie said. "I ran to the office supply store to buy industrial-strength staples."

"That's okay, but you might have missed the delivery of Dr. Lilly's books."

Sadie shook her head. "No chance of that. Dr. Lilly's inside —"

"Then why didn't she answer?" said Seymour. "I pressed the doorbell *twice* already!" He paused. "Hey, that's funny. I'm the postman. And I rang twice!"

"I pressed it once myself," I told Sadie, ignoring the sound of Seymour laughing at his own joke, "before the councilwoman stopped by to brighten our day."

Sadie turned the key in the handle and pushed the door open. "I didn't bother with the dead bolt," she said. "Since the store's occupied."

The little bell above the door tinkled as Sadie crossed the threshold. Seymour was next, then me.

"Dr. Lilly?" I called. My voice sounded

hollow in the empty shop.

I set the donuts on the check-out counter and Seymour set down the coffee containers, then tugged a handkerchief out of his pocket and dabbed sweat from his brow.

"I think I deserve a free cup of Joe," he panted. "And another doughnut."

Sadie nodded. "Of course, Seymour. You've been such a great help."

As I entered our bookstore's Community Events room, I noticed how many chairs had been set up and suddenly worried that fifty cups of coffee and forty-eight donuts wouldn't be enough (or rather forty-four, since Bud already had two and Seymour was angling for a second).

Then I moved toward the front of the space, and donuts and coffee became the least of my worries. While we were out, a terrible accident appeared to have taken place. The six-foot stepladder had fallen, obviously slamming against the podium in the center of the low wooden platform that served as our stage.

I rushed forward, seeing the leather sandal on the ground, then the foot it belonged to. Finally my eyes traced the dangling *film noir festival* banner, mounted on the wall behind the podium, the loose material was stretched taut, still clutched in Dr. Irene Lilly's hand.

I knew the woman was dead without touching her. There was so much blood on the hardwood floor I would have to wade through it to reach the body. And it was clear that Dr. Lilly's head had struck the sharp corner of the low platform. Near the base of her skull, grayish brain matter mingled with the blood that stained her sunshine yellow dress.

"Oh, no. Oh, god . . ."

Swallowing a scream, I took two steps backward, then ran to the front of the store.

Chapter 6
Slip and Fall

That's life. Whichever way you turn, fate sticks out a foot to trip you.
— *Detour,* 1945

At some point during the investigation, Chief Ciders's size-twelve boots tramped through Dr. Lilly's blood. Now everywhere the chief walked his heels left faint, half-moon-shaped trails on the polished, hardwood floor. Objectively, I knew they were just little brownish prints, but whenever I saw those tracks I wanted to scream.

Behind the store's counter, Aunt Sadie blew her nose. "What a terrible, terrible accident."

"At least it was quick," Seymour said, attempting to console her — while simultaneously browsing our New Release table. "It was probably, just, you know. Lights out! Like that final episode of *The Sopranos.*"

Sadie glanced toward the archway leading

to the Community Events room and her expression darkened. "They've been in there for over an hour," she said softly. "What are they doing? What are they waiting for?"

For Chief Donut to get a clue, maybe, said Jack, who never was in awe of Chief Ciders's investigative prowess. *And if that's the case, it's going to be a long wait.*

Officer Franzetti stood near the front door, where the chief had posted him. Overhearing Sadie's question, he cleared his throat. "Actually, Ms. Thornton, I think the chief is waiting for a doctor to get here — a new guy, some expert from Newport named Rubino."

Any warm body would be an improvement over that lamebrain with a badge.

"Easy, Jack," I silently told the ghost.

Dismount off that high horse already, doll. I know for a fact you feel the same way about Ciders.

"The chief means well, Jack."

He threw you in the town jail last year!

"But only for one night — and it was all cleared up the next day."

Sadie blew her nose again. "Who is this doctor, Eddie?"

Officer Franzetti shrugged. "I don't know much. Only what I heard from Bull."

Seymour frowned. "Bull McCoy? He's in

there with the chief? How did I miss that no-neck's grand entrance?"

"He came in when you were fetching your mailbag from the trunk of Penelope's car," Sadie informed him.

Seymour faced Eddie. "Then riddle me this, Batman-zetti. How is it that Bull is in *there*, analyzing the crime scene, and you're out here?"

"Bull is, uh . . ." Eddie cleared his throat again. "He's the chief's nephew."

"I recall that!" Seymour threw up his hands. "I also remember that lousy sucker punch he gave me last year when I tried to stop him from hauling Pen off to the hoose-gow — but he's still a rookie! Not to mention a moron! What's the chief thinking using an experienced senior officer as a doorman?!"

Eddie folded his arms tightly but kept silent. Between Councilwoman Binder-Smith ordering him around like some lackey, and now Seymour tactlessly pointing out an embarrassing slight, Eddie was obviously having a horrific day.

Not as horrific as Dr. Lilly, Jack pointed out.

"True," I told the ghost, "but Eddie's my friend. It's time to change the subject of this conversation." I turned toward the front door, where Eddie was still standing.

"Eddie, you were telling us about Dr. Rubino?"

He nodded. "He's some hotshot Newport doctor. A couple of years ago, he did part-time work for the State Medical Examiner's Office. Last month he was recruited by Ciders to act as the local medical examiner on an as-needed basis. I understand he's doing that for other townships — anywhere the local police don't need to call in the Staties."

"Sounds like the chief is thinking ahead," Sadie observed.

Yeah, Jack said. *If this new guy is jake, maybe he can talk cabbage with the Keystone Cops in this cornpone community. Or maybe the doc can pull a Dr. Frankenstein and put a brain into Chief Cipher's thick skull — one that actually works.*

"Jack, you're not being helpful. And it's Ciders, not Cipher."

The man's a cipher to me. And I'll tell you who better be helpful: this new "expert" doctor. If he doesn't rule this crime scene hinky, he'll be batting as lousy as Chief Louie Lunkhead.

"Because?" I silently asked.

Because of last night, baby. You were there. You saw the "accident" at the theater. That's why I know this is all smoke and mirrors. A

128

*slick Houdini act meant to dazzle a dunce —
in this case, Chief Smalltown and Deputy Dull-
ard.*

"Oh, my god, Jack . . . last night . . ."

All morning, I'd been assuming that if
anyone was the target of that "accidental"
falling speaker it was Hedda Geist. But with
Dr. Lilly dead, I realized Jack was right.

"Hedda wasn't scheduled to make a
speech at the Movie Town Theater last
night. Dr. Lilly should have been standing
on ground zero when the boom dropped!"

*Do you remember what your Buddy Boy Mr.
Hardware said? He hung that speaker himself.
And he thinks somebody rigged a metal strut
to break with a small explosion.*

"You're right. And if the explosive was on
a timer, then Irene Lilly should have been
under it, not Hedda. Oh, god, Jack, if I
could have figured that out sooner, I might
have saved Dr. Lilly's life!"

*Easy, baby. Don't go taking on guilt you
don't deserve. You've done that enough already.*

"What are you talking about?"

*That lousy husband of yours, the one who
decided kissing New York concrete was a better solution to his problems than acting like a
man and sticking by his wife and son.*

"Don't bring Calvin up now, Jack. I can't

129

handle it."

There's one truth in life, baby: If someone wants to kill somebody else — or themselves, like your coward of a husband — they're going to do it. Doesn't matter what you, the law, or anyone else says or does. Half the time, killers don't even care if they get caught. They just want to pull the curtain on someone so much they think it's worth throwing their own life away. So believe me, because I'm leveling with you. You weren't the one who killed Dr. Lilly.

"But —"

The scheme failed last night, so the killer staged accident number two in your store. It's clear as day to me.

"But who did this? And why?" I paced the bookstore's aisle, passing McBain and Mc-Crumb, Paretsky and Poe. "Is the killing over now? Or just getting started?"

Listen, baby, you can't solve a puzzle when half the pieces are missing.

"People guess at half-solved puzzles all the time," I pointed out. "What about *Wheel of Fortune?* You can buy a vowel and sound out the words. You don't need all the pieces."

That's a game show, dollface. Guessing's fine when you're playing for Cracker Jack prizes, not when you're dealing out life and death — and believe me, I'm the voice of experience.

"Wait a second, Jack! Can't you . . . I don't know, *commune* with the spirit world? Maybe get in touch with Dr. Lilly? Ask her what happened when she was alone in the store?"

Sorry, baby, but this tomb's all mine. Unless you take me places, I'm a prisoner in this glorified library. And as far as "communing" with my fellow dead, nobody's ever stuck around here to tell me squat. I wish I could call up some company, doll. I can think of a few hot skirts from my past I wouldn't mind looking up.

"And are you sure you don't have any idea what happened in the store while I was out on the sidewalk?"

I'm a ghost, baby, not a magician. My awareness can't be more than one place at one time. When Dr. Lilly bought it in this store, I was with you — in that bakery, in Buddy Boy's van, then out on the sidewalk with the Ticket Issuing Witch of Cornpone County.

I sighed, slumping back against our complete collection of Robert B. Parker. "We don't even know why Dr. Lilly was singled out."

But we can assume a few things . . . like it's a pretty good bet the killer wasn't connected to her life back in California. Punching her ticket on the West Coast would have been a heck of a lot easier than what took place last night. There's also a possibility that a certified crazy is on the loose at this film festival. Maybe all of this weekend's special guests are in danger. Maybe the entire festival crowd.

"Someone's got to help us figure this out, Jack. I'd better talk it over with the chief. . . ."

The chief? Jack snorted. *That piker's not going to listen to you. I doubt he'll even rule this a homicide. And unless the medical man on his way is Dr. Watson, we're on our own proving a clean sneak bump-off.*

The front door rattled. Someone had knocked instead of pressing our doorbell. Officer Franzetti peered through the window.

"He's here," Eddie announced, unlocking the door.

A fit man in his forties squeezed through the crowd of people that had gathered in front of my store. He wore rumpled khakis, a lime-green alligator shirt, collar wrinkled and unbuttoned. Over his arm, he carried a bright yellow J. Crew Windbreaker, which seemed unnecessary, considering the weather report's forecast high for today was in the seventies.

Someone tried to follow the newcomer over the threshold, but Eddie slammed the door in the customer's startled face.

Our visitor ran a hand through his thick, dark brown hair. He had a squarish face with a Roman nose, prominent chin, and large brown eyes. On first impression, he seemed intelligent and attractive.

"Quite a mess out there," he said with a friendly smile.

"Good you got here, doc," said Eddie. "The chief's been waiting."

"I came from Newport as soon as I got the call . . . it's Officer Franchese, isn't it?"

"Franzetti."

"Anyway, the traffic was murder. Did you know there's some kind of film festival going on? The whole town's full of tourists . . ."

The man suddenly caught sight of me and his deep voice trailed off. Then he noticed Sadie behind the counter and Seymour slumped in one of our Shaker-style rockers.

"Excuse me for being rude," he said smoothly, his big, sleepy brown eyes returning to mine.

"This is Mrs. McClure," Eddie said.

"Penelope," I volunteered.

"She owns this store —"

"With my aunt Sadie," I interjected.

The man's smile seemed genuine. He was tanned and athletic — not quite as handsome as Robert Mitchum playing the leading-man doctor in *Where Danger Lives,* but very close.

Randall Rubino stood a few inches taller than I, but he was probably even taller. I was wearing low heels, while the doctor wore scuffed boat shoes with flat rubber soles. He was also carrying a large beige canvas backpack over his shoulder. Was his medical kit in there? I wondered.

He stepped forward, extended his tanned right hand. "My name is —"

"Dr. Rubino," Chief Ciders's voice boomed from the archway. "Your services are required back here immediately."

"Right, Chief Ciders. On my way," Rubino replied. He shook my hand and offered a wink to go along with it. I couldn't help but breathe a little easier — and I couldn't fault Dr. Rubino's bedside manner, either.

Sadie noticed the wink, too. She quickly sidled up to me. "Dr. Rubino seems quite nice, don't you think?"

What a stuffed monkey, Jack scoffed. *This guy's got Ivy League written all over him, which means you won't be able to tell him a thing. He'll already know it all.*

Ignoring Jack, I watched Dr. Rubino cross

the sales floor on his way to the Community Events space.

"I'm sure he's married," I quietly told Sadie.

Inside of ten seconds, Sadie was beside Eddie whispering questions. Finally, she came back to me.

"Eddie says he's divorced," she confided, "and that's why he's doing this work for Ciders — and any other townships in the area that need his services. Apparently he used to have a lot of money; now he has a lot less, but who cares about that? I think he's quite a catch."

Go for it, Betty Boop. See if I care.

"Stop it! I'm not interested!"

Sadie frowned and I realized I'd said those words aloud.

"Well, you don't have to decide right now," Sadie replied with a huff. "Give the man a chance to ask you out for coffee!"

I squeezed my eyes shut. "I'm sorry, Aunt Sadie, I didn't intend to say that to you."

"It's all right, dear," she said, patting my shoulder. "We're all a little rattled by Dr. Lilly's fall."

Ten minutes passed, then fifteen. Sadie rearranged books on the film noir display. I moved to the window and watched the crowd thicken outside. The store's opening hour came and went without anyone emerging from the Events room. I wondered if Buy the Book was going to open at all today — though that was probably the least of our worries at this point.

Suddenly Seymour pushed himself out of the wooden rocker. "That's it! I'm out of here," he declared, checking his Wonder Woman watch. "It's after ten, and I've waited long enough for Chief Ciders to take my statement. If Barney Fife needs to reach me, he knows where I'll be — working my route, 'cause the mail is like showbiz. It must go on!"

Officer Franzetti stepped forward. "The chief told me everyone stays here until he takes your statements."

"The chief is a local yokel, Pizza Boy," Seymour shot back. "His authority stretches about as far as Quindicott Pond. The federal government's interest in an efficient mail service supersedes his meager jurisdiction."

Eddie put his hands on his gun belt. "Cut the double talk, Seymour. You're not going anywhere, no matter what you say —"

Seymour flushed crimson. "Listen, Franzetti! Step out of the way and you won't get hurt —"

"All right, all right, what's going on here?" Chief Ciders barked. He tramped into the

store with Dr. Rubino and young Bull Mc-
Coy in tow.

Yep, quipped Jack. *McCoy is Chief Donut's
nephew all right. Same sloped brow and slack
jaw. Same funny-farm stare, too.*

"Look, Chief, I've got a job to do, too,"
Seymour complained. "Either detain me or
let me get back to it."

Ciders nodded to Eddie. "Let the man go.
Tarnish has mail to mis-deliver. I'll get his
statement later, for what it's worth."

"So, you're finished with your investigation?" Seymour asked as he inched toward
the front door.

"The preliminary phase," Ciders replied,
giving Seymour his back.

Seymour stopped. "Well?"

Ciders frowned, looked up from the clipboard in his hand. "Don't you have work to
do?"

Seymour nodded.

"Then get the heck out of here!"

Seymour shrugged and opened the door,
smacking into the crowd of film festival fans
waiting for the store to open. "Clear a path,
people! Official government employee coming through!"

"Hey, in there, are you *ever* going to
open?!" someone yelled from the crowd.

Eddie closed the door.

I faced Chief Ciders. "Well? Have you completed your investigation?"

The beefy man sighed. "We're finished. And you can open, once we're sure you're providing a safe working environment. What was this woman, Dr. Lilly, doing on your ladder? Was she a paid employee?"

"She was an academic, a film historian, and an author. She was helping us get ready for her book signing."

"I see," said the chief. "Your store does carry insurance, right?"

"Of course, but why would that matter?"

"Because, Mrs. McClure, you allowed her to climb a ladder unsupervised. That's negligence on your part. Simply put: Dr. Lilly had a fatal accident while working in your store —"

"Accident!" I cried.

I warned you, Jack gloated.

CHAPTER 7
A DOCTOR
IN THE HOUSE

My, my, my. Such a lot of guns around town and so few brains.
— Philip Marlowe, *The Big Sleep,* 1946

"Yes, Mrs. McClure, an accident," Chief Ciders reiterated. "Dr. Lilly fell off a ladder —"

"No! She was pushed!" I blurted out.

Bull McCoy snorted. "You were right, Uncle . . . I mean, *Chief.* You said she was gonna try and call it murder!"

"Shut up, Bull," Ciders warned.

"How do you know it wasn't murder?" I demanded.

"As I see it, Dr. Lilly tried to fix the banner," Ciders said. "She lost her balance and fell. She died when she slammed her head against the corner of the stage."

"It *looks* like an accident," I replied, "but that's the diabolical part. Don't you see? Someone attempted to drop a speaker on

Dr. Lilly last night —"

"You've got your facts wrong there, Mrs. McClure," said the chief. "Brainert Parker reported to me that it was a former actress — someone named Hedda Geist — who almost got clobbered."

"It was Dr. Lilly who was supposed to be on stage. Hedda was under the speaker when it fell, but she only came up to the stage at the last minute —"

"That's enough, Mrs. McClure," the chief interrupted.

"At least let me finish explaining!"

The chief waved his hand. "What happened at the theater last night was an accident, too, that's all. Clearly the result of faulty construction." Ciders rubbed his fleshy chin. "Makes me wonder if the Movie Town was built to code. Better check in with the Town Council on that one. Marjorie's sure to be interested —"

"Two accidents in two days? One nearly fatal, the other deadly. And both involving the same woman?" I shook my head. "That's too much coincidence for me. And it should be for you, too. I want another official opinion —"

"That's why I'm here, Mrs. McClure," said Dr. Rubino, stepping forward before I could suggest that the state police be

140

called in.

"I thoroughly examined Dr. Lilly's body," Rubino continued. "While I still have to perform an autopsy to be absolutely certain, my preliminary findings confirm Chief Ciders's theory. Dr. Lilly appeared to have died of an injury to the skull. The scene itself makes it clear the injury was inflicted by the edge of your stage. We have a fallen ladder at the scene, and we have a witness in your own aunt, the last person to see the deceased alive. She mentioned to the chief that Dr. Lilly was indeed trying to hang a banner, and wasn't it true that your store was locked from the inside?"

I wanted to scream, but I knew it wouldn't give the man confidence in my sanity.

"Mrs. McClure?" Rubino pressed. "Was the store locked?"

"Yes," I said, clenching my fists. "The store was locked, but Dr. Lilly could have let someone in herself. The dead bolt wasn't thrown, and the killer could have relocked the door simply by setting the handle on lock from the inside and slamming it shut when departing —"

"If I had to render an opinion right now," Dr. Rubino interrupted, "I'd say Dr. Lilly's death was a tragic *accident*. Nothing more."

"You're wrong."

You tell him, baby!

Dr. Rubino's dark brown eyebrows lifted in absolute surprise. Clearly he was used to having the last word at a crime scene. Having his conclusions so directly and adamantly challenged was an obvious shock. He glanced at Ciders, who shrugged and looked away.

"Mrs. McClure . . ." The doctor stepped closer. He lowered his voice. "If Dr. Lilly were *actually* murdered — that is to say, if a person had entered this store and killed her, there would have been clues that I would not have missed."

"Such as?" I folded my arms and tapped my foot.

"Dr. Lilly would have resisted an attack, you see?" he explained in painfully slow syllables. "If she fought and the killer had to subdue her, there would be marks on her arms, perhaps her throat."

The doctor made gestures to his arm and neck, as if I were still learning the names of body parts. "These bruises or scratches are called 'defensive' wounds." He put air quotes around "defensive."

Will ya tell this clown you've learned the alphabet already? Didn't I tell you Ivy Leaguers are the worst?

"Yes, yes," I told the doctor (and Jack). "I

know what defensive wounds are. But what if someone pushed Dr. Lilly off that ladder? Or pulled the ladder out from under her?"

Dr. Rubino rubbed his forehead. He glanced at Chief Ciders, who suddenly looked our way again with a questioning expression.

I congratulated myself. Now at least the chief was considering the possibility of foul play!

"Well . . . I suppose it's *possible*," Dr. Rubino was forced to admit. He frowned and rubbed the back of his neck. "But it would be a one-in-ten chance that Dr. Lilly's head would strike the platform. For someone to push her so she landed in just such a way as to cause death . . ." His voice trailed off and he shook his head. "No, I just don't see that as likely."

Chief Ciders sighed and looked away again.

"But someone could have pushed her," I quickly countered, trying to pry the chief's mind back open. "That same someone could have dragged Dr. Lilly to the stage and *made sure* her head struck it before she had a chance to fight back."

"Chief, the ambulance is here," Officer Franzetti called.

Ciders slapped his knee with the clipboard. "Good. We've spent enough time here."

"But —"

"That's enough, Mrs. McClure," said the chief. "You're letting your imagination run away with you." He glanced around at the novels on our shelves. "It's no wonder," he muttered condescendingly, "the business you're in."

"I didn't *imagine* last night's attempt on Dr. Lilly's life —"

"It was an *accident*," Ciders shot back. "Last night and this morning, and that's how I'm reporting both incidences." The chief moved to the front door, and then turned to face me. "If I were you, Mrs. Mc-Clure, I'd forget about trying to sell that cock-and-bull story of yours and hire a good lawyer. Your business is likely to get slapped with a lawsuit over this. So brace yourself for more bad news: My accident report will probably send your insurance premiums soaring."

A short time later, Chief Ciders and his nephew were parting the crowd in front of my store to make way for a grim procession. Along with everyone else, I watched the paramedics carry Dr. Lilly's bagged-up body to the waiting ambulance. Her remains would be delivered to the local hospital, where Dr. Rubino was scheduled to perform an autopsy later in the day.

Officer Franzetti lingered behind and, to my surprise, so did Dr. Rubino. "You don't mind if I browse a little, do you?" the doctor asked me. "It's my day off, and I haven't read a good book in awhile."

"Be our guest," Sadie called when I failed to answer.

The doctor nodded then put a hand on my shoulder. "Would you like a prescription, Mrs. McClure?" he said quietly. "I can write one for you, just something to calm your nerves. I'm actually a little worried about your reaction to all of this."

I fixed a level gaze on him. "I'm not in shock, Doctor. And I'm not delusional, either, despite what Chief Ciders thinks."

You tell him, baby.

I swallowed my reply to Jack. I couldn't risk a non sequitur now.

Good idea, doll. The doc's already sized you up for crazy pills. Better not give him cause to send you to a cackle factory.

"A what?" I asked the ghost.

A cackle factory. Don't you have those nowadays?

"Have what exactly?"

A funny farm? Nut house? Mental hospital?

145

Insane asy—

"Okay! I get it!"

The doctor frowned. "Mrs. McClure?"

I blinked. "Yes?"

"Events like this can be very stressful for a person. Perhaps you should take a rest. The chief mentioned that you and your aunt live upstairs. Maybe if you lie down, take a nap for a few hours —"

I shook my head. "Thank you for your concern, but I'm fine. And I have a business to run."

"I understand . . . well, you do have a very nice store, I must say." He smiled and made a show of glancing around. "I'll just browse a little then. You don't mind?"

I folded my arms. "Be our guest."

While the doctor began browsing the store, Eddie approached me. "You okay, Pen?"

I took a shaky breath, still upset over my clash with Chief Ciders. "Life goes on," I told Eddie. I glanced in Rubino's direction. He was leafing through a frontlist Tess Gerritsen in the New Release section. "Looks like I've already got one customer . . . and we've got to open the store for the others waiting out there, even if we don't have a guest speaker for our morning event."

"You don't have a place to *put* a guest

speaker, either."

I squeezed my eyes shut, considering the physical state of the Community Events room. It would have to be cleaned before the public could come into the store. But the thought of cleaning up all that blood made me shudder.

"I guess I'd better get started," I said softly. When I tried to walk away, however, Eddie gripped my arm.

"No, Pen, let me do it. It's the least I can do for writing you that littering ticket this morning."

"Oh, Eddie, that's very sweet. But I couldn't ask you —"

"It's Saturday night to me," he said with a shrug. "You have no idea what I see on that highway after the bars close. It's nothing I haven't seen before."

"But —"

"Thank you, Eddie," Sadie cut in, stepping up to us. "It's above and beyond the call of duty, and Pen and I appreciate it. Just come with me, and I'll show you where we keep the cleaning supplies so you can get started."

Eddie smiled, squeezed my shoulder, and then followed Sadie into the Community Events room, which led to the restrooms, store room, and supply closet.

When they were gone, I noticed that Dr. Rubino had discovered our Film Noir Festival display near the front window. He appeared to be quite interested in one book in particular, *Portraits in Shadow,* a coffee-table book written by Hedda Geist-Middleton.

The oversized book of photos featured dramatic black-and-white stills from Hedda's Gotham Features years. The small amount of accompanying text amounted to short anecdotes from Hedda about shooting her movies and working with leading men and directors.

Dr. Rubino looked up suddenly and caught me staring. "This is an older book, isn't it?" he asked.

I nodded. A small New England publisher had released the book about two years before, without any publicity. It sold few copies, according to the publisher's sales rep, who'd confided in Sadie and me that Hedda was lucky they'd kept the book in print. This weekend's film festival was a chance for her to move out their inventory and, with the help of Barry Yello's Web site, maybe even get some national buzz going.

"Hedda Geist herself will be signing these books in the Community Events room, at five o'clock today," I told Rubino.

He smiled. "Hedda mentioned coming to Quindicott for a film festival, but I lost track of the date. I hadn't realized it was this weekend."

"You *know* Hedda? Personally?" I asked, more than a little surprised.

"Yes, she and her . . ." Dr. Rubino paused. "Well, the long and short of it is that Hedda is a patient of my Newport practice."

I was about to question him further when the delivery bell rang. "Excuse me, I have to get this."

I unlocked the front door to find Vinny Nardini, our DDS delivery man, standing there in his brown uniform beside several boxes on a dolly.

"Hi-Yo!" Vinny said with a grin. "Opening the store late today, Pen? You and your aunt party too hearty at that Finch Inn last night?"

I frowned down at the boxes. They were marked *San Fernando University Press,* and I realized with a shiver that these were the very books Dr. Lilly was supposed to be signing for us at noon. The shipment had finally arrived, safe and sound, and I felt tremendously guilty that I'd failed to keep the book's author that way inside my own store.

Vinny scratched his brown beard. "Penelope?"

"Come in, Vinny, come in!" called Aunt Sadie, walking up behind me. "You know where to take those, don't you?"

"Sure thing," said Vinny, whistling as he wheeled the dead author's books toward the back of the store.

CHAPTER 8
DEAD SPEAKERS
DON'T TALK

Funny how gentle people get with you once you're dead.
> — *Sunset Boulevard,* 1950

Standing beside me, Sadie put her arm around my shoulders. "What shall we do with Dr. Lilly's books, do you think? Put them on the selling floor with some sort of note?"

I shook my head. "To tell you the truth, I'd feel terrible hawking them today."

Sadie nodded. "You're right. Let's hold them in the storeroom for now. I'm sure Dr. Lilly would want her book available to the public, but I think it's best if we let Brainert handle the announcement of what happened. We'll just focus on other books today and let the poor woman rest in peace."

"Aunt Sadie," I said in a quiet voice, "what do *you* think about Dr. Lilly's death? You heard what I said to Chief Ciders. Do you think her death is suspicious, too? Or do you believe Ciders is right, and that she simply fell by accident?"

My aunt's arm fell away from my shoulders and she actually looked a little miffed. "I can't believe you just asked me that, Penelope!"

"I'm sorry," I said quickly. "I didn't mean to put you on the spot —"

"Chief Ciders is the biggest blowhard in this town! His opinion isn't worth a hill of beans, and you've proved it more than once in the last few years. That's what's eating him, Pen. He's obviously determined never to let you get the best of him again. Well, I believe you, dear, and I believe *in* you."

Sadie smiled at me then; and, boy, did I need that vote of confidence.

"Thank you," I whispered.

"Sweetie, you're a wonderful niece, and a very sharp young woman." She put her arm back around my shoulders and squeezed. "Don't you think I feel terrible about leaving that poor woman in our store alone? Whatever I can do to help, you let me know. And for goodness' sake don't you go letting Ciders's idiotic bluster discourage you from following your instincts. They've been good in the past, and I have no doubt that whatever track you're on, it's the right one."

Bang, Bang, Bang!

Sadie and I jumped at the noise, then looked up to find a twentysomething with tattoos, a nose ring, and a SIN CITY T-shirt knocking on the glass window of our front door. "Open up already!" his muffled voice demanded. Then he turned back to his group of young friends and they all laughed.

I sighed. The ambulance, cops, and mysterious body bag wheeled out of our store had made us a local spectacle. The crowd out front was even bigger now, snaking down the sidewalk, spilling into the street. Waiting customers were gossiping with curious tourists. Some were laughing and pointing.

I stepped closer to the front window, overheard some snippets of conversation. "I can't believe it, but I think these people believe we just staged a publicity stunt."

"That's awful!" said Aunt Sadie. "Who would think we'd do such a thing?!"

"It's Film Noir week. Dark and cynical are the words of the day."

"Then I guess we'd better open soon," said Sadie, shaking her head, "or we're liable to get another ticket from the councilwoman for unlawful assembly."

"What do we do about the twelve o'clock signing?" I studied the crowd, hoping to spot Brainert. "Should we just send the

153

people away? I don't relish announcing our store's noontime speaker is now a corpse on its way to an autopsy."

"There are a lot of authors scheduled for signings this weekend," said my aunt. "Perhaps we can call someone, ask him or her to step in."

"Isn't that Maggie Kline out there, speaking to a group of college kids?" I pointed to the sixtysomething woman with the red glasses and bouncy, scarlet-streaked, cocoa-colored curls.

"The screen and television writer?" Sadie peered through the plate glass, into the crowd. "Oh, yes, that's her. I spoke to her briefly at the party last evening. She's quite smart and articulate. And we have at least three of her suspense novels in stock. She penned them years ago, but their backlist sales have held up well. Do you think, since she's here now, she might step in for Dr. Lilly?"

I checked my watch. "Ms. Kline's already scheduled for a Saturday signing, but there's such a huge crowd here now, I bet she wouldn't mind doing a little Q and A for us. How do you feel about introducing her?"

"I'd love to!" said Sadie. "I've read her books, of course, and seen most of those television shows she used to write for . . .

Let me see now . . . there was *The Brutal Streets, Manhunt, Shield of Justice.* I can certainly think of a few good questions for her if the audience can't."

In the next few minutes, our spirits brighter, Sadie and I helped Officer Eddie finish cleaning the Community Events room, and our young part-time clerk, Mina Griffith, arrived to start her shift.

"I think we should call Seymour, too," I told Sadie. "We'll really need him for crowd control."

She nodded, dialed his cell, and got right through. "He'll be here in ten minutes," she said.

Finally, Mina braced herself behind the counter; Aunt Sadie positioned herself inside the Events room; and I opened the front door. The murmuring, laughing people flowed in like a river released from a dam, many of them heading right into the adjoining space to grab seats for our noontime event.

I stood near the front of the store, watching for Maggie Kline — until a large man in a Hawaiian shirt of neon pink and lime green blotted out my view of practically everything else.

"Good morning . . . you're Pen McClure right?" asked the man. "You run this store?"

"Yes, with my aunt," I said, weaving and bobbing to see around the man's bulky form.

"I'm here for the film festival, and I was just wondering what the deal was? With the ambulance and police, I mean. Somebody have a stroke or heart attack in here or something?" He lowered his voice. "It wasn't Hedda Geist, was it? The corpse they wheeled out looked pretty small, like a woman."

I moved my gaze north of the large, Hawaiian-shirted obstruction and immediately recognized the round baby face and blond ponytail of the famous Webmaster Barry Yello — the young guy who'd introduced Dr. Lilly the night before.

"Oh, my goodness," I murmured. "You're Barry Yello, aren't you?"

"Rumor has it."

I quickly pulled him aside. In hushed tones, I told Barry that his colleague Dr. Lilly was the one who'd died in our store. "She fell from a ladder."

"God, that's awful." Barry shook his head. "I better get the news out on my Web site."

"Oh, no! Don't do that! Not until we're sure her family's been notified."

"Oh, yeah. Right." Barry frowned. "Sorry, but I didn't know her that well. I mean, I learned a lot from her books. And she seemed like a nice lady, but as far as her personal life?" He shrugged. "I think she's married, but I don't have any contact info or anything. Wish I could be more helpful. You're better off tracking down Dean Pepper for that . . . or Professor Brainert Parker . . ."

"I will."

"Like I said, I'm sorry about what happened; but I'm glad it wasn't Hedda Geist." He glanced around the store. "You haven't seen her around this morning, have you?"

"Hedda? No. She's not expected here for her signing until five."

"Her *signing?*" Barry squinted. "What's she going to sign, publicity stills?"

We were standing near the Film Noir Festival display, so I just pointed to Hedda's oversized photo book.

"Oh, yeah. *Portraits in Shadow.*" He grabbed a copy off the stack. "I forgot about this thing. But then it was pretty forgettable. The text is disappointingly minimal . . . more like extended captions. She should have hired someone like me to write a real book for her. It's no wonder it didn't make any waves. I mean, she didn't do much to promote it, either."

"Well, she's promoting it *now,*" I pointed out.

"True." Barry nodded. "This weekend's pretty much Hedda's first public appearance since her film career ended back in the day. That's why I'm looking forward to interviewing her on stage this afternoon. I'm streaming the whole thing on my Web site and uploading a choice segment onto YouTube . . ."

Oh, yeah? Jack said in my head. *Then why don't you ask her the sixty-four-million-dollar question: whether she knifed Irving Vreen by accident or let him have it in cold blood.*

"Jack, be quiet," I shot back. "I'm in a jam here!"

". . . anyway, Mrs. McClure, you can see why I was stressed about the corpse and wanted to make sure that it wasn't Hedda . . ." As Barry continued to yammer on, I realized that he had a book to hawk this weekend, too.

"Listen, Barry," I interrupted, "I have a thought. Since you're here now, would you mind taking the book-signing spot left by the late Dr. Lilly? You could even say a few words about her since you enjoyed her books on film history —"

"Oh, no," Barry said quickly. "I'm sorry, Mrs. McClure, but I wouldn't know what

158

to say. I mean, I'm great at writing on the 'Net, but speaking at length right off the top of my head with nothing written down first?" He shrugged. "Not good. I'll just stick my foot in it. And my signing's already set for Sunday. Let's keep it that way, okay? I've already announced it on my site and . . ."

As Barry kept talking, I went back to frantically searching the crowd for Maggie Kline. It wasn't that we couldn't just cancel the noon event. Sending the crowd away would be easy to do. But it would be a shame, considering this was the first festival event our store was hosting. We might not ever get the people to come back to our store again. And we had too many books in stock to let potential book buyers slip away. I was sad about Dr. Lilly, but I still had a boy to feed and clothe and put through college.

"Ms. Kline!" I called out, interrupting the beefy Webmaster. "Excuse me, Barry. I'm not usually this rude, but I'm a little desperate right now. Ms. Kline, over here!"

As I waved the woman over, Barry's expression soured. "Why are you calling *her* over here?"

"What's the matter?" I whispered. "Are you two having some sort of feud?"

"No," he said shortly. "I've never even met the woman."

Maggie Kline strode over to us, an expression of curiosity on her broad face. Her features weren't delicate or conventionally pretty, yet she had a very attractive air about her, a glowing confidence. She had a fit figure, too. She was tall and slender, and despite being in her sixties, looked great in her youthful clothes.

Over the years, I'd seen older women try to dress younger and fail miserably at it — usually because their skirts were too high, their dresses too tight or too revealing of flesh that just wasn't as elastic, smooth, and blemish-free as it once was. But Maggie's red-framed glasses, snug red T-shirt, and low-waisted khaki pants made her look carefree and approachable. Even her shoes were whimsical — instead of heels or boots, she wore black Keds.

"Hello," she said, walking up to me. "Do I know you?"

I introduced myself and explained that Dr. Lilly just expired in a freakish accident. I didn't see the need to go into my theories on how and why — not yet, anyway.

Maggie Kline's face fell at my news. "That's awful! The poor woman . . ."

"Yes, well, you see, Ms. Kline —"

160

"Call me Maggie."

I nodded. "The reason I called you over here, Maggie, wasn't just to tell you the bad news. I'd like to ask a huge favor."

"Name it."

"The store needs another speaker at noon. Would you mind very much appearing in Dr. Lilly's place?"

Maggie's expression went from expectant to puzzled. "I don't know," she said, clearly taken by surprise. "It's a little creepy, isn't it?"

She glanced at Barry standing beside me, as if to see what he thought of this idea. He just shook his head and shrugged.

"We have such a big crowd here," I explained, "and so many authors scheduled this weekend already. My aunt and I just felt it made sense to see if anyone would want to step in . . ."

Maggie shifted. "I don't know if I'm prepared. I mean, the crowd's expecting Irene Lilly to speak —"

"You wouldn't have to give a prepared speech or even say anything to the crowd about Dr. Lilly," I assured her. "My aunt will handle that. Then she'll introduce you, tell everyone about what you've written and done, and then she'll start a Q and A off and throw it open to the audience. It should be fun. And we already have your suspense novels stacked up in the Events room for you to sign."

"Holy crow," Maggie muttered, obviously put off. "You people don't miss a beat, do you? Dr. Lilly's not even cold yet, but the show must go on, huh?"

I blinked, a little stunned — and embarrassed — at Maggie's bluntness. "Oh, well . . . I, uh . . . I'm sorry you see it that way . . . maybe we're asking too much —"

"Mrs. McClure just wants to keep the crowd happy," Barry Yello loudly spoke up. "You don't have to bust her chops over it, Kline."

"Excuse me, Mr. Yello," said Maggie. "Did anyone ask *you* to speak?"

Barry folded his thick arms and narrowed his eyes. "As a matter of fact, Mrs. McClure here asked me to do exactly that *before* she asked you."

"What's that supposed to mean?"

"Do the math," said Barry.

"Oh, I see," Maggie replied. "You're saying that I'm sloppy seconds?"

"Oh, no," I cried, "that's not true at all. Please, *please* don't argue."

"Whatever," said Barry with a wave of his hand.

Maggie put her hands on her hips.

"Clearly, Yello here thinks he's hot stuff. Well, go ahead, Bad Barry . . ." Maggie tapped her wristwatch. "It's almost noon now, and you obviously don't have anything better to do."

Barry looked away. "Actually, I *do*. I'm sorry, Mrs. McClure. I wanted to catch Dr. Lilly's speech, but now I can't, *obviously* . . . so I'll be going . . ."

"If you must," I said. Although my remark was meant rhetorically, Barry went on as if Maggie and I were hanging on every moment of his afternoon schedule.

"Oh, yes, I must," he replied. "There's the showing of *Double Indemnity*. They're only showing it once this weekend, and I don't want to miss it. Then I've got to get back to my room at the Comfy Time Motel to launch the discussion of the film on my Web site. Then I have to review my questions for Hedda Geist's appearance on the Movie Town stage. So you see, I do have better things to do."

"Fine!" Maggie Kline said. "Then zip it already and go!"

The rivalry between these two was more than obvious, but I couldn't imagine what was behind their animosity. Barry claimed they'd never met before. Was his claim a lie? And if it was, why would he bother lying about it?

"All right, Mrs. McClure," Maggie said after Barry left. "I'll step in for you . . . for Dr. Lilly, I mean. I guess it's the least I can do, considering you bothered to stock my books."

"Oh, thank you! Thank you so much!"

"Really, it's no big deal. I just had to get used to the idea. The shock of hearing about that poor woman and all . . . so where do I go for this public appearance?" She glanced around. "This is the first time I've been in your store, so you'll have to show me the way."

"Of course." I led Maggie through the archway and into the Community Events room. "If you don't mind my asking," I said as we walked, "what's the beef between you and Barry? He said he'd never met you before, but you two were talking as if you did know each other."

"Oh, we *know* each other — over the Web. We've just never met in person. Yello's taken shots at everything I've written — TV, movies, books. I've fired back with my own review of his ridiculous *Bad Barry* book. He's an absolute jerk, in case you haven't noticed."

I didn't know what to say to that. So I just quickened my steps to the front of the room and introduced my aunt to Maggie.

While they were talking, I thought about what Maggie had just said. Barry Yello struck me more as young and awkward than an "absolute jerk." In her own way, Maggie herself was rather a difficult personality. On the other hand, she could have a legitimate grievance. I'd never read Barry's reviews of her novels and teleplays. They could have been unduly vicious and personal. The World Wide Web didn't always bring out the best in people.

You got it wrong, doll, Jack quipped in my head. *There's plenty of people who never had any "best" inside them to be brought out in the first place.*

Jack's voice got me to thinking again about our case. "Barry was on that stage, too, last night. He used the microphone before Dr. Lilly."

You're right, baby. And I know what you're thinking. There might be a whole lotta people like Maggie out there, who aren't too keen on seeing Barry write another World Wide word.

"Hey, Pen!" Seymour Tarnish called, coming in to help with the event. "I need to talk to you." Pulling me aside, he told me that there was some sort of problem out front.

"Great, that's all I need." I followed him to find three people in formal clothing

165

standing near our entrance: two men in suits and ties, and a tall blonde woman in pressed black slacks and a blue blazer.

"They're press," Seymour whispered.

"What?"

I talked with the small group and discovered that earlier in the week, Dr. Lilly had invited them personally to attend her lecture today.

"So what's going on?" said one of the men from a Newport newspaper. "This gentleman" — he pointed to Seymour — "told us that Dr. Lilly isn't speaking today, or any day. What's that supposed to mean?"

"Yes," said the tall blonde. "We're here to cover the publication of her book. Aren't you hosting a signing with her?"

I glanced at Seymour. He shrugged.

"I'm so sorry . . ." I explained that Dr. Lilly had had an accident, but that I couldn't release much more information than that until the authorities contacted her family. "Would you care to stay for our stand-in author? She's had quite an accomplished career as a novelist and screenwriter."

The press people glanced at each other, shook their heads, and turned to go. "Sorry, not interested."

I glanced at Seymour again as we watched

them leave. "How odd," I said. "Is that a news van out there?"

Seymour nodded. "Yep, I can see the TV satellite antennae."

"Maybe I misjudged how well Dr. Lilly is known," I murmured.

"What do you mean?" Seymour asked.

"I mean, her backlist is respectable, but it's never sold any better than any other film historian's work. She's an academic not a media personality. This is the first I've ever heard of a wonky film studies book getting press attention."

"Mrs. McClure!" Mina called from the check-out counter. "I'm having that scanning issue again!"

"Sorry, Seymour, it's back to work for me — and for you, too." I jerked my thumb toward the Events room. "Get yourself in there and make sure the audience behaves."

Seymour saluted. "Aye, aye, captain! Your crowd control expert's in the house!"

CHAPTER 9
DARK DOINGS AT
THE LIGHTHOUSE

You think you know something, don't you?
You think you're the clever little girl who
knows something. There's so much you
don't know . . .
— *Shadow of a Doubt,* 1943

About ninety minutes later, the clapping in
the Events room signaled the end of the
program. Then the author signing began,
and Seymour marshaled the crowd in his
own inimitable fashion.

"Come on, people, make a line! Don't you
remember your kindergarten fire drills?
Nice and straight please, so you can buy
one of Ms. Kline's pretty books and have
her sign it for you!"

I helped with the purchases, and before
long the crowd of nearly one hundred
people dwindled to less than ten. That's
when Mina called me over to the check-out
counter again. Only this time it wasn't a

scanning issue.

"Mrs. McClure! Phone!"

I left Sadie with the remaining people and went to pick up the call. "Hello?" I said. "Buy the Book. Penelope Thornton-McClure speaking."

"I know!" replied a woman on the other end of the line. It was the slightly scratchy soprano voice of Fiona Finch, co-owner of Finch Inn. "Pen, I need to speak with you urgently because I'm worried about interrupting her appearance. And I don't how she'll react to this news. I hope you can break it to her easy."

"Whoa, slow down, Fiona. What news? And who's 'she'?"

"Dr. Lilly," said Fiona.

I tensed. "What's wrong?"

"Someone's broken into her suite and robbed her!"

I took a breath. "Fiona, are you sitting down?"

"No. Why should I?" she asked. "I was the one calling you with the shocking news. Isn't Dr. Lilly at your store, giving a speech right now?"

"Fiona, sit down."

"Okay, okay, I'm sitting!"

"Dr. Lilly isn't giving a speech right now because Dr. Lilly is dead."

"What!"

"Listen to me, Fiona, this is very important. Do you know what's missing from her suite?"

"No, I don't. Dr. Lilly wasn't staying in the main house. She wanted more privacy, so she took the bungalow in the converted Charity Point Lighthouse."

"Are you sure someone broke in?"

"Oh, yes. One of my maids came running back to our main house. She was frantic because the front door was obviously broken open and things were scattered about. She knew right away someone had violated the room, and she didn't want to be accused of stealing."

Hear that, baby? Jack purred in my head. *The dead dame's hotel room was tossed. If that's not a lead, I'm the Spirit of Christmas Past.*

"Stay put, Fiona, I'll meet you at the inn!" I said and slammed down the phone.

Seymour and I arrived at the Finch Inn around two that afternoon. Fiona greeted us at the front desk and took us to the parking lot, where the inn's guest transport vehicles were all neatly parked in a row. Seymour moved for the driver's seat, but Fiona immediately blocked him.

"Come on, Fiona," Seymour whined. "Let *me* drive."

"No way!" Fiona told the off-duty mailman as she vigorously shook her head. "I've seen the way you handle your ice cream truck. I don't have enough insurance to let you get behind the wheel."

Slight and brown-haired, Fiona was a fastidious, middle-aged woman with small, sharp features. I always thought of her as birdlike — an opinion reinforced by Fiona herself, given her vast collection of pins shaped like the feather vertebrates. Today, she wore a decidedly spring ensemble: a crisp white blouse under a pale yellow pantsuit, an enameled pink flamingo preening on its lapel.

Hearing Fiona's "no" on his request to drive, Seymour's next move was to lunge for her keys. Smaller and faster, Fiona easily sidestepped his lumbering move and hugged the keys to her chest. They clanked against the enameled flamingo pin.

Seymour threw up his hands. "For the love of Guffman, it's only a golf cart! And you have three more."

"I *had* four more," Fiona shot back, "until a guest drove one into the duck pond."

Seymour smiled. "Yeah, I heard about that. But I'm not some bum driving along a badly lit path with a snoot-full. I'm a bona fide government employee."

"All the more reason not to let you near private property." Fiona pointed to the cart. "You have two choices, Tarnish. You can climb into the backseat or you can walk to Charity Point."

"Come on!" Seymour protested.

"Just follow the path along the pond for about a mile," Fiona said, climbing behind the steering wheel. "You'll reach the lighthouse in twenty minutes, *if* you walk faster than your typical snail's pace when you deliver my mail."

Seymour squinted at the diminutive yellow cart with its white-and-pink polka-dotted canvas top. "I need leg room. Why can't Penelope squeeze into the back? Then I can ride in the passenger seat."

"How gallant of you," Fiona replied dryly. "The answer *again* is *no*. Frankly, I don't wish to sit that close to you."

Seymour glared at the older woman, but he knew he'd met his match. Grumbling, he climbed into the back of the tiny golf cart. It took him a moment to settle in. I sat down, too, and we were on our way.

"Enjoying the ride?" Fiona asked as we sped by a small hand-painted sign for Chez Finch, the Finch Inn's brand-new gourmet restaurant.

"I feel like a set of Tiger Woods's golf clubs," Seymour muttered from the back, his knees around his ears.

The afternoon was luminous, with wispy high clouds in a cobalt sky. The landscaped and manicured grounds around Fiona Finch's Victorian inn smelled of lilacs, mingled with the salty tang of the ocean.

Situated on the shores of Quindicott Pond, the town's only bed-and-breakfast was owned and run by both Fiona and her husband, Barney. In less than a decade, the couple had turned a dilapidated mansion into a historical showplace, and a thriving business. Since then, they'd added the Chez Finch restaurant and a second, smaller rental dwelling called the Lighthouse, which was where we were headed right now.

"Have the police been here?" I asked.

Fiona nodded. "Right after I reported the burglary, Officer Womack showed up. He was all by himself, with a fairly rudimentary crime kit, which he didn't bother using. All he really did was look around, then rope off the area with yellow tape."

"That's it?" I said, surprised.

Fiona shrugged, eyes on the narrow trail. "Officer Womack said he thought the crime was committed by teenagers out to make trouble. He said fingerprints would be use-less since the fingerprints of cleaning staff and other guests would make identification of the burglar nearly impossible. He also told me another investigation was going on in town and resources were tied up. I never imagined the two crimes were connected. Obviously, neither did Officer Womack."

I arched an eyebrow. Fiona was an avid reader of true-crime fiction and one of my best customers. She also had good instincts, and the curiosity and persistence of a natural-born investigator.

"So you do think there's a connection?" I asked.

Fiona gave me a sidelong glance. "Odd coincidence if they're not."

I stared in thought at the trail ahead. "When did Dr. Lilly check in, exactly? Yesterday morning? Or the day before?"

"Much longer than that. She's been here a full week already, and she booked the Lighthouse for a second week, too."

I was surprised at that. "Dr. Lilly was in town for a week? It's odd that she never dropped by my store once. Last night, she made a big announcement about the post office losing her book delivery. Yet she'd never checked in with me or my aunt about it."

"She seemed pretty busy, if that's any help," Fiona said.

"Busy doing what?"

"One day, I saw her with a laptop in our restaurant, and another day it was a tape recorder and notebooks. I asked her what she was writing, and she said she was working on a new book."

Busy dame, that Dr. Lilly, Jack remarked. *The ink's not even dry on her new book, and she's already scribbling the next one.*

"That's not unusual, Jack," I silently replied. "Some authors are prolific. They have a lot to say. And most of them don't make much money, so they have to write a lot to make a living."

So what else is new. Every typewriter banger I knew had to hustle for every plugged nickel, too.

We'd come to the end of the pond and the golf cart's tiny engine really began to chug as we moved toward higher ground. Now the trail was bordered by a thick wooded area on one side, the rocky shore of the Atlantic Ocean on the other.

The only signs of civilization were the foot-tall, solar-powered lamps that Barney Finch had planted ten feet apart, along both sides of the trail to light up the path at night.

As we continued on, I began to spy

patches of torn-up earth and deep tire tracks. I wondered about those tracks — the trail was far too narrow for a car to negotiate. I pointed out the damage to Fiona.

"Oh, I know," Fiona said in an exasperated tone. "This is private property, from here to the Lighthouse and a little beyond, but we get trail bikers racing through here some nights and almost every weekend. The noise is awful and there's been damage."

"Vandalism?" I asked.

Fiona sighed. "Probably not deliberate. A few of Barney's solar lights have been knocked over. I've spoken to Chief Ciders about getting a patrol up here, but he claims he hasn't enough manpower. He says the only way to do it is on a motorcycle, and he hasn't got any."

"That's the best he can do?" I asked.

"Oh, he suggested I hire my own security."

"When exactly did you discover the robbery?" I asked.

"No more than an hour ago."

A moment later, I spied the top of the conical tower. We were almost there. Clearly, the area was isolated, so breaking into and entering the Lighthouse bungalow and making an undetected search of the premises would have been a pretty easy proposition for any burglar.

"How do you get your guests out here?" I asked.

"If someone wants a ride to or from the Lighthouse, they just have to call the front desk. Barney, our valet Pedro, or I will give them a lift. But honestly, unless they're checking in or out and have luggage, hardly anyone asks for a ride, except at night. Most of my guests enjoy strolling to the inn or the restaurant."

Finally we pulled up in front of Fiona's newest restoration showplace. The Lighthouse was situated on a rugged cliff that overlooked an area of jagged shoreline known as Charity Point. Below us, waves crashed violently on the millennia-old rocks, kicking up white froth before withdrawing back into the dark blue Atlantic. Gulls cawed nearby as they circled on rising thermals. Across the path from the structure was a stretch of dark woods.

"How Gothic," Seymour quipped.

"Isn't it?" said Fiona with a wistful smile. "I've always told Barney is reminds me of *Wuthering Heights*."

Seymour rolled his eyes. "Guess all you have to do is get Pedro to change his name to Heathcliff, and you're all set."

This was my first visit to Charity Point in

at least fifteen years, and the transformation of its lighthouse was astonishing. The century-old structure had never been used as an actual lighthouse in my lifetime, and for safety reasons, the main building had been bricked up decades ago.

Covered with teen graffiti, scorched by illegal bonfires, and ravaged by the elements, the lighthouse had become a real eyesore. The Town Council began debating whether to tear the place down. That's when the Finches stepped in and purchased the site — for a bargain price, too. But they had their work cut out for them. Clearly, they'd spent a small fortune to make this spot the romantic showplace it now was.

"The brickwork is pristine," I observed.

"Goodness, yes!" Fiona cried. "It took days of sandblasting to get rid of the graffiti and that garish orange paint. You can't imagine the mess we found inside when we broke through the bricked-up entrance." She shuddered at the memory.

"Well it's certainly lovely now," I said, climbing out of the cart.

The lighthouse tower was impressive. Three stories high, it was capped by a shiny brass-and-glass octagonal compartment that had once held the light itself. But the most noticeable change was to the blocky base, which had been turned into a charming cottage with bay windows, a sundeck, and a winding flagstone path that led up to the front door.

We walked through a rose-covered trellis, and I immediately spied yellow tape on the door, its thick strands emblazoned with the warning: POLICE LINE — DO NOT CROSS.

Without hesitation, Fiona tore away the tape. "Officer Womack said someone jimmied open the door."

Seymour examined the brass knob on the thick, polished door. He scratched the surface with his thumbnail and shook his head. "No way," he said. "There are *scorch* marks on the doorjamb, and some of the finish on the wood has actually blistered."

"From heat?" Fiona asked.

"You bet," Seymour replied. "I'd say a small explosive was used to break the lock open."

You taking notes, baby?

Jack's old buffalo nickel was in my pocket, his voice still strong in my head. "I hear you, Jack. And if Seymour's right, then this burglary and last night's near-fatal accident at the theater are connected. And if they're connected, then ruling Dr. Lilly's death an accident without further investigation would be idiotic."

179

Talk to your Buddy Boy first chance you get, commanded Jack in my head. *Ask him if he found any evidence of an explosive device — pieces of a timer, chemical residue, anything — when he inspected the theater earlier this morning. If the same stuff was used there as here, you'll have hard evidence to take to the Staties.*

I cleared my throat and turned to Seymour. "Are you sure about what you're saying? There could be a lot riding on it."

"I'm sure." Seymour nodded. "Back in the day, I sweetened an M-80 —"

"A *what?*" Fiona asked.

Seymour rolled his eyes. "A firecracker, okay? I used petroleum jelly as an accelerant and added a touch of cordite. *Ka-BOOM!* Blew the door to shop class right off its hinges!"

Fiona grimaced. "Ugh."

"Good lord." I tensed, motherhood momentarily eclipsing my sleuthing. "*Please* do not repeat that story to Spencer. I'm anticipating girl troubles during his high school years, not random explosions."

"Don't worry, Pen. Times ain't what they used to be. A kid who tries that these days will probably be investigated for terrorist connections and end up at Gitmo. Then Spencer would spill that he learned his

180

methods from his uncle Seymour, and *I'd* be on the hook."

"Very funny," Fiona said.

Seymour shrugged. "Anyway, I'm pretty sure the statute of limitations is up for that minor act of vandalism."

"Maybe," I said. "But Mr. Kelly is still Quindicott High School's shop teacher. And he has a memory like an elephant."

"Oh, yeah? I haven't thought about 'Big Bear' Kelly in years." Seymour shuddered. "That guy still freaks me out."

"Listen, Seymour," I pressed. "Can you find any proof of an explosive? Debris. Residue, maybe?"

"There's not much left of an explosive after the blast," Seymour explained. "Maybe if we had a spectrometer or something, we could detect residue."

Fiona huffed impatiently. "Sorry but there are no spectrometers on my golf cart, so I suggest we go inside!"

Chapter 10
A Babe
in the Woods

Better to be a live coward than a dead hero.

— *Key Largo,* 1948

Fiona pushed through the front door of the lighthouse and we followed, entering a bright, tastefully appointed two-bedroom bungalow. The cozy living room had a working fireplace, the walls were lined with aged oak paneling, and a massive plateglass window overlooked the Atlantic shoreline.

A stiff breeze from an open side window brought in the tangy smell of ocean air, and I could hear waves splashing against the rocks below. It seemed the perfect hideaway for well-heeled vacationers who enjoyed privacy along with sweeping, dramatic views.

Just off the living room, near the door to one of the bedrooms, I noticed a circular wrought-iron staircase. "Does that go up to the lighthouse beacon?" I asked.

"It's a sunroom now," Fiona explained. "Before you go, you simply must see the view. We even placed an antique brass telescope up there."

Who needs a telescope in this joint? Jack quipped in my head. *Nothing to spy on but seawater.*

"I'm sure guests would enjoy looking at passing ships and seabirds." I told him.

Seabirds? Jack grunted. *The only animal I ever cared about watching through a telescopic lens had four legs, a jockey, and ran around a racetrack.*

I turned to Fiona. "I'll check out the scenery before we leave, but first I want to see what was disturbed by the burglar."

Our first stop was the bedroom Dr. Lilly had been using. The room was lovely, with a Victorian flower pattern, and a large antique bed with a lace canopy, also Victorian. Pretty much everything was Victorian, including a large standing mirror set in an ornate frame. On the bed, the sheets were rumpled. Dr. Lilly's robe hung on a wall rack beside a nightgown.

Adjacent to the bedroom was the bath; its tiled floor was littered with damp towels. On the basin I found a hairbrush, hair products, makeup, and a toothbrush.

I noticed a small jewelry box had been dumped on top of the dresser. A few necklaces made of hemp, beads, and other natural materials were scattered about, but little else. If there'd been any jewelry containing gemstone, gold, or silver, it had been taken.

While Fiona moved on to the next room, Seymour lingered to examine a framed painting of a sea battle. I was about to follow Fiona when I spied a piece of white paper on the nightstand. The corner of the paper had been deliberately tucked under the heavy Tiffany lamp, probably to prevent it from being sent flying by the brisk ocean breeze pouring through the open window. I tilted the lamp, pulled the paper free, and unfolded it.

"What did you find there?" Seymour asked.

"An invoice of some kind," I replied. "Looks like a printout of a PDF file, the kind a company would attach to an e-mail."

I saw the letterhead — San Fernando University Press — and realized that this was a confirmation for a shipment of Dr. Lilly's new book, the ones that were delivered to Buy the Book earlier today. I noticed a box marked *special instructions,* and a block of text under it.

"Wait a minute!" I cried. "There are specific instructions here from Dr. Lilly to the publisher demanding that the shipment arrive on Friday morning — *this* morning, and *not* before."

"Yeah, so?" Seymour said with a shrug.

"Don't you remember what Dr. Lilly announced to the Movie Town theater audience last night? She claimed that the 'late' arrival of her new book was caused by an 'error at the post office'?"

"Oh, yeah, that's right!" said Seymour. "Lilly even apologized to the crowd for the mistake." He shook his head. "Blame the mailman! That's *sooo* typical."

"This must mean something," I murmured.

"But what?" asked Seymour.

"Seems obvious to me," said Fiona, overhearing us. "Dr. Lilly didn't want anyone reading her book until today."

"Yeah, but why?" asked Seymour. "What's the big deal?"

"I've read a lot of true crime and stories of investigative journalism in my time," Fiona said. "Believe me, there are plenty of books out there that can set off explosions."

I frowned at Fiona's choice of words, but in my head Jack became excited.

Your Bird Lady's onto something, baby.

185

When you get back to your shop, you better break open those boxes of Lilly's books in your store room, and take a good, hard look at what the dead woman wrote in those pages.

"Perhaps the book Dr. Lilly just published is going to expose something or break some sort of news," Fiona went on. "In that case, she might have wanted to control where and when it was released. What's the book's title, Penelope?"

"Murdered in Plain Sight."

"My goodness," Fiona said, "that does sound incendiary! Do you know anything about its subject?"

"I assumed it was going to be another film noir study. That's what she's known for . . ." I blinked just then, remembering the reporters showing up at my store.

"Pen? What is it?" Seymour asked.

"There are hundreds of film studies on the shelves already," I said. "Those reporters showed up today for something more."

"Reporters?" said Fiona, stepping closer.

I nodded. "They came to the store to cover Dr. Lilly's lecture. When they saw she wasn't there, they turned around and left."

"What do you think her book's about?" Fiona asked.

"Hey, wait a minute," said Seymour, snapping his fingers. "Last night, didn't Dr. Lilly say something about her book covering the details of Hedda Geist's life and career like never before?"

I tensed. "Yes, that's right . . . she did."

Seymour scratched his head. "You think maybe she was going to expose something about Hedda's involvement with the Pierce Armstrong trial?"

"A trial?" Fiona said. "You *must* tell me more. What's that all about?"

As Seymour told Fiona about Irving Vreen's untimely death at the point of a steak knife sixty years before, I continued searching Dr. Lilly's bedroom. Unfortunately, I turned up nothing more. Seymour and I canvassed the living room next; and, in the middle of our search, Fiona called us into the second bedroom.

She pointed to a round table. A heavy porcelain vase had been slid to the side to make room for *something* but there was hardly anything there: just some small cassette cases and several pens scattered about. There was no laptop computer, no notepad or notebooks, and no tape recorder with which to play the audiotapes.

"She must have been using this desk for a workspace," Fiona said.

I picked up one of the cassette cases and discovered it was empty. I moved to the next one, and the one after that. All five cassette cases were empty!

"Either the tapes are somewhere else in this cottage or they've been stolen," I said.

Fiona and Seymour quickly tossed the room but came up empty.

I looked for a tape recorder, but that appeared stolen, too.

Anyone with peepers can see the dead dame was scribbling something, Jack said. *Maybe that's the something that got her iced.*

I looked around. "Fiona, you said that you saw Dr. Lilly writing in notebooks, listening to tape recordings, and typing on a laptop. None of those things are here. So if there was a working manuscript among all that, it's missing, too."

Along with the jewelry, Jack noted. *But I'm betting that was just a con to make it look like your average smash-and-grab burglary.*

Fiona stepped up to me. "Try to remember, Penelope. Did Dr. Lilly bring any of those things with her to your store this morning?"

I closed my eyes, tried to conjure every detail. "Dr. Lilly arrived at Buy the Book on foot, with a small clutch purse and nothing else."

"I don't get it," said Seymour. "What

188

value could an unfinished manuscript have?"

Fiona threw up her hands. "If it's an exposé, it could have plenty of value, even unfinished!"

"I've *got* to read *Murdered in Plain Sight* as soon as possible," I said. "It might have clues to whatever you saw her working on. I'd better try to get in touch with Brainert, too. And if he doesn't know anything, he might have contacts at Dr. Lilly's home or at her university. Someone must know more."

"That seems very logical to me," Fiona said, "and I know you have to get going. But do take a quick look at the top of the lighthouse before you leave. I doubt there are any clues up there, but it may be your last chance in a long while to see the view. We're booked solid for months. I've even got people on a waiting list to take over Dr. Lilly's remaining reservation time, now that she's . . . well, now that she's gone."

I headed for the spiral staircase. Behind me, Fiona compulsively straightened up the pillows on the couch while Seymour studied the nautical paintings on the walls.

"Hey, Fiona, I actually like these. They remind me of the Hornblower series. Any of them for sale?"

Fiona exhaled with obvious annoyance. "It took me months to find exactly the right local artwork for this room. Why in the world would I want to sell it to you?"

"Name your price for the set."

"All right, one million dollars."

"Sounds fair for a set of paintings rendered by a *nobody*. So I'll tell you what, how about I write an IOU?"

"An IOU from Seymour Tarnish! That's rich. Why don't you just lose the check and tell me it's in the mail?"

Their voices grew fainter as I moved up the spiral staircase, one hand on the iron railing. At the top of the tower, I found a cozy space with wicker chairs and a matching table. The glass chamber was warm and stuffy, but I popped one of the windows and the stiff sea breeze quickly cooled things down. I looked around but found nothing. If Dr. Lilly spent time up here, she hadn't left anything behind.

My elbow bumped something — an antique brass telescope on a swivel base. For the heck of it, I considered peering through the lens, but I really didn't want to waste too much time, so I turned, ready to descend the spiral staircase again . . . and that's when I caught sight of him.

A man was ascending the rocky steps that

190

led from the shoreline below to the high bluff where the lighthouse sat. When he reached the top of the cliff, he paused in surprise at the sight of our golf cart on the isolated trail.

The trespasser scratched his dark head, staring at the cart. He seemed puzzled for some reason.

Was it possible this man was our burglar, returning to the scene of the crime? Maybe Fiona's maid had scared him away and he was hiding out until the place was deserted again. At the very least, he could be a witness to something that had happened here earlier!

The antique telescope was set up for a view of the ocean, which meant I had to kick-slide the heavy tripod across the floor so I could get a better look at the stranger. It was tough work, but by the time the man furtively crossed the trail, I'd gotten my first good view. I'd simply hoped to be able to describe the man to the police at some later date. I didn't expect to *recognize* him!

It was Dr. Randall Rubino, carrying the same beige canvas backpack over his shoulder that he'd been holding in my bookstore earlier. He was wearing the same clothes, too — only now he was actually wearing his yellow J. Crew jacket, probably to ward off the stiffening wind coming off the ocean.

I took a closer look at his bag. It seemed more stuffed than ever — so stuffed it actually bulged.

I froze with a thought.

I hear you, said Jack. *That pack just might be filled with cassette tapes and Dr. Lilly's missing computer and manuscript.*

As I spied on the doctor, he crossed the trail and entered the thick woods. He must have found an easy path into the brush, because Rubino quickly vanished from sight, even from my high vantage point.

But I couldn't let him get away. If he was carrying the stolen stuff, I had to catch him red-handed. And this was my chance!

I bolted down the spiral staircase so fast my low heels set the wrought-iron structure to wobbling. Standing near the picture window, Fiona Finch grinned like a proud parent.

"So, how did you like the view? Spectacular, isn't —"

I raced to the front door without a word, thrusting Seymour aside to get there.

"Yo! Pen? What's up?"

"Follow me! Important!" I cried.

In seconds, I was outside and down the flagstone path. Once through the trellis, I ran to the spot where I thought Dr. Rubino had entered the woods.

"Slow down, Pen!" Seymour called, huffing and puffing far behind me.

I found a path immediately, right near one of the Finch Inn's PRIVATE PROPERTY! NO TRESPASSING! signs that were posted all over the area, and followed it for perhaps twenty or thirty yards. Then it forked into two paths leading off in opposite directions.

Stymied by the fork, I looked for footprints, or any sign of Rubino's passing. I saw nothing.

Then I heard Seymour again. "Pen! Where are you?"

"Over here!" I yelled back. "I'm at the fork, just keep following the trail!"

I couldn't wait around for Seymour to catch up. Dr. Rubino already had a good head start. Even if I picked the right path, I'd have a hard time catching up with him.

"I'm going left!" I yelled to Seymour. *"you go right!"*

Then I took a deep breath and plunged down the left-hand path. I proceeded along for five minutes. It was still, cool, and dark under the canopy of trees — a little too dark, I thought, looking up. Through a break in the leaves, I saw clouds gathering. The wind had picked up, too, swishing the branches over my head.

I pressed on. The path wound around a deep ravine strewn with fallen trees. There was another fork and I thought I saw footprints down the right-hand trail, so I took it.

"Seymour!" I yelled behind me. "If you can hear me, I'm taking the right path on the second fork!"

As I ran forward, I began to hear a rumbling vibration. It was faint at first, but it quickly grew louder. "What's that?"

An engine, dollface, Jack replied in my head. *A big one.*

I recalled Fiona's complaint about dirt bikers, and realized I was probably smack-dab in the middle of a popular trail. I was stuck here, too. Thick thorn bushes had grown high between rows of giant oaks in this area of the narrow path, so there was nowhere to go but forward, or back. But I couldn't tell which direction the bike was coming from, only that it was getting closer.

Within seconds, the rumble became a roar. Bouncing off the trees, the mechanical growl seemed to come from everywhere.

Get out of the way! Jack yelled in my mind.

Instead of listening, I turned. Eyes wide, I spied a motorcycle barreling right at me along the path. Like a doe caught in a Hummer's headlamps, I froze, paralyzed!

I said move!

I'm not sure what happened in that final, critical second. But I must have instinctively leaped aside just as the big, Darth Vader of a motorcyclist reached me because I narrowly avoided getting run down. As the bike and the biker roared past me in a cloud of dirt; however, I wasn't able to avoid the stout tree trunk. Slamming headlong into the rough bark, I saw an explosion of searing white light.

After that, everything went blacker than *noir.*

CHAPTER 11
WRONG TURN

SAILOR: Where are we?
SAM MASTERSON: In a small accident.
SAILOR: What happened?
SAM MASTERSON: The road curved but I didn't.
— *The Strange Love of Martha Ivers,* 1946

New York City
May 10, 1948
"It's so dark . . ."

"There's a good reason for that, baby. We're under the East River."

"What?"

I opened my eyes. My black-framed glasses were gone again, but I could see just fine. Around me was a mass of metal. In front of me stretched a dashboard with big, clunky gauges that looked like something out of the Smithsonian. Above it, a windshield framed a dim roadway, and on the driver's side of the front seat was Jack Shepard — only not in spirit.

The PI's sandy brown hair was neatly trimmed, his iron jaw was freshly shaved, and his broad-shouldered form was draped in what looked like a brand-new, deep blue, double-breasted suit. He even had a matching blue fedora, which rested between us on the seat.

"Where are we again?" I asked Jack's granite profile.

"We're in the new tunnel," he said. "Well, kinda new. They opened it about ten years back. It's the tube that connects Manhattan with Long Island City."

"We're driving through the Queens Midtown Tunnel?"

"Bingo."

I studied the roadway in front of us. The car's headlights were on — and they needed to be. The weak yellow light bulbs that ran along this concrete tube's ceiling gave less illumination than a mausoleum.

"Jack, I don't understand. Why did you bring me down here?"

"Well, gee, for a dime, I could've gotten us both across the river by subway, but where we're going isn't exactly the safest part of town for a dame to hoof it, so I scared up some wheels for us instead."

Slumping back in the monster car's big

front seat, I put a hand to my head. "Why do I feel like a truck hit me?"

"Because you should have listened to me, doll, and jumped sooner."

"When?"

"On that wooded trail, which you shouldn't have been on in the first place." Jack's jaw worked a moment. "Dames like you make me crazy. Always trying to be good girls and get along and accommodate and make everybody happy. Then the one time you decide to grow a backbone and dig your heels in, you nearly get yourself run over."

"I don't have the foggiest notion what you're talking about."

Jack's slate gray eyes glanced at me. "I just don't like worrying about you."

"You worry about me?"

"In life, I never worried about anybody's hide but my own. I figured that's the way it'd be for me in death, too."

"Guess you figured wrong then."

"Guess so."

The tunnel was coming to an end and Jack's gaze returned to the road ahead. He pulled up to a toll booth and paid. Then we were off again, backtracking toward the other side of the East River, only this time above ground. As we drove along, I watched the sun sinking below the Manhattan sky-line. Blue twilight was settling over New York's five boroughs.

"Welcome to Queens, baby. Home of the 1939 World's Fair, the Steinway piano, and Harry Houdini's final resting place."

I'd been to Queens only a few times when I lived in New York City, mainly to travel back and forth to LaGuardia Airport. I'd never been to this part of the borough, so I wasn't altogether sure what Long Island City looked like in my time. In Jack's time, it was obviously a major manufacturing zone. Hundreds of factories were jammed together along the streets. I read the signs as we passed them: machinery parts, paint, shoes, bread, sugar, even spaghetti.

As we drove closer to the river, smoke-stacks rose up like sooty tree trunks. Be-tween their dirty silhouettes, I spotted tugboats, container ships, and barges full of coal moving along the water, beyond a col-lection of busy docks.

Traffic on the road was pretty heavy, too. Delivery trucks roared by as Jack did his best to circumvent the gridiron of elevated subway lines, railroad yards, and bridge ap-proaches. He signaled a lane change but someone behind him didn't notice because a horn blasted and a bakery truck suddenly swerved, narrowly cutting us off. Jack cursed as his hands jerked the wheel. I slid across the seat, slamming into him.

He straightened the car out again. "You okay, doll?"

"Whoa, don't you have any seatbelts in this tank?"

"Seat *what?*"

"Seatbelt, Jack. It locks around your waist to keep you from sliding all over the place, or worse slamming your head into the —" I frowned at the dashboard. "That thing's solid *metal,* isn't it?"

"What thing? The dashboard? This is a 1939 Packard, honey. What else would it be?"

I shuddered at the idea of cracking my forehead open against that thing. In fact, my head felt like it already had.

"Good lord, Jack. No seatbelts, no shoulder harnesses, no airbags, and a dashboard of solid metal! How did your generation stay alive on the road?"

"Well, let's see now, baby . . . when my generation wasn't struggling to survive a nationwide Depression, we were trying to keep from dying in a world war. Vehicular safety wasn't high on our list of concerns. But if you're that worried about smash-ups, I have an idea how to keep you from bouncing around in my car —"

He dropped one hand off the steering wheel, snaked a muscular arm around my waist, and pulled me playfully against him. "How's that, doll? Nicer than a crummy old seatbelt, isn't it?"

"That's all right, Jack," I said, fighting a warm flush of embarrassment. "I don't need a seatbelt. I'll just make do."

As I extricated myself from his grip and slid to the other side of the car, Jack laughed. It was an amused, highly infuriating sound, as if he knew exactly how I'd react to his pass. That's when I noticed his smashed fedora sitting on the seat between us. I picked up the mangled hat and waved it in front of his nose.

"See what you get for teasing me. Your headgear's as flat as a pancake."

He snatched it from my fingers and tossed it into the backseat. "It's okay, baby. Feeling your heart skip a beat over me was worth it."

He laughed again, and I attempted to regain my dignity by roughly straightening my outfit. That's when I realized I was no longer wearing my own clothes. Once again, Jack had chosen an outfit for me, only this time I wasn't decked out in a slit-skirted gown with four-inch heels. My current forties costume consisted of a tweed suit with a cinched waist, a knee-length skirt, and brown shoes with a nice low, *sane* amount of heel.

I was about to thank Jack for the wardrobe improvements when I caught my reflection in the sideview mirror. My auburn hair was curled into a lovely, sleek pageboy, but my face was displaying quite a lot of makeup. The colors looked strange.

"What's on my lips?" I murmured.

"Lipstick," he said. "Hokey-Pokey Pink."

"You've got to be kidding."

"What's your beef?" Jack said defensively. "I saw it in a magazine. It's the most expensive brand on the market: one whole dollar, plus tax."

"Redheads don't wear bright pink lipstick."

"Why not?"

"They just don't."

"Well if you're worried about how you look, baby, it's a waste of brain cells. You're cute as the lace panties you're wearing under that getup. I picked them out of a magazine, too, along with your bra, stockings, and garter belts."

My cheeks now matched the Hokey-Pokey Pink lipstick. "Can we please get *off* the subject of my underwear?"

Jack snorted. "Forget getting off the subject. I'd rather just get off your —"

"Jack!" I interrupted, "I'm *sure* you didn't bring me back here just to talk about my panties. So I'd appreciate it if you'd —"

"Okay, okay," he said. "I'll get down to business."

And he did, promptly filling me in on what I'd missed since our night at the Porterhouse Restaurant. Irving Vreen, the Gotham Studio head, had expired from his stab wound (no surprise), and Hedda Geist's actor boyfriend, Pierce Armstrong, had been taken into custody.

"But not Hedda herself?" I asked.

"The tabloids are hounding her every day, but she's still free as a bird."

"Can we find out more about the case?" I asked.

"Which one?"

"What do you mean, which one?" I said. "Vreen's death, of course."

"You forget, baby, Vreen wasn't my case. The reason I took you to the Porterhouse in the first place was because I was tailing Nathan Burwell at the time. That's why I'd witnessed Vreen's stabbing — it was in my memories. I've told you before: I'm a ghost, not a magician. I can't take you anywhere I didn't go in life."

"Yes, Jack. I understand." I sat up straighter as it all came back to me. "Burwell was your cheating-husband case. But wasn't that case a little dicey, trying to get evidence on someone as powerful as the city's district attorney?"

Jack checked his rearview mirror, gave a little smirk. "Why do you think I'm wearing a new suit?"

"Oh, I get it. Burwell's wife is paying you enough to make it worth your while?"

"Bingo, doll, only I ran into a little roadblock."

"What do you mean?" I worriedly glanced around. "You wrecked the Packard?"

Jack sighed. "I was talkin' figuratively, baby. Try to keep up. See, I was tailing Burwell and his chippy for a few weeks before Vreen got the big knife in the back. I'd been taking notes on the DA's trysts, getting photos of the two together when I could — on the street, in a diner, in front of the Hotel Chester. Then all of a sudden . . ." Jack snapped his fingers.

"What?"

"Over. Burwell's back to his old routine. No more cheating. No more visits with the chippy. After about a week, I figure that's okay. Maybe the stabbing spooked the hubby, and he thought it best to end the affair. So I still think everything's jake because I know where the girl's staying. I go to her hotel — but she's not there."

"She checked out?"

"Gone. Lammed it on May sixth, the morning after Vreen's murder. The clerk at the Chester gives me a name and address, but they don't exist. So now I'm holding the bag."

"Why?"

"Because I need that girl . . ." Jack checked his rearview again. "I need her in the flesh."

"Why? You've got evidence, haven't you?"

"My notes can be disputed. Even photos can be explained away. But the actual girl can be subpoenaed to testify under oath. Burwell's wife needs that assurance before she tries to put the screws to her husband. Without the chippy's real name and address, I can't even verify that she was underage, which would have been the lynchpin to getting Burwell to settle out of court."

"You have any leads on her?"

"Two — *maybe*."

"What are they?"

"First one's you, baby."

"Me?!"

"Yeah. When you first saw that girl in the restaurant, you said she looked familiar."

"I did . . . but I don't remember where

I've seen her before. I'm sorry, Jack."

"Well, keep working on it, because I can use all the help I can get right now."

"What's your second lead?"

"A 1941 gull gray Lincoln Continental Cabriolet with spode green wheels."

"Excuse me?"

"That's the only lead I've got on the DA's chippy. The bellboy at the Chester remembered taking her suitcase out to that make and model car. I remembered a car like that outside the hotel when Burwell went upstairs to . . ." Jack paused abruptly and cleared his throat. "When he went upstairs with the girl."

"I understand."

"I know you do. Anyway, I got its plate number in my notes so I had a friend at my old precinct run the license. Got an address in Queens along with a name — Lester Sanford."

Jack was driving as he talked, moving us north along the East River. The sun had completely set by now, and night was creeping across the sky. As stars appeared in the darkening purple, Jack turned abruptly and zigzagged through an area of warehouses and garages. Finally, we ended up on a large, brightly lit avenue, where every few blocks rough-looking men spilled out of dive bars. There were dock workers, stone cutters, sailors, and factory men — some of them were falling-down drunk, others were shouting or starting brawls.

Jack was right, I realized: This wasn't a safe neighborhood for a dame to hoof it. I was about to mention this when I noticed him checking the rearview again.

"You're looking in that mirror an awful lot," I noted.

"That's because a third lead just showed up."

"What do you mean?"

"We're being tailed —"

I began to spin in my seat.

"Don't look!" Jack warned. "Keep your eyes ahead. I've been onto this car since we left the tunnel."

We turned down Thirty-fifth Avenue, where a box truck partially blocked the road. Jack slowed to a crawl so we could inch by without stripping the car's paint. As we did, I watched men in overalls unloading what looked like fake palm trees and carrying them into a huge building. I would have guessed the place was a factory, but its exterior was too clean, and there were very large windows on the upper floors.

"What is this building?"

"Astoria Studios," Jack said. "Paramount

Pictures runs it now . . . used to be Famous Players Lasky Corporation. They shot silent films there once, then started shooting talkies . . . Marx Brothers comedies, *The Emperor Jones.* That's also where Gotham Features rents its sound stages when they aren't shooting on the street."

"Is that where we're going?"

"No, but Lester Sanford's address is only a few blocks away."

By the time we reached our destination, night had fully descended. Jack's tall figure cast a long shadow as we exited the Packard and walked between streetlights.

The area was obviously mixed zoning. One- and two-story brick row houses sat next to warehouses and garages. As we walked, I got the feeling someone was following us. I was itching to turn around and look, but Jack quietly warned me not to swivel my head.

"Just keep walking, baby. Don't worry. I've got my rod on me."

"What, are you kidding? Guns are what I'm worried about."

"I can shoot straight."

"Yeah, but what about the other guy?"

"Do me a favor, don't crack wise. Just keep moving those pretty lace panties of yours."

I gritted my teeth but didn't argue, kept my focus on the task at hand. The address itself wasn't an apartment building or home. It was a very large building that looked like a factory warehouse. A parking lot sat beside it, and Jack immediately spied the gull gray Continental Cabriolet. There were actually two that looked exactly alike, right down to the green wheels. They were parked together. He checked the plates of each one, and pointed.

"This is the one — the car I spotted idling that night outside the Hotel Chester. It's the same description the bellboy gave me of the car that picked up the DA's girl when she checked out."

"Why are there two cars here that look exactly alike? Don't you find that strange?"

"Maybe not, baby. Let's have a little talk with the folks inside."

Jack didn't bother knocking, just reached for the door handle.

"Do you know anything about this place?" I asked.

"It's a storage facility for Gotham Features."

The door opened and we walked right in. Despite the hour, the place was lit up and buzzing with activity. Men in overalls were milling around, talking. I could hear hammering and sawing going on somewhere in the back. Boxes were stacked sky-high. Shelves were filled with odd items — lamps, books, kitchen appliances. Pieces of furniture for every room in a typical home were jammed into corners with fake plants and giant rocks.

Jack didn't seem phased by the chaos. He scanned the area and the men working and walked right up to a short, stocky guy wearing glasses, pinstriped pants, and suspenders. The stocky man was holding a clipboard, shooting orders to a younger, fitter man in overalls.

"We'll need those chairs painted over by morning. And scare me up a Victrola, will ya? We have one in the back, next to the fake radios."

I tugged Jack's sleeve. "Who's the man giving orders?"

"Property master and studio manager."

"Is he Lester Sanford?" I asked.

"No," Jack said.

Just then, the property master turned, saw us, and grinned from ear to ear. "Jack! Jack Shepard?! Where've you been, you big lug!" He walked over with his hand out. Jack pumped it.

"Hi there, Benny."

"Who's the little lady?" Benny asked.

"She's my, uh . . ." Jack glanced at me.

"Partner," I whispered.

"New secretary," Jack declared. "Just hired her. Ain't she a looker?"

"I'll say." Benny smiled, looking me up and down like a prize racehorse. "I just don't get why you hired her when you could have married her." He laughed and finally addressed me. "Don't you think it's time your boss settled down?"

Settled down? My eyebrows rose at that one. From all the wild stories the ghost had told me, I just couldn't see the living Jack Shepard smoking a pipe in the suburbs with his feet up. Even in death, the expired gumshoe was climbing the walls of my bookstore, eager to glom onto the merest hint of excitement in our "cornpone" little town.

"I'm sure Jack's happy as a bachelor," I told Benny. "Besides, any woman he married would have to put up with —"

Jack loudly cleared his throat, shutting me up with a pointed stare. Obviously, he preferred that I refrain from speaking during this particular meeting.

"So how've *you* been, Benny?" he asked the stocky man.

"Good, good . . . things around here could be better, though. You know about Irving?"

Jack glanced at me. "Yeah. I read about

what happened in the not-so-funny papers."

"We can't believe it around here. Pierce Armstrong arrested for murder?" Benny shook his head. "He would never do anything to hurt Irving. Pierce wouldn't hurt a fly! Do you know he could get the gas chamber for this?"

"Yeah, Benny, I know."

"Are you here for Pierce then?" Benny asked, almost hopefully. "Did he hire you to help fight the charges?"

"No." said Jack. "I'm looking for a guy named Lester Sanford. Know him?"

"Sure, I know Sandy. He's been with us almost eight months now. He's not here at the moment though."

"What's his title?"

"Title?" Benny shrugged. "On the credits it's assistant producer."

"Which translates to?"

"Transportation manager, truck driver, and senior grease monkey."

Jack stepped closer. "Does he own those two gull gray Lincoln Cabriolets in your parking lot?"

Benny paused then. He seemed to be considering Jack's tone. "What's this about?" he asked, his own voice suddenly less friendly.

Jack quickly backed off. "Oh, nothing

important. It's just that I need a favor, see? I'm on a divorce case, and I'm trying to find a witness. I spotted one of Sandy's cars at the scene, and I thought if maybe I talked to him, he'd help me out with a lead."

Benny scratched his ear with his pen. "Well, Sandy might be listed as the owner of those cars, Jack, but he wouldn't have been driving them. Those particular cars are being used for a six-week shoot."

"A shoot of what?"

"Movie's called *East Side Serenade.* We're wrapping it next week."

Jack's jaw worked silently. "Then anybody at the studio could have used those vehicles?"

"Oh, no. Not anybody," Benny said. "Those are expensive automobiles. Sandy keeps a strict log. And when those keys aren't on the shoot or with a driver who signs them out, then they're with me." Benny reached into his pocket, pulled out a massive key ring, and jingled it like Santa Claus shaking his sleigh bells.

"You wouldn't mind if I took a quick look at Sandy's log book, would you?"

Benny smiled. "Not if you got another hot tip for me from that jockey friend of yours at Aqueduct. You do and she's all yours."

Jack nodded. "I'll ring you inside of a

week. And that's a promise."

"Good enough for me." Benny waved his hand. "Come on over to my desk."

Benny rifled through a stack of clipboards and paperwork and found Sandy's log. "What do you wanna know?" he asked, opening the log book.

Jack pulled out a slender notebook from inside his jacket pocket, riffled backward through some pages.

"First date I'm after is April sixteenth."

Benny's thick finger moved down a page in the log. "Here we are. Shooting wrapped at sunset and the car was signed out by an actor."

Jack frowned. "You let actors borrow these vehicles?"

Benny shrugged. "Part of the perks if you're a principal player. Irving doesn't pay much, you know, so he lets them borrow the studio's cars, as long as they keep them clean and bring them back with the gas tank full."

"Who's the actor that signed it out?"

Benny glanced at the large, bold block letters. "Pierce Armstrong." He frowned. "That's bad luck. I mean, you can't very well talk to him about being a witness to anything when he's already in the hoosegow for a capital crime."

"Check another date for me, would you?" Jack asked.

"Sure."

"May sixth."

Benny nodded. "There was filming early that day, on location in Manhattan. Looks like a principal checked the car out again."

"Who?"

Benny adjusted his glasses, squinted at the small, fluid script. "Pierce Armstrong."

Jack frowned. "But it couldn't have been. Armstrong was taken into custody the night of Vreen's stabbing, which was May fifth."

"That's odd," Benny admitted.

"Then you didn't witness the sign-out yourself?" Jack asked.

"Not when they're on location. You'd have to talk to Sandy or the director, young guy named Delahunt." Benny checked his watch. "Delahunt's somewhere out on Long Island shooting workarounds. Now that Pierce Armstrong's in jail, he's trying to finish the film without him."

"What about Sandy?" Jack asked. "He out on Long Island, too?"

"Yeah, but not for the same reason. His wife just had a baby girl. He'll be off work for a few days at least."

Jack nodded. "Okay, when will Delahunt be back here then?"

"Tomorrow morning. But I doubt he'll remember what happened that day with the car." Benny shook his head. "Everyone's pretty frazzled right now with Irving dead and Pierce arrested, and when you're trying to wrap a picture one day just melts into all the others. That's why we keep logs and lists." Benny pointed to the clipboards stacked on his desk.

"I understand," said Jack. "But I'd like to talk to the man anyway. Oh, and one more thing, Benny . . ."

"Sure, Jack."

"Is Hedda Geist on that picture, too?"

"Of course. She's under contract. Every film she's been in has been a hit for us. No way we'd make a movie without her in a leading role."

"So she's out there on Long Island, too?" Jack asked.

Benny nodded.

"Guess I'll come back tomorrow." Jack smiled. "That is, unless you've got another case for me tonight? How's the security around here since I solved your little problem a year ago?"

"Tell you what, Jack, you did me a real favor finding that Larry Lightfingers on my staff. Put the fear of God into everybody. We haven't had one more disappearing prop

216

since. The only thing's gone missing in months is a piece of wardrobe, and I'm pretty sure it just got misplaced."

"What was it?" Jack asked.

Benny shrugged. "Just one of Hedda's costumes. The silver gown she wore in *Wrong Turn.* We had two made exactly alike, 'cause one Hedda wore for the poster and the other we had to rip at the shoulder for the opening sequence. The ripped one we still got. The other one's lost." He waved his hand. "Believe me, Jack, it's no big deal. Nothing we'd need to hire you for. That thing looked expensive on screen, but it was actually pretty cheap goods."

Jack's eyebrow arched, he glanced down at me. "Sounds a little like Hedda herself."

We exited the building and headed back toward Jack's Packard.

"Okay," I said, as we walked by a line of row houses. "What was the DA's mistress doing wearing Hedda's gown? Who gave it to her? And what was Pierce Armstrong doing in a car outside the girl's hotel? Was he sleeping with her, too? Do you suspect this Delahunt character of anything? Or Lester Sanford? And can you trust Benny?"

"Keep your voice down, baby," Jack whispered. "We're being followed."

My eyes widened as I realized Jack already

had my back. He'd positioned himself directly behind me, shielding me from any blow or bullet that might come our way.

"What are you going to do?" I whispered.

"Well, I'm not waiting for him to decide," Jack replied. "You see that sharp turn off the sidewalk up ahead?"

"The alley?"

"Turn down it, baby."

"What? Why?"

"Question me again, and the next time I bring you back to my time, your gumshoe work will be limited to typing and filing."

I got the message and kept moving forward. The sidewalk was deserted, the street quiet. The only sound was the click of my heels along the broken concrete. Jack's footsteps were silent as the grave, and apparently so were the steps of the man taillng us.

A single car rumbled down the road. It cruised by us quickly. I waited for it to pass and then I turned into the alley.

"Wait up, sweetheart!" Jack called loudly enough for our tail to hear. "What about that kiss you promised me?"

We were between streetlights, so the shadows were pretty thick and the darkness overwhelmed me as I moved farther down the narrow passage. Suddenly, Jack's hot breath grazed my ear. "That's good, baby." His hand pressed my backside. "Keep walking." Then the warmth of his body vanished.

I gnawed my lower lip as I continued walking forward. What I wanted to do was turn around and ask him what he planned on doing. But I knew a good detective wouldn't question his partner in a situation like this. A good shamus would assume his partner had a plan — and trust it.

And that's exactly what I did: I trusted Jack and kept walking. My heels clicked loudly along the alley's cobblestones, echoing up the walls of brick on either side of us. It smelled rank back here between the buildings, like spoiled food. I bumped a metal garbage can. Farther down the alley, a cat meowed loudly. I heard scurrying. Mice? Rats? I shuddered in the dark but kept going until I heard —

Smack! Thwack! Smack!

Fists were hitting flesh behind me. There was a loud grunt, a body fell, and I worried whether Jack was okay. But when I turned around, it was Jack's dark silhouette that was still standing.

I backtracked quickly to get to Jack's side. The man who'd been following us was now crumpled against the alley wall.

"Do you know him?" I asked.

Jack shook his head. He crouched low and patted the man down, coming up with two handguns. "Here," he said, shoving one at me and then another. The first was a snub-nosed revolver. The second had a long, narrow barrel. I think it was a German Lugar.

"Whoa, Jack," I said, holding up my palms. "I don't know how to shoot these —"

"Good because I just want you to *hold* them, okay?"

"Oh, okay." I juggled the weapons, finally getting a firm hold of each gun butt.

Jack noticed my awkward maneuverings. "Fingers *off* the triggers, okay?"

I vigorously nodded.

Jack turned back to the man. He was groaning now, coming to, and Jack started his interrogation. "Who are you?"

The man shook his head. "Buzz off."

Jack searched the man's pockets, pulled out a wallet, and flipped it open. "Well, well, well . . . this little license says you're a private dick, just like me . . . Egbert P. King."

"Bert," the man muttered. "Nobody but my mother calls me Egbert."

"Okay, *Egbert,* who sent you to tail me?"

The man snorted, rubbed the back of his head. "You got it all wrong in the tail department, fella. I wasn't tailing you."

Jack squinted. "Oh, you weren't?"

"No. See, I saw that piece o' tail you're with —" he pointed at me — "and I thought I'd grab me some, too. She's not too expensive, is she? Looks like cheap goods to me."

Jack's meaty fist cocked back. "You son of a —"

"Jack, don't!"

Too late. He'd knocked the other PI unconscious.

I sighed. "That wasn't too smart, Jack. Now he can't tell you a thing."

Jack grabbed the guy's lapels and shook him. "Wake up, shitbird."

The man groaned.

As Jack shook him again, I heard something suspicious. In the street beyond the alley, a car was rumbling closer, only it wasn't rolling at a normal pace. It was cruising slowly, as if the driver were looking for something or *someone.*

"Jack, listen," I whispered.

"You made a mistake, Shepard," muttered the PI named Egbert. "A big one."

Just then, three gunshots came in succession. Someone was opening fire on us.

It was too dark to see anything but a few white flashes from a dark car window. Above us, an old fire escape pinged as bullets ricocheted off the rusting structure.

Jack reacted instantly. While I was still gaping in shock, he was pulling out his own weapon, returning fire, and pushing me farther into the darkness.

"Move, baby! Go!"

I did, stumbling farther down the alley a few feet before I realized I was holding weapons, too! I dropped the revolver into my pocket, and pointed the Lugar with two hands.

Before I could fire, Jack was next to me, pushing the gun's barrel toward the ground. "I said *run*. Not shoot!"

"But —"

"Let's go!" Jack hustled me the length of the alley and we turned down the next street. Then he stashed me in a dark doorway and told me to stay put until he returned. A few minutes later, he was back.

"They're gone," he told me, returning his weapon back to the shoulder holster inside his jacket. "Egbert and his ride both hightailed it out of here. But I'm not surprised."

"Why?"

"Those shots landed a mile over our heads. Whoever fired them didn't want to hurt us. They just wanted to scare us."

"But who hired them?"

"Something tells me I'll find out soon

enough."

"Here," I said, holding out Egbert's weapons. "You want these?"

Jack took them from me. He checked the safeties then pocketed them both. "You did good, sweetheart. Stop shaking."

"I thought we were dead."

Jack touched my cheek, gave me the slightest smile. "Only one of us is dead, Penelope. And I'm glad about that."

I was, too, because life was short. I forgot sometimes, but this moment reminded me.

Jack reached over and drew me into his arms. His touch wasn't playful, like it had been in the car; it was tender, his expression ardent. This time, I didn't pull away; and when his mouth covered mine, I closed my eyes and let him drive. . . .

CHAPTER 12
MURDER
BY THE BOOK

Hmm. Next time I come out with you, I'm gonna bring along an extra set of nerves.
— *Kiss Tomorrow Goodbye,* 1950

"Pen, wake up! Come on, wake up!"

Someone was patting my hand. I tasted dirt, felt a sharp pain in my back and a dull throbbing in my head. "Where am I?"

"You're in the woods beyond Charity Point," a male voice replied. "Don't you remember?"

"What year is it?" I murmured, wondering where Jack had gone.

"Uh-oh, she's acting goofy, Fiona."

I opened my eyes to find Seymour crouched over me, his face pinched with concern. I tried to sit up.

"Wait, maybe you shouldn't move," he said. "Something might be broken."

"I've got to sit up, Seymour. Rocks are digging into my spine, and I think I have a bug in my blouse!"

Seymour called over his shoulder. "I think maybe Pen has a concussion."

I pushed Seymour away. "I don't have a concussion. And who are you talking to, anyway?"

I sat up, did a double-take.

Fiona was pale faced, standing beside the mud-splattered golf cart. Grass stains streaked the cart's bright finish. Torn vines clung to the headlights and dangled from the rearview mirror. A low-hanging branch had ripped a ragged hole in the pink-and-white pokka-dotted canvas top. Taking the golf cart off-road and into the woods had obviously exacted a toll on the fragile vehicle.

"Let me guess," I said. "Seymour was driving."

"No, it was me," Fiona replied. "I saw Seymour follow you into the woods. I knew I couldn't catch up unless I had wheels. I drove up the trail and picked up Seymour first. We heard you calling in the distance, but we couldn't find you. Then we heard you scream."

"That's when I grabbed the wheel and made Fiona go off-trail, right through the brush," Seymour said. "And we finally found you."

"I appreciate it."

Seymour and Fiona helped me to my feet. I gingerly touched my head, groaned when I felt the lump above my forehead.

"No blood," Seymour said, inspecting my skull. "Just a jumbo-sized egg." He stepped back, pulled a twig from my auburn hair.

"I think I'm okay," I said.

Seymour frowned. "What the hell happened, Pen? Why did you run into the woods like some nutcase?"

I told them about seeing Dr. Rubino from the top of the lighthouse, then following the man into the woods. I glossed over the part about getting lost. Left out the crazy dream of tracking down clues with Jack Shepard in 1948 Queens, New York, and simply told them that a speeding biker ran me down.

"I'm going to speak with Chief Ciders again," Fiona said angrily. "This is unacceptable. It's trespassing. How long before one of these careless dirt bikers runs down one of my guests!"

Fiona helped me brush off the remaining dirt and leaves from my hair and clothes. "Did you recognize the biker?" she asked. "Someone you maybe saw around town?"

I shook my head. "I don't know . . . it happened so fast."

Fiona pressed. "What do you remember?"

I closed my eyes, massaged my throbbing temples. "Darth Vader," I said.

Fiona whispered to Seymour. "What does she mean, do you think? That he was all in black?"

Seymour snorted. "Well, I doubt she means he was waving a lightsaber."

"He was a big man," I continued, my eyes still closed as I struggled to replay that split-second flash of memory. "He wore a black leather jacket. His head was completely covered with a darkly tinted visor, and his motorcycle was big. I don't know what brand it was, but it was black and chrome." I sighed and opened my eyes. "That's really all I remember . . . hey, wait a minute!"

I turned to Seymour. "Do you remember seeing Hedda's granddaughter, Harmony?"

"Sure." Seymour smirked. "I'm a man and I'm breathing. How could I forget seeing her?"

"I meant, do you remember when we saw her at Mr. Koh's fruit bins this morning? Do you remember what happened?"

Seymour's eyes bulged. "Oh, right! A big motorcyclist in a black leather jacket was flirting with her." He paused and then shrugged. "Of course, there are a lot of motorcyclists in the area, especially in the spring and summer. He might be the same guy, or he might not. We need more to go on."

I nodded. "Right now we just have to *go*."

Seymour blinked. "Go where?"

"Back to the store." I rubbed my forehead. "I may have taken one in the cranium, but I haven't forgotten that we need to take a look at Dr. Irene Lilly's brand-new book."

It was nearly four o'clock when Seymour dropped me off in front of Buy the Book. We'd taken his car to Finch Inn because mine was still crippled by a dead battery.

"I'll be back as soon as I find parking," Seymour said and pulled away from the curb.

The store was crowded with customers, which was certainly gratifying. But I felt a little guilty for having left Sadie and Mina alone for so many hours on such a busy day. On the other hand, Sadie was all for my investigating Irene Lilly's death, and that's what I'd been doing.

As soon as I entered the store, Brainert Parker cornered me. His brown hair was neatly combed and his scarecrow frame was dressed as smartly as ever. He had no bow tie today, but his khaki pants displayed a knife-sharp crease and his salmon-colored button-down appeared to be pressed within an inch of its life beneath his favorite blue blazer.

"Pen, you've got to tell me what happened this morning," he said in a whisper. "I tried to get the details out of Sadie, but she's been busy with the store. She simply told me that Dr. Lilly had a fatal accident, and I should talk to you."

"Yes, yes. How much do you know?"

"I know that the woman died in a fall from a ladder."

"And what do you know about her new book?"

"Excuse me?" Brainert frowned. "What does that have to do with her accident?"

"Listen to me, Brainert. I'm convinced that what happened to Dr. Lilly in our store this morning was no accident. I'm sure she was murdered and the scene was staged to make it appear as if she died in a fall."

Eyes wide, Brainert gripped my arm. "You'd better fill me in."

"I will. But first we have to take a look inside Dr. Lilly's new book. I'm betting it will give us a clue why someone wants her dead."

Brainert scanned the sales floor. "Where is the book? I don't see it on display."

"Because of what happened to her, we decided to keep the shipment boxed up in the storeroom." I waved at Aunt Sadie and called to her. "If you need me, I'll be in with the stock."

She nodded and went back to ringing up a customer's purchases. When I turned back to Brainert, Seymour was walking up to us.

"Hey, Parker, did she tell you?" he called. "Pen was run down in the woods by a mad biker!"

A few customers curiously looked our way.

"Keep your voice down, Seymour," I whispered.

"I call it as I see it," he said with a shrug then glanced at Brainert. "So? You in on the case?"

Brainert frowned. "It's a *case,* is it?"

"Sure," said Seymour. "Pen's running the investigation, and I'm her right-hand man."

Brainert rolled his eyes. "You *have* a right hand, Seymour. That's all I'm willing to concede."

"I have a *fist,* too, Parker. You want me to show it to you?"

"Stop bickering!" I commanded. "Just be quiet, both of you, and follow me."

I led the pair into the stock room and closed the door behind us. The cramped space smelled of ink, paper, and cardboard. The boxes delivered from San Fernando University Press were stacked where our

230

delivery man had left them. I ripped open the top carton, gave one book to Brainert, one to Seymour, and took one to look at myself.

The three of us fell silent for the next five minutes as we examined Dr. Lilly's newly published work. As she'd promised in her speech at the theater, the dust jacket of her book featured the poster from *Wrong Turn,* which meant Hedda Geist's strikingly beautiful image dominated the cover. Her blonde hair flowed over her hourglass curves, encased in the shimmering silver gown she'd worn in the movie — the one that had gone missing from Gotham Features's wardrobe, if I could trust the dream that Jack had given me.

I flipped the book over. There was no text on it, only a large color photograph of Dr. Lilly — very unusual for an academic book. I opened the front, read the flap copy, and my jaw dropped.

"This isn't a film study," I said, finally breaking the silence.

"Yeah," agreed Seymour. "Looks like a biography of Hedda Geist."

"You're both mistaken," said Brainert. "It appears to me that *Murdered in Plain Sight* should be filed under true crime."

"What are you talking about, Brainiac?"

Seymour asked.

Brainert shook his head. "You two don't know the first thing about speedy evaluation. Contents reveal the outline, then skip to the last few chapters for the conclusion." He tapped his copy of the open book, his finger running down the middle of one page after another. "From what I gather, Dr. Lilly has written an exposé that accuses Hedda Geist of the calculated murder of Irving Vreen back in 1948. She claims Hedda planned and executed the entire murder."

"But Pierce Armstrong was tried and convicted of manslaughter for that crime," I pointed out.

Brainert squinted at the page. "Dr. Lilly seems to be saying that Hedda Geist manipulated Pierce Armstrong and Irving Vreen into the confrontation. Her goal all along was to see Irving Vreen dead and Armstrong convicted of his murder."

"I knew it!" Seymour cried, slapping his knee. "Pierce Armstrong was a fall guy. He was railroaded. Hedda was the real vixen. She arranged everything."

Brainert shook his head. "This is quite disturbing. And, frankly, it's very difficult for me to believe that the Hedda Geist-Middleton I've gotten to know could be capable of this. As a young woman she was a gifted actress *playing* femme fatales to perfection, but I can't believe she actually was one. Look at the quiet, respectable life she's lived for decades. She's been an esteemed member of the Newport community for years. She's a beloved mother and grandmother. She's given tens of thousands to charity —"

Seymour snorted. "Not to mention your own pet project: restoring your movie theater."

Brainert put a hand on his hip. "What are you implying?"

"That you have an agenda."

"I'm an *academic*. I need to see evidence. My own observations tell me that Hedda's a class act. This *alleged* crime she committed was sixty years ago. Pierce Armstrong was tried and convicted of manslaughter for that crime. How in the world could anyone *prove* that conviction was false after all these years?"

"Dr. Lilly was an academic, too, Brainert," I pointed out. "I doubt she would have published a book without new evidence. She invited members of the press to our store today. I think she must have had solid facts to present. We just need to read them." I held up the book. "Consider this exhibit A."

"Exhibit A, huh?" said Brainert, paging through the final chapters. "All I see here related to the letter 'A' are *Allegations*." Brainert was silent for a minute, continuing to skim. Finally, he sighed and shook his head. "I don't even see a motive for Hedda to have supposedly perpetrated this heinous crime."

Seymour grunted with skepticism. "It sounds to me like you're more than willing to overlook your business partner's past. Obviously Dr. Lilly saw things differently."

Brainert smirked. "Obviously."

"What are you saying, Brainert?" I asked. "Do you believe Dr. Lilly based an entire book on unsubstantiated gossip?"

Brainert sighed. "If there's any *real* evidence in here, I'll be willing to consider it. Until then, I'm putting this theory about Hedda on the level of Frannie McGuire's story that she sold Elvis Presley take-out quahogs at the Seafood Shack in 1992."

"What's so hard to believe?" Seymour said with a wrinkled brow. "Everybody knows Elvis staged his own death."

"Now you're being ridiculous," Brainert sniffed.

"And you're being naïve," Seymour charged, "to trust a spiderwoman like

Hedda Geist —"

"Wait one minute," said Brainert, loudly snapping shut Lilly's book. "It's one thing to speculate about a woman's past. It's quite another to insult her with a name like that. I'll not have you slander a major contributor to the history of motion picture arts, not to mention an upstanding member of our community —"

"*Our* community?!" Seymour cried. "The old bag lives in Newport. Since when can we afford to live in Newport?"

"Hold the phone," I said.

"What?" they asked together.

"Hedda Geist may live in Newport now, but she didn't come from money. Not even close." While the two men were bickering, I'd continued to skim Dr. Lilly's book. I pointed to one of the early chapters. "It says here that Hedda was the fourth daughter in a family of seven. Her father was arrested for robbery when she was nine and died in a prison brawl. Hedda's mother cleaned houses to make ends meet."

"Then how'd she get into the movie business?" Seymour asked.

I continued skimming the text. "Seems Hedda's two older sisters were known to make, uh . . . 'dates' with men for money. They encouraged Hedda to do the same."

"That's a libelous accusation!" Brainert cried.

"Dr. Lilly claims it was one of Hedda's 'boyfriends' who got her a break at sixteen, a bit part in a Gotham Features film that was shooting exteriors near Hedda's neighborhood. Apparently, Hedda worked hard after that first break. She took speech lessons, dance lessons, and kept on moving up the Gotham ladder of players until she finally landed a leading lady role at twenty. You know the rest."

Brainert frowned. "*The rest* is an unsubstantiated charge of cold-blooded murder. And I still don't believe it."

I exhaled, trying to puzzle out a next step. How could I or anyone else prove — or disprove — Dr. Lilly's theory of Irving Vreen's death? Irene Lilly herself was dead, so we couldn't ask her to back up her accusations. And the crime happened so far in the past, pretty much everyone connected to the crime was dead. Everyone except Hedda and —

"We could talk to Pierce Armstrong!" I exclaimed.

"And ask him what?" Brainert demanded.

"We can ask him if Dr. Lilly's charges are true!" Seymour replied. "That's a great idea, Pen!"

I vigorously nodded. "If Pierce Armstrong was railroaded, then he has a powerful motive for wanting to see the truth about the past come out and Hedda Geist brought to justice."

"I suppose so . . ." Brainert reluctantly admitted.

"It would also prove that Hedda Geist had a reason to want Dr. Lilly out of the way," Seymour said.

Brainert frowned. "Surely you're not suggesting that frail old woman murdered Dr. Lilly?"

"Okay, maybe she didn't do it herself," said Seymour with a shrug, "but she is rich enough to buy an accomplice."

"Or keep it inside the family by using someone like her granddaughter, Harmony," I noted.

Seymour shook his head. "So sad to think that a hottie like that could actually be a hellion. But I guess rotten apples don't fall far from the tree."

Brainert tightly folded his arms. "I don't like this."

"Then there's something else you won't like," I said and informed Brainert about the break-in at Dr. Lilly's rented bungalow. "Her laptop, tape recorder, and a number of audio cassettes appeared to have been stolen. I'm betting Dr. Lilly had damaging evidence in her possession — all the more reason we should speak with Pierce Armstrong as soon as possible."

Brainert nodded. "I suppose Mr. Armstrong could shed some light on all this. He'll be at the festival sometime this weekend. He's a surprise guest, you know. It was my colleague who arranged his appearance."

"Which colleague?" I asked.

"The dean," said Brainert. "Dr. Wendell Pepper."

Seymour blinked. "Dr. Pepper? The man named after the soft drink that uses prunes for flavoring?"

Brainert exhaled in disgust at Seymour's relentless needling.

"We should strike while the iron is hot," I quickly suggested. "Has Armstrong even arrived in Quindicott yet?"

Brainert nodded. "Oh, yes. By now he should be here."

"Great!" I said. "Where's he staying?"

"With Dr. Pepper," said Brainert. "He has plenty of room. He owns a very large house on Larchmont Avenue and —"

"He's the most original soft drink ever in the whole wild world —"

"Stop it, Seymour!"

Seymour laughed. "It's just too easy to

get a rise out of you, Parker. So, Pepper lives on Larchmont, eh!" Seymour clapped his hands and rubbed them together. "Man I'd love to see the inside of one of those giant old mansions. Ring Dean Soda Pop up and get us an invite."

Brainert wrinkled his nose at Seymour's disheveled postal uniform, now stained with grass and dirt. "Shouldn't you go home and change your clothes?"

"That's a great idea. I want to look my best when I meet Pierce Armstrong — Big Mike O'Bannon — in the flesh," Seymour said, grinning. "Lucky for me, I don't have to go home. I have civvies packed in the trunk of my car."

"But don't you still have *mail* to deliver?" Brainert pressed.

"I already called in a favor, asked a colleague to finish my route for me," Seymour replied. "I'm free to pursue this case for the rest of the weekend. I'll just run along and fetch my clothes, and we can be off."

Scowling, Brainert pulled his cell phone from the pocket of his blue blazer. Before he could dial Dr. Pepper's number, however, Aunt Sadie stuck her head through the stock room door.

"Sorry to interrupt," she said softly.

"Aunt Sadie!" I approached her with a

copy of *Murdered in Plain Sight.* "Do me a favor. Is Spencer home from his Little League clinic?"

"Yes, he just got back. He headed upstairs to play a video game, but he asked for permission to go to his best friend Danny's house tonight for dinner and a sleepover in Danny's new tent. Sounds like fun. Apparently, Mr. Keenan just set it up in their backyard."

"A sleepover in a tent . . . ?" I frowned, my mind shifting gears to mother mode. I couldn't help worrying about everything Spencer might need for an outing like that — PJ's that were warm enough for a May evening, his sleeping bag, toothbrush, underwear. It might get pretty chilly so he'd need extra blankets, a sweatshirt. And all of that would be hard to carry. I checked my watch and shook my head. I couldn't drive Spencer over to Danny's house! My Saturn's battery was still dead, and —

You're being a real Killjoy Jane, you know that?

"Excuse me, Jack," I silently told the ghost, "but this doesn't concern you —"

That kid's no infant. He can carry his own kit across town, for cripes sake. What's the problem? He got an invite from his best friend. Let him play Davy Crockett for a night if he wants to.

"The problem is . . ." I started to argue, but then I stopped myself. "Wait. Did you just say he got an invite from his *best* friend?"

Wake up, Wanda.

I blinked. Spencer never had a best friend before. Oh, he'd been friendly with classmates back in the city, but he'd been so shy and morose when Calvin was alive — wilting in his father's depressive shadow.

Things were different now. And Spencer was different, too. He'd been in the same class with Danny Keenan for the past year, but it was only lately, since Little League had begun, that the two had become really tight. I hated to admit it, but Jack was right. This invitation was important. And it was exactly the reason I'd moved back to Quindicott, so Spencer could get away from his worries, make friends, enjoy the world around him, enjoy *living.*

I faced Aunt Sadie. "Do you think Danny's mother or father could pick Spencer up? My car's battery is still dead."

Sadie smiled. "I'm sure they'd be happy to do that."

"Well, if not . . . I can always ask Seymour to help out and drive him over. Either way, it's okay." I nodded. "Tell Spencer he's allowed to spend the night at Danny's."

Nice call, baby.

"Thanks, Jack," I whispered to the ghost — and then I remembered Dr. Lilly's book in my hands. "Oh! Aunt Sadie, one more thing: Ask Spencer to run this book over to Fiona Finch. She'll know what to do with it."

Overhearing me, Brainert groaned. "You're not bringing Fiona into this?"

"She's already involved, Brainiac," Seymour informed him.

"And she's a true-crime expert," I added. "I want her opinion of what Dr. Lilly's written."

"Good idea," said Aunt Sadie, taking the book from my hands. "But the reason I came back here wasn't to tell you that Spencer was home."

"What's up?"

"I wanted to let you know that Ms. Hedda Geist-Middleton has just entered the bookshop with her granddaughter, Harmony."

CHAPTER 13
ONCE A DIVA

She was the greatest of them all. In one week she received seventeen thousand fan letters. Men bribed her hair-dresser to get a lock of her hair. There was a maharajah who came all the way from India to beg one of her silk stockings. Later he strangled himself with it.

— Sunset Boulevard, 1950

I hurried onto the bookshop's selling floor. Hedda Geist-Middleton was standing near the front door, surveying the crowded aisles with the regal mannerisms of a minor monarch.

"I'm ready for my signing," she announced after I introduced myself.

And her close-up, Jack quipped in my head. *I see the old broad's returned to the scene of the crime.*

"If she's guilty."

True . . . if . . .

Jack's jaundiced tone made me take a closer look at Hedda. As I shared pleasantries with the former actress — asking about her stay at the Finch Inn, explaining how our signings work — I tried to assess what the woman was capable of.

Despite her advanced age, Hedda Geist still glowed with charisma and energy. She was tall, lean, and didn't appear particularly delicate or fragile. Mostly, she projected class and elegance. Her silk blouse of emerald green perfectly matched her famous catlike eyes. Her cream-colored crepe slacks draped like filmy curtains; a wide belt of hand-tooled leather cinched them fashionably at the hip. Her silver-white hair was neatly pinned back to show off platinum earrings.

Even her perfume was unique and elegant — a distinctly delicate scent of orange blossoms. I'd never smelled a scent like it.

It was hard not to admire the elderly lady. Her confidence was magnetic and she spoke with eloquence and power.

"Could Brainert possibly be right?" I quietly wondered.

Right about what? Jack suddenly challenged. *Spill, baby . . .*

"It's true that Hedda was reckless when she was younger. She threw over her actor boyfriend for the married head of her studio, and when the two men confronted each other, she was caught in a horrifying position. But that doesn't necessarily make the woman a murderer, does it?"

Go on . . .

"What if the real femme fatale here isn't Hedda Geist? What if Brainert's right? What if it's Dr. Lilly?"

"What if" don't pay the rent, baby. You've got to sell me.

"Think about it, Jack. For years Irene Lilly's been living in the academic shadows. Her backlist film studies were never big sellers — there are hundreds of books like them, carrying the same sorts of essays and retrospectives. Perhaps Dr. Lilly wanted to come out of the shadows for once in her career, not to mention make certain her retirement nest would be well feathered."

You're saying Dr. Lilly was peddling pabulum and knew it?

"A PhD at the end of your name doesn't grant you a halo. Publish or perish is an academic credo, and I know for a fact that stress can drive some professors to rather unethical ends —"

Just a guess, baby, but I'm thinking my idea of "unethical ends" may be a tad different than yours.

"I'm talking about professors who hire professional writers to ghost their papers, even entire books. And I'm not saying Dr. Lilly did that. I'm simply saying she *might* have chucked academic honesty out the window. Maybe she never had any evidence about Hedda Geist's past. Maybe Irene Lilly simply wanted to use that dark moment at the Porterhouse restaurant to gain media attention for an otherwise ordinary biography."

So you think our dead Lilly just wanted big headlines?

"Today's news business is a pretty hungry monster: 24/7 cable news, thousands of Internet sites globally. Leveling sensational charges would have gotten the book some sort of attention, even if the charges were ultimately unsubstantiated."

I flashed back on the image of what Jack had showed me at the Porterhouse. When Irving Vreen had fallen on that steak knife, the young Hedda's horrified reaction appeared real enough to me. She seemed genuinely shocked that she'd stabbed the man.

Sure she did, baby, Jack whispered in my head, *but then Hedda was one of the best actresses around, wasn't she?*

"True."

Appearing as anything the script called for was her specialty. Just like now . . .

"What do you mean?"

Queen Hedda of Newport, daughter of old money. It's an act, baby, just another part. Remember what you read in that book about her childhood? The broad wasn't born the daughter of royalty or privilege. Back in my time, the dame grew up with a fishmonger's accent, in the shadow of those Long Island City smokestacks we drove by.

"True . . . Dr. Lilly did bring up some pretty ugly details from her youth. With Hedda and her family trying so hard to maintain the upper-class image, the book could prove embarrassing . . ."

Yeah, baby. It could.

I swallowed uneasily, seeing a brand-new motive for Hedda to want Lilly killed — along with the book's publicity.

But could Hedda have done away with Dr. Lilly all by herself? Brainert had characterized Hedda as frail and old. While her age was obvious, I wondered how "frail" she really was.

Time to go fishing, sweetheart.

"Right," I told Jack. Then I turned to Hedda.

"We have quite a lot of customers queued up for your signing in the Events room, Ms.

Geist. How's your strength? Do you feel up to this?"

Hedda waved her hand, flashing more platinum on two diamond rings. "I still ride two hours every day on my horse farm," she said with a proud little smile. "I think I can handle scribbling my name on a few books."

She gestured to someone behind me. I turned to find her granddaughter, Harmony, standing there. The young woman looked as stunning as ever in a belly-baring white tank and a low-riding skirt of designer denim. Her layered blonde hair was loose, her pretty feet at the end of long, tanned legs, were manicured with pink nail polish and caressed by sandals of Italian leather.

I greeted her, counting at least three small groups of young men who were either gaping openly in her direction or glancing furtively at her backside while whispering among themselves. I didn't see Dixon Gallagher among the admiring males — and none of them looked big enough to be that Darth Vader biker who'd run me down in the woods near Charity Point.

Ignoring the lump that still throbbed high on my forehead, I clapped my hands and brightly suggested, "Shall we move into the Events room?"

Both women followed me into the large

space, where a crowd had been marshaled into a civilized queue, thanks to Seymour Tarnish. "Don't push, people! There are plenty of Hedda's books available. I *said*, don't push! That means you, buster!"

The fans were all ages and they began to applaud and whistle when they saw Hedda enter the room. The old actress smiled, obviously pleased, and gave her adoring fans a royal wave. I showed her where to sit.

She took her time settling herself into the padded armchair behind the polished walnut table. "Is there water, Mrs. McClure?"

"Yes, of course." I presented her with a sealed bottle. She eyed it with a frown of obvious disapproval. I got the hint, opened it, and poured it into a paper cup.

Hedda took a sip and cleared her throat. "Now . . . where are my special pens? Harmony!"

Harmony stepped up and provided them. "Here you are, Grandma."

"Thank you, Harmony. You're such a dear! Enjoy yourself now, darling. Why don't you select some books for your summer reading. My treat."

Harmony smiled, nodded at me, and wandered off toward the selling floor — the eyes of just about every male in the room watching her leave.

The signing went fairly smoothly after that, with the exception of a plump older man in a sports jacket who attempted to monopolize Hedda with gushing tales of his fandom.

". . . and I have every poster on my wall and a signed photograph from the publicity department of Gotham Features. Oh, how I treasure that photo. I can't believe I'm here talking to you. To finally smell your perfume is a thrill for me." The man made a show of inhaling the air. "Ah . . . that delicate orange-blossom scent. I read in your book how a French admirer sent you a bottle of Vouloir from Paris, and it's the only perfume you've ever worn since. Your signature scent. I can finally smell it for myself. Intoxicating! Now, let me ask you about playing opposite Pierce Armstrong in —"

"Okay, buddy!" Seymour shouted. "Hedda signed your book. Now move along! Give someone else a chance!"

As the crowd dwindled down, I stepped up to Hedda.

"More water, Ms. Geist?"

"Yes . . . unless you have a good bottle of California Sauvignon Blanc handy?" She smiled. "My late husband had friends who owned a vineyard in Napa. I'm a sucker for a good Sav."

"Sorry, no wine," I said. "We tried serving alcohol once at a signing but our local councilwoman fined us for not having a liquor license."

"What a shame."

I opened a fresh bottle of water and cleared my throat. With the signing almost over, I knew this was the best chance I had to ask the former actress a few more questions.

"I was wondering, Ms. Geist," I began, as I refilled her cup. "Did you hear about Dr. Lilly?"

"Terrible business . . ." Hedda shook her head, but her eyes remained down, focused on the table and the book she was signing. "A tragic accident to be sure . . ."

"Just like last evening," I replied. "That large, heavy speaker falling onto the stage."

"Oh, yes!" She straightened immediately and met my eyes. "I was quite put out. It could have killed me!"

"*Or* Dr. Lilly," I noted.

"Oh, no!" Hedda frowned. "You're mistaken, Mrs. McClure. Dr. Lilly stepped aside to let *me* speak. She was completely clear of danger when that speaker *careened* toward the stage and nearly finished me!"

With wide dramatic eyes Hedda stared at me a moment, then she turned back to the crowd, her expression instantly transforming into a warm smile as she waved the next customer forward.

"Come, come!" she said brightly. "Step up!"

"Okay," I silently told Jack, "that was weird."

Jack snorted. *Once a diva, always a diva.*

"Or drama queen . . ."

A rose by any other name . . . still wants the spotlight.

Clearing my throat, I stepped closer to the former actress. "I was wondering something else, Ms. Geist," I said quietly as she signed the next customer's book. "Did you know about Dr. Lilly's new publication?"

"What's that, Mrs. McClure? You say Dr. Lilly had a new book?"

"Yes, but it wasn't a film study like her other titles. This book was a biography of your life and career, and it made quite a few rather sensational charges at the end of it."

"Is that so?" Hedda finished signing and handed the book back to the young woman. She waved the next customer forward, a young man wearing a St. Francis College T-shirt.

"You know, it's sad." She glanced at me, then back down at the book she was signing. "There are so many desperate writers out there like Irene Lilly, hacking out some story that wouldn't have existed in the first place if it weren't for people like *me,* people with innate talent who risked and toiled to become recognized figures. They're rather like parasites, don't you think?"

"Dr. Lilly claims in this new book that Irving Vreen's death wasn't an accident. She claims that Pierce Armstrong was set up and betrayed. She claims that what happened at the Porterhouse restaurant in 1948 was calculated, premeditated. Cold-blooded murder."

Hedda ignored me for a moment, handed the book she'd just signed to the young man and waved at the next person to step up. It was another young man, a very handsome one wearing a fraternity jacket. She winked flirtatiously at the boy and laughed.

"What do you think, young man?" she teased. "Have I still got it?"

He laughed and nodded vigorously, his cheeks reddening. She giggled like a young girl, then opened his book and began to sign.

"You know, Mrs. McClure . . ." She looked my way, then back to the book. "Another ambitious writer once tried to stir the pot, just like Dr. Lilly. This was back in

1966, before you were even born."

"What happened?" I pressed.

"This young man, a magazine journalist, tracked me down, tried to shock me with allegations and pointed questions. I had nothing to say, of course. He dug and dug but found nothing and simply gave up. Nobody really cared anymore, you see? It was all played out already. Irving Vreen was long dead by then. And nobody really cares about the dead. To the living, they're just . . . irrelevant."

Speak for yourself, you old bag!

"Easy, Jack."

I'll show the self-satisfied biddy how irrelevant the dead are!

"No, Jack. No more haunting the customers! You promised!"

Just a little levitating table action, baby. Maybe blow some frigid wind up her pristine pants.

"Jack! Behave!"

Why? If I give her a heart attack, maybe she'll finally see how irrelevant she really is.

Hedda smiled and shook her head, as if amused. "Later, in the seventies," she went on, "there was a famous episode of an old television police show that was a thinly disguised version of what happened that night at the Porterhouse. The show cast me

254

as the kind of femme fatale I played on screen, tried to say that I planned Irving's death. But that was a television show. Complete fiction. Just like Dr. Lilly's book . . ."

My brow wrinkled. "I thought you said that you didn't know about her book."

"I don't. I just . . ." Hedda shrugged. "I simply assumed from what you've told me that she was trying to do what that journalist had tried to do: dredge up an ugly incident for her own gain."

"I haven't read the entire book yet," I admitted. "But Dr. Lilly may have found proof to substantiate her charges."

Hedda sighed. "Well, if she didn't put it in the book, I guess we'll never know, will we? I mean . . ." The elderly actress fixed her cool green gaze on me. "We can't very well ask her *now,* can we?"

"No," I said, holding Hedda's fixed stare, "we can't."

The actress nodded and turned back to her signing.

"But," I added after a moment, "I'm sure someone will be asking Pierce Armstrong about it this weekend."

Hedda froze the moment I mentioned the name of her former leading man. Her pen stopped moving. *Hedda G—* was as far as her small, fluid script got. It took a few more seconds for her to finish writing her own name.

"Pierce Armstrong?" she finally repeated after clearing her throat. "I'm sorry. What's that you're saying, Mrs. McClure? I think I misheard you."

"Pierce Armstrong is going to appear at the Quindicott Film Noir Festival sometime this weekend. He's a surprise guest."

"But . . . how can that be? Nobody's heard from Mr. Armstrong in decades . . . I mean . . . his name disappeared off the guild lists, and . . . I . . . I didn't realize that he was even still alive."

"I haven't seen him yet myself. He's in town though. Professor Brainert Parker told me he's staying as a guest in Dean Pepper's home."

"Well, it's been years, I must say. More like a lifetime. I can't imagine what Pierce would think, seeing me after all these decades . . . but I'd be very interested in saying hello to him. . . ." Hedda's smile appeared tight. She lowered her voice. Through gritted teeth, she asked: "How many *more* books must I sign here, Mrs. McClure?"

I glanced up at the crowd. Only about a half-dozen more people were lined up. I signaled to Seymour. "That young woman in the blue shirt is the last one in line. Let's keep it that way, okay? We're done after her."

Seymour saluted. "Aye, aye, Captain."

Hedda signed two more books and then an attractive, dark haired man stepped up — he had sleepy eyes and a yellow J. Crew Windbreaker draped over his arm. I recognized him instantly. And I noticed with interest that he was no longer carrying his bulky canvas backpack.

"Hello there, Hedda." The man's voice was as smooth as I remembered. "Would you mind signing a book for your biggest fan?"

"Dr. Rubino!" Hedda immediately brightened. "What a delightful surprise!"

"The delight is seeing you here," he said. "I was in town on business, and I almost forgot that this weekend was the film noir festival you were telling me about at your last appointment." Randall Rubino's sleepy dark eyes glanced up at me then, and he smiled. "Penelope here was good enough to let me know about your signing." He handed the book over. "Would you mind?"

"Mind? I'm flattered! And more than happy to oblige with a *personal* inscription . . ."

Rubino nodded and set down the book.

As Hedda went about scribbling a note in her small, fluid handwriting, I suddenly remembered something.

"Jack?" I silently whispered.

Yeah, baby?

"Have you noticed how small Hedda's handwriting is?"

Yeah, baby, an hour ago. I was waiting to see how long it'd take you.

"In the dream you gave me, Benny had to squint to make out the second signature in the Gotham Features log book. The first Pierce Armstrong signature was in big, bold block letters, the second was small, fluid script."

So either Armstrong likes to write his name two different ways, or Hedda signed out the second car herself and wrote down Pierce's name to keep herself out of the written record.

"So what was she doing picking up the DA's mistress at the Hotel Chester? Was she a friend of the girl's? Isn't that a little coincidental — since the DA was at the Porterhouse the very night of Vreen's stabbing? And what's with Dr. Rubino showing up here after his run in the woods? I still think it was strangely coincidental that I spotted him near the lighthouse so soon after the burglary."

After a few more charming but fairly insubstantial remarks to Hedda, Dr. Rubino gave me another smile, then picked up his signed book and stepped away. I watched his back as he wandered toward the Event room's exit.

Why are you just standing there, baby? You're not letting him go, are you? Get your panties in gear, and go brace the man!

My eyes wide from Jack's balling-out, I hastily excused myself from Hedda's side and rushed across the room to catch Rubino.

"Doctor? Pardon me! Dr. Rubino, I'd like to speak with you in private."

Randall Rubino turned around and calmly nodded, as if he wasn't one bit surprised to be collared. "Of course, Penelope, of course."

He almost sounded resigned. I pointed to a quiet corner of the Events room. We strolled over there, and Rubino immediately started talking.

"I can't say that I'm surprised by this, Penelope."

"Really?"

"I don't think you should be embarrassed, either."

"I'm not."

"Good. What happened earlier was quite

a shock. Anyone would have reacted the way you did."

I blinked, hardly able to believe getting the man to talk was going to be this easy. "That's nice of you to say, Dr. Rubino, considering the situation."

Strangely enough, Dr. Rubino then handed me Hedda's book to hold while he reached into his jacket pocket for a pad and pen.

"Oh, Doctor. You don't have to write it down. Just talk to me, tell me everything. Get it all off your chest."

The doctor froze. "What are you talking about?"

"What do you mean? I'm talking about seeing you at the Charity Point Lighthouse and running after you into the woods. I wanted to question you then, but I lost you. I assume you have something to confess, and I'm glad you're making it easy."

"Now I *really* don't know what you're talking about," said Rubino.

"Well what were *you* talking about?"

"Writing you a prescription for Valium, of course!"

"I thought you were going to explain *why* you were running away from a recently burglarized bungalow. A bungalow belonging to a woman who you declared died of an accident — when it was not an accident at all."

"Penelope, I really do think you need some medication." Rubino began scribbling on his prescription pad.

"Don't evade the question, Doctor. What were you doing at the Charity Point Lighthouse?"

"If you must know, I was hiking the area, looking for a good spot to *fish.* I did notice a *no trespassing* sign near the lighthouse and that's why I hurried away. I had no idea I was on private property." He shook his head. "I'm surprised to learn you saw me — or that you were trying to chase me down."

I studied Rubino's knitted brows. "You fish?"

"Yes, the area near your town has some of the best oceanside fishing in the state. When Chief Ciders called me here today, I packed my gear."

"Oh, you packed your gear, did you? Then where is it?"

"In the trunk of my car. Where else?" Rubino ripped off the prescription and handed it to me. "Now if you'll give me back my signed book, I'll be on my way."

"But . . ."

Dr. Rubino snatched the book from my

hands. "I'd advise you to get that prescription filled right away, Penelope. The stress is obviously getting to you." Then he turned on his heel and began to walk away. "And don't take it with alcohol," he tossed over his shoulder.

Congratulations, baby, your gumshoeing just got hinky.

"Well, you weren't exactly a big help."

There was no saving that interrogation, honey. It was about the absolute worst I've seen in all my years — and I'm including the dead ones.

"You don't need to rub it in."

Tell you what: I'll make it up to you.

"What? Another night tailing cheating husbands while drinking martinis stirred not shaken?"

No baby, another lead. Turn around and take a look at who else seems to be Dr. Rubino's friend.

Through the archway connecting the Events room to the store's selling floor, I saw Randall Rubino speaking with someone. I took a few steps closer to the room's exit and finally saw who: Harmony Middleton. The two were standing very close, their heads bent together in private conversation. As I watched, it appeared the good doctor was growing impatient, even angry.

A lover's spat? Jack proposed.

"Could be," I replied.

Suddenly, Rubino stepped back, grasped young Harmony's upper arm, and pulled her away from the crowded part of the store.

Get closer, baby. Follow them.

I did. Careful to stay clear of their sightline, I tailed them to a quiet aisle near the back corner, where I stocked a collection of children's and young adult mysteries for the families in the area. I peeked around the endcap display of Encyclopedia Brown books — the ones Spencer had devoured back in fourth grade.

"Come on, Randy . . . you know I need it."

It was Harmony's voice and it sounded whiney, like a brat who wanted candy.

"Let's not go down that road again, Harmony. You remember what happened the last time."

"You're being difficult. Can't you see my side?"

"Let's table this discussion. It's not the time or place. Talk to me another time, all right?"

"When?"

"Whenever you need to. Ring my cell, and we can straighten this out."

The two parted then, and I quickly moved

263

away from the aisle.

"What do you think, Jack? Seems awfully suspicious," I noted.

Jack agreed then reminded me of one more suspicious thing. *Dr. Charm says he was looking for a fishing spot when you saw him hiking near the lighthouse with a backpack, right?*

"Right."

When you saw him out there, he was carrying a pack and nothing else. Where the hell was his fishing pole?

Chapter 14
True Crime

It was a great big elephant of a place, the kind of place crazy movie people built in the crazy twenties.
— *Sunset Boulevard,* 1950

I returned to the front of the store, resolving to keep Randall Rubino high on my "suspects with hinky alibis" list. I noticed Brainert finishing up a call on his cell. I walked over to him.

"Have you spoken with Dr. Pepper?"

Brainert closed his phone. "All I get is his voice mail. I've tried his home, the college, even the box office at the theater, but I can't locate the man." He sighed. "I'm sure Pierce Armstrong is settled at Wendell's house by now, but the old man might be reluctant to answer someone else's phone —"

"Then let's drive over. Surely Armstrong will answer the door if he's there."

Brainert nodded. "My thoughts exactly.

I'm parked right across the street, and it's a short drive to Larchmont Avenue."

"Let's go."

I gave Sadie a heads-up, grabbed my purse from behind the sales counter, and hurried back to Brainert, who quickly scanned the room. "No sign of Seymour," he said, and started for the door.

"Wait! I'm sure he's around. He was helping me with Hedda's signing, but we're all through with that now, so he's probably changing out of his uniform —"

"No, no, Pen. You misunderstand," Brainert whispered conspiratorially. "Seymour's absence is a good thing. We don't need him fawning over Pierce Armstrong while we try to interview the man, or poking fun at Dr. Pepper's good name and embarrassing us both."

Suddenly a large arm snaked around Brainert's neck and a beefy hand mussed his neatly combed hair.

"That's what I love about you, Brainiac," Seymour said. "Always a stickler for etiquette."

Brainert quickly extricated himself from his friend's bear hug and smoothed down his neatly cut brown hair. He whirled to face Seymour and gasped.

"What's the matter?" Seymour said, arms

wide. "I told you I was going to change into civilian clothes."

Seymour's large T-shirt sported a vintage Mighty Mouse flying over a cartoon skyline, tiny cape fluttering in the breeze. His hairy legs stuck out of khaki shorts that ended just above his dimpled knees. Size-twelve feet were tucked into clogs, which he wore sans socks.

Brainert groaned. "How old are you?"

"Old enough," Seymour replied.

"Except for your lack of a baseball hat — worn backward, of course — you could pass for one of my college students' younger siblings."

Seymour reached back, yanked a ragged Red Sox cap out of his back pocket, and donned it *backward.*

"Let's go," he said. "I can't wait to meet Pierce Armstrong."

Larchmont Avenue was a quiet, shady boulevard at the top of a picturesque hill on the edge of town. The homes were large three- and four-story structures surrounded by expansive lawns and lush topiaries. Each house was unique. Many had flagstone paths, balconies, even widow's walks circling their roofs. The oaks, elm, maple, and chestnut trees that dotted the lawns and hugged the walls of the homes were well over a century old. And no home here was built later than the 1920s. That was about the last time most people in our little town of Quindicott had been able to afford a new house as large as these.

The dean of St. Francis's School of Communications lived here, too, in a sprawling three-story building of sand-colored stone, red roof tiles, arched windows, and wrought-iron balconies.

On the drive over, Brainert had explained that the dean's large house was a repository for his lifelong interest in certain collectibles.

"It's practically a museum dedicated to Hollywood of the 1940s through the '70s, chiefly related to film noir. I'm sure you'll both be impressed. It's a superb collection. The Smithsonian has expressed interest in obtaining certain pieces after his death."

Brainert parked at the curb. He tried his colleague's home phone one more time, but only connected with the answering machine.

With a sigh, he closed his cell phone. "Let's go."

We followed a winding stone path through a manicured lawn trimmed in dark green shrubs and bright red tulips. At the large front porch, we paused in front of the door.

"I hope someone's here," Brainert said as

he rang the bell.

I heard movement in the house on the second ring. The lock clicked and to my surprise screenwriter and novelist Maggie Kline opened the door.

"Parker! What a surprise!" Laugh lines creased the edges of her eyes as she gave him a big smile. She adjusted her red-framed glasses and put a hand on the hip of her low-waisted khakis. "And you brought friends, I see. Is this a party? Did Wendell invite you over? Come on in."

We entered a high-roofed foyer with bright yellow walls and a slowly rotating ceiling fan. The space was dominated by a huge framed poster for the film *Taxi Driver.* The central image of Robert De Niro as Travis Bickle was framed by a yellow border, which matched the walls. Below it was a glass case, displaying a pistol rigged on some kind of sliding rail — a prop from one of the movie's scenes, I assumed.

"The man in the Mighty Mouse shirt is Seymour Tarnish," Brainert told Maggie. "Seymour is our local mailman, and a big fan of Pierce Armstrong's."

"Oh, I see. You came to pay him a visit. I'm so sorry, he's not here. Wendell just took Pierce over to the Movie Town Theater for his first talk of the weekend."

Brainert sighed. "I'm sorry we missed him, too. I called several times but —"

"Uh-oh, my bad. I've been ignoring the phone. This is kind of embarrassing, but . . ." Maggie made a pained face. "Wendell's ex-wife has been calling and calling. I didn't want to complicate matters by picking up the phone again and getting into a conversation with the woman about who I am and why I'm staying with Wendell. We had one brief, unhappy conversation, and frankly I don't care to go through a repeat performance. But let's not dwell on that. Come in! Come in!"

Maggie led us into the living room. Here the bone-white walls were lined with three-foot-tall posters, framed under protective glass. On one wall, Humphrey Bogart was facing off with Mary Astor in *The Maltese Falcon;* Fred MacMurray was passionately kissing Barbara Stanwyck in *Double Indemnity,* the words *You can't kiss away a murder!* emblazoned across their clinched bodies; and Veronica Lake's stunning image smoldered away in *This Gun for Hire* — her first film with Alan Ladd, who was destined to become her leading man in the classic noirs *The Blue Dahlia* and *The Glass Key.*

I walked the length of the room, taking in more legendary images: the ravishing, raven-haired Faith Domergue clutching a gun as sleepy-eyed Robert Mitchum grabbed for her in *Where Danger Lives;* Robert Montgomery's finger squeezing a trigger in *The Lady in the Lake;* trench-coated cop Dana Andrews appearing completely smitten with the bewitching Gene Tierney in *Laura;* and Bogart facing off with yet another woman, this time his legendary lady love, Lauren Bacall, in *The Big Sleep.*

"Wow," I said. "These old movie posters are absolutely amazing."

"They're actually called one-sheets," Maggie said.

"One-sheets?"

"That's right." Maggie pointed to the faintest traces of creasing in the *Double Indemnity* poster. "Until the 1960s, one-sheet posters were printed on uncoated paper and folded into rectangles for shipping. That's why it's so hard to get them in good condition. Wendell's done a magnificent job preserving these."

A few of the framed one-sheets were surrounded by smaller posters, displaying entirely different scenes from the films. "And what are these called?" I asked, pointing to the smaller posters.

"Oh, those aren't posters. Those are lobby cards," Maggie informed me. "They're printed on heavy cardstock instead of paper, and they were usually sent by the studios in sets of eight. Theater owners placed them in the lobby — hence the name. They were very similar to window cards."

"Okay," I said, "you got me again. What exactly are window cards?"

Maggie gestured to a 14-by-22 inch card advertising the 1945 film *Detour.* "Window cards were printed on heavy cardstock, too. You can tell the difference between a window card and a lobby card by this blank strip at the top of the card. See?" She pointed to the top of the card. "The local theater would use that space to write its name. In this case, it was the Empire, in New York City."

Waddya know, my old haunt, said Jack, obviously amused. *Of course, back then I charged a per diem for my haunting. 'Cause I wasn't dead yet.*

"Oh, Jack . . ." I privately groaned. "That is so bad . . ."

"So, Maggie," Brainert spoke up, "you *and* Pierce are both staying here?"

Maggie nodded. "This house is large enough to put up five guests, let alone two, but I guess you know that."

Seymour's bulging eyes had been bugged out in awe since he entered the living room.

"Mind if I have a look around?" he asked.

"No problem! Enjoy," Maggie replied.

Seymour wandered off — I presumed in pursuit of any Fisherman Detective memorabilia — and Maggie continued to chatter away.

"Wendell's so proud of his movie mementos. He tells me his ex-wife would only allow them in *certain* rooms. Now that she's gone, he's put things all over the house. It's wonderful! Reminds me of when I was growing up. My father was in the movie business. It was so exciting. He saved every poster his studio ever put out. Unfortunately, it was all lost after he died. Anyway, there aren't many folks in this area who really appreciate the scope of a collection like this. Things would be different on the West Coast —"

"Excuse me," Brainert finally interrupted, "but you mentioned that Wendell took Pierce Armstrong to the Movie Town Theater?"

"That's right."

Brainert scratched his head. "I wasn't aware that a talk was scheduled for this afternoon."

"It wasn't. It's kind of a last-minute thing," Maggie explained. "Pierce agreed to a lengthy appearance on stage tomorrow, as well as an autograph session. But when he found out there was a screening of one of his short-subject films today, he expressed an interest in seeing it. So Wendell suggested an impromptu Q&A after the showing. I'm sure it will be quite a shock for the audience to see the Fisherman Detective in the flesh. But then Pierce is supposed to be one of the weekend's special 'surprise' guests." Maggie laughed. "Surprise!"

Maggie's face fell after that. She touched Brainert's arm. "Frankly, I think Wendell wanted to cheer the old man up. Pierce took the news of Dr. Lilly's death very hard."

I blinked. "Pierce Armstrong *knew* Dr. Lilly?"

Maggie nodded. "Dr. Lilly taped an extensive interview with him for her next book."

"Her *next* book," I repeated. "Not the one that was just published?"

"That's right," said Maggie.

I stepped closer. "Did Pierce Armstrong say what the unpublished book was going to be about?"

"Haven't a clue." Maggie removed her red-framed glasses and cleaned them with the edge of her T-shirt. "He claimed Dr. Lilly's project was top secret. Funny, huh?"

"More like puzzling." Brainert frowned. "Dr. Lilly's current book is about Hedda

Geist's life and her career at Gotham Features. I wonder why she didn't interview Pierce Armstrong for that one?"

"That I can tell you," said Maggie, popping her glasses back on. "Apparently, Dr. Lilly caught up with Pierce only a few months ago. He was living incognito in a Florida retirement community. That's how he got on board with your film festival — through Dr. Lilly. I have to admit, I was shocked to learn the man was still alive and kicking. There are very few actors of his generation still breathing."

"Did you say Pierce Armstrong was living *incognito?*" Brainert asked.

Maggie nodded. "At the time Dr. Lilly found him, he was living under his given name, which is Franklin Pierce Peacock. He changed it to Pierce Armstrong for his Hollywood career, but there's nothing unique about that. In Hollywood, people's names are about as authentic as your average anorexic starlet's C-cup breasts."

My mind was racing. "Jack?" I silently called. "Are you hearing this?"

Yeah, baby. I always pay attention when the conversation turns to women's breasts.

"Are you joking?"

Jack laughed.

"What's gotten into you?"

275

I don't know. An entire house dedicated to pretend stuff sort of strikes me as funny.

"Well, I'm not laughing. I'm thinking about all those missing tapes in Dr. Lilly's bungalow."

I know, baby. If your friend Maggie here is right, then Dr. Lilly has been secretly interviewing Pierce Armstrong, which means those tapes are probably the ones that are missing. In fact, I'd be willing to bet the ranch . . . if I had a ranch.

"Pierce could be the key, Jack. He could be the reason Dr. Lilly was working on a second book. He could be providing proof that the allegations made in her first book are true."

Not necessarily, doll. Our dead Lilly could have been working on a simple biography of his life. Just like she wrote of Hedda's — only at the end of the book, she could have lowered the boom on Pierce, just like she did with Hedda, making him look like a heel. After all, he did time for manslaughter, but if Lilly charges that he'd planned the murder with Hedda, then he'll come off as a cold-blooded killer who should have gotten the gas chamber.

"Oh, my god, Jack, I hadn't thought of that. But it's exactly what Truman Capote did to get his story for *In Cold Blood*. He duped the murderers into trusting him, so he could get the inside story of their crime from their point of view."

I blew out air and gnawed my thumbnail, pretending to admire the one-sheet for *Out of the Past* while considering Jack's theory. "Dr. Lilly could have *duped* Armstrong into giving her interviews, pumping him up with tales of glory. But her ultimate goal might simply have been to publish another sensational biography about a scandalized actor."

And if Pierce got wind of that new book of Lilly's, Murdered in Plain Sight, *he might have figured that out. And he might not have been too happy.*

"So Pierce could be the one who killed Dr. Lilly, or *had* her killed, and her tapes stolen . . ."

It's a possibility. And although I'm no fan of Queen Hedda the Diva, I have to tell you, Pierce has the strongest motive for offing her next. Hedda was the one who put the nail in his coffin by testifying against him, right?

Suddenly Seymour cried out. "Hey, in here! Come quick. You've got to see this!"

Brainert, Maggie, and I immediately dashed off in the direction of Seymour's call. We raced down a hallway filled with more film memorabilia and found him in the house's large dining room. The space was dominated by a huge tropical fish tank.

"Check it out," Seymour said, pointing above the tank.

I followed his gaze, hoping for some sort of clue about Pierce from the Fisherman Detective series, but the framed one-sheet on the wall featured another actor, from an entirely different decade. Three action-packed images were punctuated by a blurb that read "Look up! Look down! Look out! Here comes the biggest Bond of them all!"

"This is an original Robert McGinnis poster for *Thunderball!*" Seymour exclaimed. "There's Sean Connery with the famous jet pack on top; beneath that he's battling thugs underwater. At the bottom, he's surrounded by the signature Robert McGinnis babes."

"Who's Robert McGinnis?" Brainert asked.

"Who's Robert McGinnis?" cried Seymour in outrage. "Only one of the greatest illustrators of the 1960s. Not only did he paint a slew of James Bond posters, McGinnis also did the poster art for *Barbarella* and practically all the paperback covers for the Mike Shayne mysteries."

"Mike who?" Brainert asked.

"Mike *Shayne,*" I replied. All eyes turned toward me. I shrugged. "Shayne was the star of those old hard-boiled detective novels written by Brett Halliday. Aunt Sadie knows the rare book market, and she always said it was the cover art that made them collectable."

"And look at this!" Seymour exclaimed, pointing to a narrow sideboard.

In my experience, dining room sideboards were used to display soup tureens and crystal vases. But this narrow cabinet of polished mahogany was completely dedicated to displaying what looked like a strange-looking long-barreled weapon.

"What is that?" I asked, not quite trusting my eyes.

"It's an original speargun prop from the *Thunderball* movie!"

Seymour's eyes were bugging. He carefully lifted it off the metal display stand. "Wow, it's heavy, too. Must be at least seven pounds."

He aimed it at the fish tank.

"Man, think of it: one of Largo's men actually pointed this spear gun at James Bond in the big underwater battle, just like this!"

"And who is Largo?" Brainert sniffed.

"*Emilio* Largo was Bond's arch-villain in *Thunderball*! Sheesh! Don't you know anything, Brainert?!"

"I know *other* things, Seymour. *Important* things."

"Right, like how many biblical references Melville packed into *Moby Dick*? Five hundred and twenty-four was my last count. Or what year Franz Kafka first published a novella about a traveling salesman who turns into a giant cockroach? Nineteen-fifteen."

"What are you driving at, mailman?"

"Trivia by any other name is still trivia."

Brainert threw up his hands. "So that's why you called us back here? To impugn higher education while you play with a movie prop?"

"I wanted you to see the *Thunderball* poster! It's got legendary art on it. I thought even an egghead like you could appreciate it. Apparently not."

Brainert exhaled in exasperation. "I don't even know why Wendell *has* a James Bond poster and speargun prop, and in his dining room of all places." His nose wrinkled. "It's in bad taste!"

Brainert and Seymour were still arguing as we walked out of the dining room and back into the hallway. While we strolled toward the living room, I took a closer look at the memorabilia that we'd raced past on our way to Seymour.

There were more posters as well as props and pieces of costuming either framed or in glass cases. I noticed a one-sheet and lobby cards hanging near an arched alcove and stopped dead. A familiar face was staring back. The actress in the picture was very young and no raving beauty — more like the girl next door with caramel-colored curls and a dimple in her chin.

"My god," I cried aloud. "That's —"

It's her, doll! District Attorney Nathan Burwell's paramour. The chippy from the Hotel Chester!

"Ah," Maggie said, obviously responding to my outburst. "You're admiring the restored one-sheet for *Man Trap*."

"Oh, uh . . . y-yes," I stammered.

"It's really something," Maggie continued. "There's only one more like it in the whole world. That one resides at San Fernando University's film history archive . . ."

As Maggie talked, I pretended to examine the *Man Trap* one-sheet, but I was really checking out the scene on one of the eight surrounding lobby cards. The face on the scantily clad girl standing next to Sybil Sand was unmistakable. It was the same girl I'd seen in my dream of Jack's past, the girl at the Porterhouse with Nathan Burwell.

"Who's this actress?" I asked aloud.

Seymour stepped closer. "I think she's in the nightclub scenes in that movie. Yeah, a cigarette girl with a few lines. She speaks to Hedda Geist, and then another actor makes a comment about how the girl's way too young to be working in a place like that. Never saw the actress before or since. Just some extra, I guess."

"Hey, look at this," Brainert said, pointing to a yellowing booklet resting inside a glass case. "This is an original souvenir program for *Man Trap.*"

"It's unusual to have one for a film like this," Maggie said. "But the studio wanted to promote Hedda —"

The doorbell buzzed, interrupting her. Maggie excused herself and headed for the foyer.

"Quick," I hissed when the woman was out of earshot. "Open the case and let me see that booklet."

Brainert's eyes widened in horror. "What!"

"Open that case," I insisted. "Even if you have to break it open."

Seymour reached out a hand and lifted the lid. "Relax, it's unlocked."

I gently removed the crumbling press book from its display case and carefully turned the brittle pages. The complete cast list was on the third page.

"Cigarette Girl played by Wilma Brody," I read aloud.

Seymour blinked. "So what?"

"I concur," Brainert said. "Who is this Wilma Brody and why should we care?"

Before I could make up an explanation, we were interrupted by a woman's voice, shrill with anger. Maggie's reply came in a reasonable but icy tone.

"Oh God," Brainert said, cringing. "It's Virginia . . . the former Mrs. Wendell Pepper."

I placed the press book back into its case and closed the lid. In the living room, the voices became louder.

"I think we'd better do something," Brainert said. "It's turning into an argument."

Seymour backed away, palms high, head shaking. "Count me out. Ex-wives scare the crap out of me."

"All right," Brainert said. Squaring his shoulders, he led the way to the living room. I followed, Seymour brought up the rear.

"I'm looking for Wendell," cried the shrill voice from the living room. "Not his latest mistress!"

"I'm nobody's mistress, Mrs. Pepper," Maggie civilly replied, "and I told you, Wendell is not here. Try calling him at —"

"I've *tried* calling him, dozens of times! He's ducking me, the worm, but I won't tolerate —"

Virginia Pepper looked up when we entered the living room. The ex-wife of the St. Francis dean was tall and willowy with a long, slender neck. Her blonde hair was pulled back tightly, exposing a great deal of Botoxed forehead. Her eyebrows appeared to slant demonically when she spied Brainert, Seymour, and me. Then her gaze began to bounce back and forth among all of us, as if she were trying to decide who to target first.

"Hello, Virginia," said Brainert, boldly stepping into the line of fire.

My gay, academic friend may have had a physique like Ichabod Crane's, but he had the heart of a Round Table knight, always willing to withstand slings and arrows for his friends.

The woman's predatory eyes narrowed. "Busybody Brainert," she said, her voice dripping with contempt. "Showing gawkers around this mausoleum, are you?"

Brainert's eyes narrowed. "No need to be rude, Virginia. I really don't think —"

"I recognize *her*," said Virginia, moving on to me. "You're that shopkeeper, the woman who runs that bookstore with her old aunt on Cranberry Street. My friend the councilwoman's mentioned you."

"Councilwoman?" I said. "Which one? You don't mean Marjorie Binder-Smith?"

"Yes, of course. There are *other* women on the council, of course, but *she's* the only one with any vision in this backward little town. She says you're a real troublemaker. Probably stupid, too, if you're involved with my ex-husband."

Cripes, this dame's one annoying harridan. No wonder ol' Wendell's not returning her calls. Who'd want to talk to a broad with a stick up her —

"Stop being a bitch, Virginia," Brainert snapped, stepping even farther forward. "Just tell me what you need from Wendell, without the insults."

"A check!" she cried, veins flashing blue in her pale neck.

I cringed, stepping back in an autonomic response. This was the first time I'd met the woman, but her barely contained neurosis reminded me too much of my wealthy, pill-popping, perpetually dissatisfied in-laws, the ones Calvin had looked to for providing a functional foundation in life.

And look how well that worked out for him.

"Oh, God, Jack."

You want me to handle this, baby?

"No. Let her go."

Okay. Jack snorted. *If you say so.*

Virginia stomped her foot. "Wendell promised he'd help with our son's graduation party! Now June's almost here, and I haven't seen a cent! He keeps crying poverty, but just look at all this junk he's put around the house! Maybe I should just come in here one day, take a few things, and sell them on eBay. Then I'll have my money!"

"I'm sure it's an oversight," Brainert calmly replied. "Wendell's very proud of his son. He's mentioned setting up a generous trust fund for him. I'm sure he means to give you the money for the party. It's just that he's been busy with the theater opening and the festival —"

"That theater. That damn theater!" Virginia sneered. "I wouldn't be sorry to see it burn down."

For a moment, you could hear a pin drop. Then Maggie Kline stepped forward.

"You've gotten your answer, Mrs. Pepper," she said. "Wendell's not here, and frankly, we have things to do, so I'll show you to the door."

Virginia purpled. "I used to live here," she cried with a toss of her head. "I know where the front door is."

Maggie's eyes locked with hers. "Then use it."

With a huff, Virginia Pepper whirled on her flats and strode to the exit. All of a sudden she stumbled, awkwardly careening right into the closed door, her Botoxed forehead hitting the wood with a sharp thump. With a string of curses that would have made the Fisherman Detective blush, she opened it, stormed out, and slammed the door behind her.

Oops, said Jack. *Guess there was a wrinkle in the carpet that wasn't there before.*

"Jack! What did you do?"

I let her go, like you asked, doll. Right into the front door.

"Well, that was pleasant," Maggie said, her eyes dancing with amusement.

"Now you see why I'm a bachelor," Seymour said.

Maggie glanced at her wristwatch and faced Brainert. "Could you give me a lift to the Movie Town? It's a nice walk, but I'm running late."

"Of course," Brainert replied. "Are you rushing to catch a film?"

"No," she said, with a raised eyebrow. "I want to be there for Hedda Geist's appearance. It's scheduled right after Pierce Armstrong's. If she arrives on time, the two of them will finally meet after all these years. Now *that* would be something worth seeing, don't you agree?"

We all did agree. And as Maggie ran around, looking for her keys and handbag, I moved toward the house's vestibule. With the front door closed, I noticed an alcove off the entryway that I hadn't seen on our way in. It was the sort of recessed niche where a homeowner would typically display an antique grandfather clock. But there was no clock here.

A thin, rectangular glass case the height of a coffin occupied the space. Inside it hung a full-length evening gown, clearly a preserved piece of wardrobe. I moved closer, my eyes widening, as I realized the dress was made of shimmering silver satin. It had a plunging neckline and a tiny bow at the bodice.

"Jack, I can't believe it," I whispered. "It's the silver gown from *Wrong Turn,* the one that wasn't ripped at the shoulder!"

The one that turned up on Wilma Brody the night Irving Vreen was stabbed to death. Yeah, baby, I can see that. I just have one question.

"You don't have to tell me, Jack. I have the same question."

Good. Then maybe you can ask Wendell

Pepper where the hell he found Hedda Geist's missing gown.

CHAPTER 15
TRAPDOOR TRAP

I killed him for money and for a woman. I didn't get the money. And I didn't get the woman.

— *Double Indemnity,* 1944

An explosion of laughter followed by a burst of applause greeted our ears the moment we entered the lobby of the Movie Town Theater. The noise came from inside the auditorium, where Pierce Armstrong was speaking to a boisterous crowd of loyal fans.

Brainert's grin stretched from one ear to the other. "Sounds like a packed house," he crowed.

"Sounds like Pierce Armstrong is on stage right now," Seymour cried, racing ahead of us.

Maggie Kline laughed. "That guy is really into the Fisherman Detective thing."

"Seymour is a particularly odd individual," Brainert muttered.

Maggie smiled. "In Hollywood, he'd fit right in."

"Mr. Parker! Mr. Parker, sir . . ." A tall young man was waving Brainert over to the concession stand. He wore a white cap and white shirt with *movie town theater* emblazoned across the pocket in bold red letters.

Brainert frowned. "Excuse me. Our head of concessions is calling me. I'm afraid I have some important managerial business to attend to."

"Thank goodness you're here, Professor Parker," the young man called, "we're almost out of Raisinets again!"

Brainert glanced unhappily at me. "I'll join you shortly."

As he headed to the stand, Maggie and I followed Seymour into the crowded auditorium. On the way I glanced at the gold-framed bulletin board, where the day's schedule of events was posted.

Hedda Geist had appeared on stage earlier in the day for a Q&A with Barry Yello. She was due to speak again in less than fifteen minutes, providing a short personal introduction to *Tight Spot,* another of her Gotham Features films.

Another ripple of laughter from the auditorium told me that Pierce Armstrong was still going strong. He would most likely be on stage when Hedda arrived, so it appeared the two former lovers were indeed about to meet face-to-face for the first time in sixty years.

"Hurry," Seymour called. "I can't wait to see this."

Me either, I thought.

We entered the theater during a lengthy question from a middle-aged man, who'd stood up from the second row to deliver it. On stage, the elderly Pierce Armstrong sat behind a table spread with a white cloth. His features were hidden behind oversized copper-framed glasses and his hair was white and rather long, ending in ringlets that rested on the shoulders of his red patterned shirt. The shirts collar was buttoned up and encircled by a bolo-style Western tie.

The fan's rambling question finally ended — something about location shooting. Pierce leaned forward toward the microphone, adjusted his large copper glasses, and raised a pale hand.

"We almost never went out on the ocean," he began in a strong voice. "The first time we did was for *O'Bannon Against the Bund,* where we worked off the coast of Fire Island. On the first take of my fight with Ramon Lassiter, I fell off the boat and actually had to be rescued! Can you believe it? After that . . .”

Gales of laughter drowned out the rest of his story.

“Hey, I was a cowboy, not a sailor!” Armstrong cried with a grin.

We finally found seats in the rear of the theater, but not together. Seymour sat in one row. Maggie and I behind him, right on the center aisle.

I noticed Dr. Wendell Pepper sitting beside the old man on stage. The sixtysomething dean was looking relaxed and attractive, his thick salt-and-pepper hair was casually finger-combed to the side, his white dress shirt was open at the collar, and his casual, chestnut brown sports jacket hung loosely off his broad-shouldered form.

“All of the Fisherman Detective screenplays centered around crime on the docks, and we mostly used locations near our studio’s offices in Long Island City, Queens,” Pierce Armstrong continued. “We filmed at night, not to set any kind of mood. It was because those docks were damn busy in the daytime. We were only allowed access to one pier, so that’s why you keep seeing the same scenery over and over again in every movie. We needed an animal wrangler, too. Not because we used any animals. He was there to keep the stray dogs at bay!"

The audience burst out laughing again.

"Of course, we had a mock-up of the *Sea Witch*. We used that on the sound stage at Astoria Studios, which Paramount rented out to us. The crew would rock the prop boat and toss buckets of water into the scene. Those guys really got a kick out of dousing me!"

The question-and-answer session continued for another twenty minutes. Throughout most of his presentation, Armstrong was lively and animated. Near the end, however, he seemed to tire. Finally Dean Pepper rose and called a halt to the fun. Some folks rose out of their seats to rush the stage.

"No autographs, please," Dr. Pepper warned. "Mr. Armstrong will be signing tomorrow. Check the schedule of events on the bulletin board for the exact time."

After some groans of disappointment, then big applause, Pepper stepped behind Pierce Armstrong and took hold of the man's chair. That's when I realized the former action star and stunt man was partially confined to a wheelchair.

Beside me, Maggie sighed. "No sign of Hedda. I guess the big meeting isn't going to happen. Not yet, anyway. I'm sure they'll meet sometime this weekend. Excuse me,

I've really got to use the ladies'. Do you need to?"

I shook my head. "I'll save your seat," I promised her.

Maggie got up and joined the crush. In the next row, Seymour stood up and stretched, then faced me. "Man, Pierce Armstrong was really funny. I couldn't believe that story about Howard Hawks. . . ."

As Seymour continued to chatter away, the theater partially emptied. Like Maggie, people took advantage of the break to visit the restrooms or concession stand. I spied Bud Napp in the wings: the young Dixon Gallagher was with him, and the two appeared to be tinkering with the sound system. I noticed the new speakers sat on the floor on either side of the stage. Bud was obviously determined to avoid any more falling speaker "accidents."

Dean Pepper and a young usher started transferring Pierce Armstrong's wheelchair from the stage to the auditorium floor. On stage, Pierce waited for them to finish, his wrinkled hands clutching the black vinyl handles of an aluminum walker.

Finally, big Barry Yello appeared. The young Webmaster with the blond ponytail walked on stage from the wings. He and Dean Pepper each took the old man's arm and guided Pierce down the short staircase and back into his chair. Just as Dr. Pepper began to push the chair up the center aisle, Hedda Geist-Middleton entered the auditorium.

Attired for the upcoming festival party, Hedda wore a simple but elegant black cocktail dress, belted at the waist. A string of flawless pearls hung around her neck. Her silver-white hair was down, just brushing her shoulders, the ends curled into a 1940's-style pageboy.

I saw no sign of Hedda's granddaughter, Harmony, and the elderly actress seemed momentarily flustered. Her haughty airs were gone, and she began to fumble inside her black clutch bag.

As Dean Pepper continued to wheel Pierce up the aisle, I held my breath while those around me — apparently oblivious to the drama about to unfold — chatted and munched popcorn. I was sorry Maggie Kline was not here to see this. She, at least, was aware of the significance of the situation.

Hedda finally closed her bag and looked up, right into the eyes of Pierce Armstrong. The shock of recognition registered on her face, and she took a step backward, mouth moving soundlessly. Pierce clutched the arms of his wheelchair and slowly pushed himself to his feet. On unsteady legs he took a single step forward.

"Hello, Hedda," he said evenly.

Hedda's acute anxiety appeared to vanish, as if a curtain came down — or went up — and a performance began.

"Pierce," she said, her chin raised, her voice strong and confident, "so lovely to see you after all these years."

There were no hugs, no air kisses, not even a smile. Her greeting was civil, but cold and formal. The two former lovers stood face to face for a long moment. Then Hedda broke the deadlock. Her eyes drifted away from Armstrong and over to the man standing behind the elderly actor.

"Ah, Dr. Pepper. There you are!" she declared. "I sent my granddaughter off to find you and now she's vanished."

Pepper smiled. "I'm right here."

Hedda tilted her head and forced a smile of her own. "I believe you asked me to give a little introduction before the screening of *Tight Spot*. Am I on time?"

"You are," Dr. Pepper replied, "and I see my colleague Brainert Parker is here to escort you to the stage."

Brainert appeared at Hedda's side and offered the woman his arm. She took it and without another glance at Pierce, sauntered toward the stage. Pierce sat back down. As Dr. Pepper wheeled the man away, I noticed a smirk on the old actor's face, an unmistakable look of amused triumph.

That's what it looks like to me, too, baby.

"Well, Jack, I guess if anyone knew Hedda was acting, it would be her former leading man."

Suddenly, someone rushed up to me. "Whew, I almost missed it!" It was Maggie Kline, acting like a kid in an amusement park. Her face was flushed, as if she'd crossed the lobby in a dead run. "The bathroom was so crowded, and then I heard someone say Hedda had arrived, and I raced back!"

"So you got a good look?"

"From the theater doors," she said, and then shrugged. "I'm a little disappointed. I guess I was expecting more. Fireworks, explosions, something . . ."

Maggie's reference to *explosions* suddenly cast Pierce Armstrong's smirk in a whole new light. Tensing in my seat, I flashed back on that giant audio speaker sparking and flashing above the stage and nearly crushing the elderly Hedda Geist, right in front of her adoring fans.

"Jack? Peirce is such an old man. You

don't think he could be a threat, do you?"

The ghost grunted. *Back in '46, a cop I used to work with went to arrest an eighty-two-year-old man for smacking his wife around. The guy didn't shine to a buttoned-up yancy telling him what he could or couldn't do with his little woman.*

"What happened?"

Long story short, the cop was clocked twice with a ball bat before his partner iced the old fart.

"Excuse me!" I told Maggie.

"Change your mind about the ladies'?"

"No, the *man*."

"What?"

I climbed out of my seat and hurried down the aisle to the far end of the stage, where I called to Bud in the wings. Smiling, he approached me.

"Hey, Pen. What's up?" he asked, crouching down on one knee.

I jerked my head toward Brainert and Hedda, who were locked in conversation at the bottom of the steps that led up to the stage. Harmony had arrived, too. She looked stunning tonight — a photo negative of her grandmother in a white summer dress, a choker made of shiny black gemstones, and her blonde hair pulled into a high ponytail.

"Listen," I said softly, "you remember

what happened the last time Hedda was on stage. Have you checked this place out thoroughly?"

Bud frowned. "You don't think —"

"Oh, but I do."

To my relief, he didn't question me. While I watched, he checked the curtains, walked the length of center stage while peering up, into the catwalks. He checked the microphone wires, the chairs. Bud even glanced under the tablecloth, presumably for anything that looked like an explosive device. Then he stepped behind the chairs and walked toward the staircase, using small, cautious steps while following the path Hedda would take to her seat.

Suddenly, Bud froze. He took a step backward. His head jerked in my direction, and when Bud's eyes met mine, I knew he'd found something.

While I watched, Bud called an usher, whispered something to the teenager. The kid took off backstage, returned a moment later with an aluminum easel under his arm. He and Bud set the display up so that its tripod legs straddled the spot where Bud had paused. The usher ran off again, and returned with the sign advertising Hedda's appearance that had stood in the lobby. He placed it on the easel.

Bud approached me, his face pale. "The trapdoor was unlocked," he said. "I felt it give under my foot. Put more weight on it and the door would have opened right up. Anyone standing on it would have fallen through. It's a fifteen-foot drop to a concrete floor. At Hedda's age, a fall like that could be fatal."

"Could this be an accident?"

Bud shook his head. "Someone had to do it. A trapdoor doesn't unlock itself —"

"When?"

He shrugged. "I don't know, but it had to have happened recently. I've been back and forth across this stage for the past two hours. The door would have popped open before."

I frowned. That spot was exactly where Pierce Armstrong had been standing while he waited for Dr. Pepper to help him down the stairs.

"Bud, do you think Pierce Armstrong was the one who unlocked that trapdoor —"

A burst of applause drowned out my words. Barry Yello had walked onto the stage to a raucous greeting. As he began his introduction of Hedda, Bud gestured for me to go find a seat. He tapped his watch and mouthed, "Later." Then he moved to the wings.

■ ■ ■ ■

Two hours later, Bud Napp was shaking his head at me. "Sorry to shoot your theory down, Pen, but there's no way Pierce Armstrong could have set that trap for Hedda."

The movie had finished playing by now and the theater was clearing out. Practically everyone was heading off to the open-air block party on the Quindicott Commons — everyone but me and Bud. I was standing on the stage next to him, listening as he shot my meticulously reasoned theory all to hell.

"Are you certain Pierce couldn't work the lock?"

"Look here," he said, moving the aluminum easel. "On this side of the trapdoor, there are no bolts, no hinges, no screws. That stuff is underneath. Otherwise people on stage would be tripping over the hardware all the time."

I studied the trapdoor; it certainly did look like part of the floor. I sighed. "So how does one go about unlocking it?"

"You have to go under the stage," Bud explained. "Which means if Pierce Armstrong is guilty of trying to harm Hedda, he had to have an accomplice working underneath this floor."

302

I nodded. "Show me."

Bud led me to the rear of the backstage area, where a narrow staircase led to an empty basement of newly whitewashed concrete. At the bottom of the steps Bud flipped a switch and a few naked lightbulbs dully illuminated the vast space. On the wall to my right, I saw a steel fire door marked *exit*.

"Where does this lead?" I asked.

"To the alley that runs behind Cranberry Street."

Bud flipped another switch, placed his hands on the door's horizontal handle, and pushed it open. Warm air streamed into the cool, damp cellar, tainted with a whiff of garbage from the Dumpster just outside the door.

"It was unlocked," I noted.

"It's always unlocked because it's a fire door," Bud explained. "It's only locked on the outside. You'll notice I cut off the alarm before I pushed it open." He pointed to a small metal circuit box that looked like another light switch. "If I hadn't, an alarm would have rung upstairs, alerting management to a break-in."

I scratched my head. "And there's no way someone could have slipped in through that door and gotten under the stage without

303

anyone in the main theater noticing?"

Bud shrugged. "Unless they had an accomplice inside who came down here and opened the door for them. That accomplice would have had to know about cutting off the alarm switch."

"How likely is that?"

"Unfortunately it's very likely. And there's something else you should see. Follow me." He led me to a spot in the middle of the empty cellar. "Look up."

I did. After gazing into the shadows for a moment, I finally made out the bottom of the trapdoor fifteen feet above me. It looked like a square in the ceiling with hinges on one side. Two dead bolts held the door in place and they'd both been opened. The ceiling was so high, the only way to reach it was the folding ladder set up right under the door.

"The wannabe killer must have set up this ladder," I said.

"The truth is, I set this ladder up myself, just yesterday, to change a burned-out lightbulb." Bud pointed to the ceiling. "But it's obvious to me that whoever unlocked the trapdoor *did* know their way around this theater."

I mulled Bud's words while he climbed the ladder and relocked the dead bolts.

"Any way to get more light around here?" I asked him from the floor.

"Try the work light," Bud replied. "It's right over the bench."

I found the fluorescent light and turned it on. Powerful beams penetrated the shadows, making this section of the large cellar twice as bright as before. That's when I noticed a small dark object on the whitewashed concrete. I dropped to all fours and picked it up.

Bud watched me from the top of the ladder. "What have you found?"

"An earring. Looks like black onyx in a silver setting. It looks new, too. There's no tarnish or dust on it. Want to see?"

Bud climbed down from the ladder and crossed to the bench. He studied the earring pinched in my fingers while he used a rag to wipe soot off his hands.

"That's not from my crew," he said. "My guys have been down here plenty, but there are no women on my work crew — and no pierced ears, noses, or lips either."

Suddenly a memory flashed into my mind — a young woman in a white dress, accented by a choker made of black gemstones, stones that may well have been onyx.

Harmony Middleton.

"Sorry, Pen, but it's getting late," said

Bud, tapping his wristwatch. "And I promised Sadie I'd meet her at the block party."

"Oh, yeah, the block party."

"Aren't you going, too?" Bud asked.

"I wasn't planning on it."

Well, change your plans, Jack immediately growled in my head. *That earring is missing off some broad's earlobe. And if you find it missing off Harmony's, then you'll know you've got your man.*

"Or woman."

Figure of speech, baby. 'Cause trouble is my business, and in my business, dames are the most trouble of all.

CHAPTER 16
CHIPPY OFF
THE OLD BLOCK

MIKE: Mind if I sit here?
KAY: Not if you can't behave yourself.
MIKE: Well, you never liked me when I did.
— Mike Shayne hitting on Kay Bentley in
Sleepers West, a Mike Shayne Detective
Mystery, 1941

New York City
May 10, 1948
"Jack, where am I?"

"In my apartment."

"Your apartment! How did I get here?"

"I gave you a ride, baby. Don't you remember when we took that trip to Queens, and those lousy two-legged rats shot at us in the alley? Then I stashed you in that dark doorway?"

"Oh, yeah . . . I *do* remember."

"You were shaking like a wet kitten, and I took you in my arms —"

"And kissed me. That's right."

"Well, it led to a few more kisses, and one thing led to another, and I drove you back here."

I opened my eyes. I was nestled against Jack's solid form on a big, lumpy sofa. The PI's apartment was small but neat with an easy chair and a coffee table. A bar stood against the wall, holding bottles of liquor. A large radio sat between two tall windows covered in drawn Venetian blinds, and a bookshelf in the corner held paperbacks and a stack of magazines. I saw a small kitchen through one door, a bedroom through another.

Jack's deep-blue double-breasted jacket was thrown over the arm of a chair. His leather shoulder holster was hanging over its back. The PI's shoes were off, too, and his sock-covered feet were crossed on the coffee table in front of us. His shirtsleeves were rolled up, revealing muscular forearms. One strong arm was now draped around my shoulders. The other held a tumbler with wheat-colored alcohol. He was sipping the drink with one hand, caressing my shoulder with the other.

I looked down, a little worried about how many pieces of clothing I'd find missing. I was still wearing the skirt of the smart tweed suit that Jack had selected for me, but the jacket was gone and my blouse's top buttons were undone, revealing quite a bit of lace bra. I pulled away from Jack's embrace and did up the buttons.

The PI smirked. He rubbed his square chin now rough with stubble. "Don't look at me like that, baby. You were the one who unbuttoned them. You said you were hot."

I arched an eyebrow, thinking about his kisses. "Oh, I'm sure I was."

"So." He yawned and stretched, set down his drink on the coffee table, then leaned back again and clasped his hands behind his head. "Now that the fun's over . . . you want to tell me what happened tonight?"

I squinted. "Am I sleeping right now? Is this a dream?"

His slate-gray eyes held my gaze. "What do you think?"

"I think you've got Hokey-Pokey Pink lipstick on your collar —"

He smiled, with a little too much satisfaction. "And?"

"And I remember something about Bud Napp helping me under the Movie Town Theater stage, finding an onyx-and-silver earring, then running back to my bedroom above the bookshop and changing for the block party."

"Yeah, baby, you changed clothes and

handbags, too. Only you forgot about yours truly."

"The nickel!"

"You left without my lucky buffalo in your purse, which left me stuck watching reruns of Jack Shield episodes on the Intrigue Channel all by my lonesome."

"I'm sorry, Jack! I remember now. When I got to the block party, I realized you weren't with me. I was *going* to go back home and get your old nickel, but then I saw Harmony and didn't want to miss my chance to surveil her earlobes."

Jack sighed. "All right, baby, so you flew solo. Tell me what I missed."

"Well, Harmony wasn't wearing *any* earrings but that actually seemed suspicious to me because —" I paused, feeling Jack's hand reaching over to sweep hair away from the nape of my neck. "Jack?" I tensed. "What are you —"

His fingers began to message my tight muscles.

"Oh, wow . . ." I rolled my head around. "That actually feels good . . ."

"Of course it does, baby. Now tell me why it was so suspicious that Harmony wasn't sporting earrings? I don't know much about the jewelry-wearing habits of dames. Enlighten me."

"Okay, well . . ." I shifted on the couch to get more comfortable. "Harmony's ears are pierced. And most women with pierced ears wear earrings. So it seemed awfully suspicious that she wasn't wearing *any*. And I thought maybe she realized that she'd lost *one* earring and simply taken the second one out before going to the party."

"So what did you do?"

"I noticed Barry Yello at the party —"

"Barry's the big guy?"

"Yes. He was the guy with the blond ponytail and the Hawaiian shirt, the one who introduced Dr. Lilly the first night of the Film Festival. Barry's also the Webmaster of FylmGeek.com, and . . . Oh, wait. I should explain what dot com means —"

"Don't bother," Jack said. "Between you and your aunt working on that computer every day, I've figured out what the Internet is —"

"An information highway."

"Another set of street corners for pervs and shitbirds to prey on the public."

I sighed. "That too. Anyway, Barry had a digital camera with him, and he was snapping photos all night, presumably to post on his Web site. I figured he would have been paying special attention to the festival's guests. I asked him about Hedda's and

Harmony's movements."

Jack's massaging fingers moved from my neck to one shoulder. His other hand joined in, taking care of the other shoulder. "Move back a little, baby," he whispered, "closer to me."

I slid backward on the lumpy couch, making the old springs creak beneath my weight.

"Go on, doll," Jack growled in my ear. "Tell me what Barry said."

I cleared my throat, trying my best to ignore the realness of Jack's hard thigh against my tweed-covered bottom, the faint male smell of undiluted whiskey on his breath when he spoke. I reminded myself that this was all a dream; warned myself not to get carried away. But the truth was, there hadn't been a man in my life for years. Even when I'd been married to Calvin, he hadn't exactly been an attentive, supportive husband. Not that a ghost could be a replacement for a husband, but I had to admit that Jack's spirit was a good companion, and a good friend. And right at this moment, what he was doing to me felt pretty darn good, too.

I knew what some people would say to that. They'd accuse me of wanting to live in a dream world. But then I considered the store I was running — and what I was selling. What were all those books providing to the people who read them?

"Baby? What's wrong? You goin' buggy on me?"

"I was just thinking that I liked being here . . . with you."

"It's all we've got, sweetheart. Don't over-think it. Dreams are a gift, you know? You should just enjoy them."

I turned around to meet Jack's eyes. "You enjoy them, too, don't you?"

Jack stopped massaging my neck. His hard face smiled. "What do you think?"

I smiled, too. Then I turned around again. "I think you missed a spot."

Jack's hands returned to my shoulders. "So? Back to Barry and your little block party . . ."

"Right. According to Barry Yello, Hedda had been holding court at a picnic table all evening. Apparently, she never returned to the Finch Inn after the showing of *Tight Spot.* Just went straight to the party on the Commons. And her granddaughter, Har-mony, had been hanging close with her all evening."

"Uh-huh. And what did that tell you?"

I detected contained amusement in Jack's voice, and sure enough when I turned my head, I found the PI smirking. He was obviously entertained by my gumshoeing tale.

"What it told me, Jack, was that if Harmony dropped that earring under the Movie Town stage, and she never went back to her hotel room to drop off its match, then I was likely to find that earring on Harmony herself."

"And did you?"

"No. I did manage to search her handbag though."

Jack's fingers stilled. "You're kidding?"

"Nope. Seymour Tarnish helped. He distracted her and I grabbed her bag, riffled through it, and returned it without her knowing. No earring. And she didn't have any pockets on her skintight dress, but I did find something very interesting inside that purse."

Jack sat up straighter. "Spill."

"A pack of condoms and three bottles of prescription medications from three different doctors."

"Well, well, well." Jack's eyebrows arched. "Keeping party favors and candy in her handbag tells me that she's the type who wants to be ready for anything — if not any man. Just like her grandmother. Guess the apple doesn't fall far from the tart."

"I think the girl's got major problems," I said. "And she's clearly having sex with a boyfriend."

"Or boyfriends, plural — one or more of whom might be willing to help her get rid of her granny, so she can inherit a fortune."

"Or part of one."

"Nice work, baby."

I could see that Jack meant it. The smirk was gone. He seemed genuinely impressed. Without taking his long, strong legs off the coffee table, he leaned forward to reach for his tumbler of whiskey.

"And what about Pierce Armstrong?" he asked.

I frowned. "What about him?"

"Didn't you brace him at the party, too?"

"Unfortunately, he didn't go to the party. I cornered Wendell Pepper, though. He told me Pierce was so exhausted that he asked for a ride back to his house. Pepper took him before returning to the block party."

"I see." Jack took a sip of alcohol then held the glass out for me. "Go on, it won't kill you."

I took the glass, sipped a little. I wasn't a drinker of straight hard liquor, but I was curious what Jack's dream-whiskey would taste like. "Ack!" I coughed. The liquid burned all the way down my throat.

Jack laughed. "It's a cinch, baby. You're even a Square Jane in your sleep."

"But you *have* to admit," I rasped, finishing my coughing fit. "I'm getting to be a good detective awake."

"Jury's still out on that one, doll. So what about that question I had for Dean Pepper — did you remember to ask it?"

I nodded, handing Jack back his tumbler of firewater. "Hedda's silver evening gown from *Wrong Turn.* I asked him about it, all right. Lucky for us, Pepper's practically an encyclopedia of trivia about every piece of memorabilia he collects. And do you know what he said about Hedda's old costume?"

"Not unless you tell me."

"He said that he bought it at an auction from a relative of the actress Willow Brody, also known as Wilma Brody. Wilma changed her name when she moved from Queens to Hollywood. It didn't help her career much. She could only ever get bit parts in big pictures, and then she died in 1966."

"Why does that year ring a bell? It's not like I was alive to remember it."

"It's the same year Hedda Geist said some journalist started digging around, trying to piece together the real story about Irving Vreen's death."

"And Willow Brody died that same year? That's awfully coincidental, baby, don't you think?"

"I'll tell you what's even more coincidental."

"What's that?"

"According to Dr. Pepper, Wilma Brody died from a *fall* while *horseback* riding in the Hollywood hills."

"Horseback riding?" said Jack. "And didn't Hedda Geist tell you that she rides horses, too?"

I nodded. "She owns a horse farm in Newport. Said she still rides two hours a day."

"But she used to live in Los Angles with her husband, the TV executive. Think she was riding horses in California back in '66?"

"I glanced over my shoulder. "To quote Jack Shepard . . . 'I'd bet the ranch, if I had a ranch.' "

Jack sat fully up, sweeping his legs off the coffee table. "One more question, sweetheart. Did ol' Dean Pepper happen to mention what age Wilma Brody was when her ticket got punched?"

"Actually, yes. He said she was young when she died, only thirty-three."

"Thirty-three in sixty-six. You know what that makes her in forty-eight?"

"Fifteen?"

"Jailbait. That's what that makes her."

Jack stood up from the sofa, began to pace

the small living room. "That means District Attorney Nathan Burwell could have been blackmailed because he was committing statutory rape with the girl. The pieces are coming together now. At fifteen, Wilma Brody was a young Gotham Features actress. Dollars to donuts, she was just a poor little nobody like Hedda once was. Young Wilma probably worshipped Hedda Geist, the studio's biggest star. She would have done whatever Hedda asked."

"So you believe Hedda persuaded fifteen-year-old Wilma to seduce New York's district attorney?"

"Yeah, baby." Jack nodded. "Somewhere down the line Hedda must have discovered that Burwell had a weakness for jailbait, so she set out to trap him using Wilma Brody. I doubt very much a girl like Wilma, working at a low-rent studio at the age of fifteen, would have had much in the way of prospects or wardrobe. Hedda probably gave the girl promises of bigger parts in her movies, gave her pretty dresses to wear on her dates with Burwell, more payoff for doing her bidding —"

"Including that slinky silver gown Wilma wore to the Porterhouse the night Vreen was murdered!"

"Exactly."

"What about the car?" I asked. "The gull-gray Lincoln Continental cabriolet? How does that fit in?"

"Easy. When I saw that car parked outside the Hotel Chester the first night I tailed Burwell and his chippy, I saw silhouettes of a man and woman inside. It must have been Hedda and Pierce Armstrong, waiting for Wilma, watching to see if she could get the DA up to her room. Using the studio's car was smart. Since it wasn't registered with either of them, someone would really have to dig to connect Hedda or Pierce with the license plate."

"And what about the morning after Vreen's murder?" I asked. "You said the Chester's valet remembered Wilma being picked up by the same type of car."

"It had to be Hedda alone who picked up Wilma that morning after Vreen was stabbed. Once again, she was taking care of her young pawn, making sure the girl was spirited away so Burwell couldn't get to her anymore — and a detective like me couldn't get close to question her, either."

"But Benny showed us Pierce Armstrong's name in the log book for that morning," I reminded him.

Jack nodded. "Since Pierce was already in custody, I'm sure it was Hedda who signed his name, just to make sure she wasn't listed on any written record. Don't you remember what those two signatures looked like? The first one was done in big, bold block letters, but the second one —"

"— was in small fluid script, just like Hedda's signature at my bookstore signing," I finished for him. Then I took a breath, trying to add it all up. "So if Hedda was in league with Wilma, then she would have known when Nathan Burwell was taking her to the Porterhouse."

Jack nodded. "And she could have arranged to have the crime happen right in front of the DA."

I met Jack's stare. "So Pierce Armstrong was in on it all, too? Even Vreen's murder?"

"He must have been, doll. The whole scene that night played out like a B-movie script, with Pierce loudly announcing he had no beef with Irving. The guy was obviously trying to set up the accidental defense. Pierce was playing a part for Hedda. And the DA was his audience."

"If all that's true, Jack, then Hedda's actions that night at the Porterhouse *were* premeditated. She killed Irving Vreen in cold blood."

"Yeah, baby."

"But why?" I threw up my hands. "What

could Hedda and Pierce, and Wilma, for that matter, have possibly *gained?* What was the conspiracy all about? When they killed Vreen, all they ended up doing was destroying the studio that employed them!"

"I can't answer that question for you, doll. Not without more pieces to this puzzle. I think, for the moment, we've reached a dead end."

I fell back against the lumpy sofa and sighed.

Jack sat down next to me again, draped a muscular arm across the sofa back. "Tired?"

"No," I said. "What I am is frustrated."

"Oh?" the PI arched an eyebrow. Then he gave me a little smile. "*That* I can take care of." He leaned closer.

"Jaaack . . . I'm not frustrated that way!"

My pathetic push against his rock-solid chest was enough to make him pause. "Then what *did* you mean, baby?" he asked with a sigh.

"I don't know . . . I guess I mean I just need more info, too. Whatever happened to your own case back here? I mean after you caught that private eye tailing you. Was he working for Hedda Geist?"

"No."

"Who then? Did you ever find out?"

Jack sighed again, leaned back a little.

"You really want to know?"

"Sure."

"Then close your eyes."

"Jaaack . . ."

"No funny business. I promise. So close 'em . . ."

I did.

Jack kept his promise. There was no funny business next. Just business. When I opened my eyes again, I found myself standing in front of a polished oak apartment door in the hall of a grand Park Avenue building.

Jack was looking spiffy in his brand-new blue suit, his face freshly shaved. He rang the apartment's bell and waited.

"Where are we?" I whispered.

"Nathan Burwell's penthouse."

"What? You're bracing the district attorney?!"

Jack smirked. "I can be wild, baby. But I'm not crazy. Nathan's not home at the moment."

The door opened. A young maid greeted us and showed us inside. "I'll get Mrs. Burwell," she said and disappeared.

The entryway where we were standing was brightly lit and stacked with trunks and suitcases. I could see a luxurious living room beyond a short hallway. Half of the room appeared to be packed up in boxes.

"Mr. Shepard, thank you for coming."

Jack gave a curt nod to the tall, slender woman. She was middle-aged, dressed in a beautifully tailored wool suit with stylishly padded shoulders, but her bobbed black hairdo looked more like it belonged in the 1920s than the late 1940s.

"I got your message," Jack said.

"Yes, well, let's not prolong this. Here you are." Mrs. Burwell held out a thick envelope. "This should end our contract."

Jack hesitated before taking the pay. "If you don't mind, Mrs. Burwell, I'd like to know why?"

"Why?"

"Why you suddenly changed your mind about having your husband investigated," Jack said stiffly. "Why you expressed no interest in seeing my report or my photographs or anything in my files."

"Well, I, just . . . don't need to . . ."

Jack glanced at the trunks and suitcases. "So you're leaving?"

Mrs. Burwell nodded. "Nathan's letting me go. There's no problem anymore. He won't fight my request for a divorce, won't fight for custody of our daughters, won't even fight me on taking my money with me. So, you see, it's all worked out."

"And what changed his mind? Did you tell him you hired me?"

"No. I didn't."

"Well, Mrs. Burwell, I've got news for you: A scumbag shamus tried to get the drop on me last night. Only I got the drop on him. The man's name was Egbert P. King. I called around and found out he works for Dibell Investigations. You know who they are?"

Mrs. Burwell blanched. "Yes," she admitted. "I do."

"So do I. They do the dirty digging for Marigold and Webster, the law firm where your husband worked before he became a public prosecutor."

The woman's eyes were wide, her expression clearly distressed. "I never once mentioned you to Nathan, Mr. Shepard. You have to believe me. The reason I'm letting you go has nothing to do with Nathan. I mean . . . it does, actually, just not in the way you think. Can't that be enough for you? Won't you go now and let things be?"

Mrs. Burwell stared at Jack. He stared back. His large form seemed to fill the hallway, and it was clear that he had no intention of moving it until the woman told him what he wanted to know. She seemed to figure that out, too, because she finally cleared her throat and admitted —

"Nathan's being blackmailed."

"By who?"

"Someone. He won't tell me; not even whether it's a man or woman. He said his hand is being forced in an official capacity. If he doesn't comply with the demands of this person, then Nathan's . . . well, his *indiscretions* will be exposed. It would ruin him. Ruin me, too. The scandal would destroy our standing completely."

"Why don't you let me uncover this blackmailing rat? You've already paid me an awful lot of dough, Mrs. Burwell. Let me find out who's blackmailing your husband."

"My husband knows very well who's blackmailing him, Mr. Shepard. And apparently Nathan has already decided to give in to this person."

"So what's the payoff?" Jack asked.

"No payoff. There's no demand for money."

"Then what does the blackmailer want?"

"A reprieve, Mr. Shepard."

"From what?"

"Apparently from being accused of murder. This blackmailer planned a murder with an accomplice. The blackmailer demanded Nathan let them both off, clearing them of any crime, but Nathan's made the blackmailer see that the public needs a fall guy. So in a few months, he'll put the accomplice on trial — for manslaughter. The black-mailer will betray the accomplice and provide testimony to help with the conviction. Nathan gets a conviction, and the blackmailer goes free."

Jack's jaw worked for a moment. "If you don't want my help, then why are you telling me this?"

"So you'll take the money and *go*. Nathan doesn't know about you, Mr. Shepard, and I want to keep it that way. When he found out he was being blackmailed, he told me everything. I told him I wanted a divorce, and that if he gave it to me I'd go away quietly instead of making things worse for him. He has enough trouble, so he's letting me go. But if he found out I hired a private eye, that you were collecting hard evidence against him to be used in court, well . . . I don't know what he'd say or do then. So please just take the money and leave."

Jack rubbed his chin, took the envelope. "All right . . . if that's what you want."

"It is. I'm flying to Miami tomorrow with my girls. I hear life's good down there. Sunny. I like the sunlight. Clears out the cobwebs . . . I've lived enough years in Nathan's shadow."

■ ■ ■ ■

We left the penthouse and headed outside. It was late afternoon; the sun was going down and the streets were getting dark. Commuters filled the sidewalks, flooding out of office buildings, flowing down to subways, rushing into train stations. Jack flagged a cab and we rode downtown toward his office.

"It had to be Hedda," I said in the back of the cab. "You know that now, right? The blackmailer was Hedda and her accomplice was Pierce Armstrong."

"Yeah, baby. It only took me sixty years — and a little snooping redhead — to break the case."

"Little snooping redhead?" My eyes widened. "You mean *me?*"

"Who do you think I mean, baby? Little Red Riding Hood? I was never able to ID Wilma Brody as the chippy at the Hotel Chester and I never came up with any leads connecting her to the starlet Hedda Geist. Now that you've done both, the pieces have fallen into place."

I stared at Jack, a little stunned. He wasn't the sort to dish out compliments when it came to gumshoeing — yet here he was telling me I'd actually helped him crack one of his own cold cases. I couldn't help grinning.

"Thanks," I said.

"Yeah, well . . . you did good, kid." Jack chucked my chin. "But don't let it go to your head or anything. You're still green as a broken traffic light."

"I may be green, but I'm far from done." I folded my arms. "And you're not off the hook, either. There's a pretty heavy situation still going on in my time."

"I know, baby. I haven't forgotten."

"Good," I said, then admitted something that was still bothering me. "There's still one thing about your case I don't understand."

"What's that?"

"Why didn't Mrs. Burwell take you up on your offer to help nail the blackmailer?"

"The lady just wanted out. And that's what she got."

"But her husband admitted to her that he was going to let a murderer walk free! How can she live with that?"

"You don't understand these cliff dwellers, baby. The threat of scandal might sound like a punch line to some floozy in the Bowery, but women with Mrs. Burwell's address would never survive the shame of a tabloid blitz. Society's circle would close her out. She'd be shunned by friends, family . . . ruined. It's a long way down from a Manhattan DA's wife to an object of pity. Alcohol and pills is the typical end for dames in that situation. I've seen it before. They're lucky if they don't get a trip to Bellevue and a nice long stay at a cackle factory."

"But Jack . . . she's buying her freedom with a man's life."

"Mrs. Burwell didn't stab Irving Vreen, sweetheart. Hedda Geist did."

"With the help of Pierce Armstrong," I pointed out. "And Wilma Brody."

"Well, Wilma's dead," Jack reminded me. "You told me that yourself. She died in 1966 in a horseback riding accident — the same year some journalist tried to open a can of worms on the Vreen murder."

"But Pierce is still alive," I noted. "And so is Hedda."

"And that's why you've got to be careful," Jack warned. "You're in the middle of a kettle that's been boiling for decades. And it just might explode in your face. Keeping watching your back, honey."

"I will. As long as you keep watching it, too."

"I always do."

"Not my back*side*, Jack. My back."

He laughed.

A few minutes later, our cab pulled over and Jack paid the fare. As we climbed onto the sidewalk, Jack touched my arm.

"Be a doll, okay?" He took a bill from his pocket and handed it to me. "Take that sweet back*side* of yours into the drugstore on the corner. Buy me a deck of Luckies and meet me upstairs in my office."

"What am I? Your secretary?"

"For the moment? *Yeah,* you are. My old one quit last week to get hitched. Just be grateful I haven't put you to work yet typing and filing."

"Ha! From the complete lack of organization in those dusty files of yours that Kenneth Franken sent over, I'd say you needed to hire a new secretary *badly.*"

"I'll take it under advisement."

We parted ways on the sidewalk. As Jack took his building's elevator up, I ducked into the corner drugstore. I bought the cigarettes for him, a candy bar for me, and took the same elevator north to his office. The clanging lift may have been new in Jack Shepard's day but to me it felt like an ancient relic. It had a hard-to-close cage and it squealed and squeaked and seemed to take forever to climb the few flights up. Finally, I arrived.

I pulled back the cage and stepped onto green linoleum. When I found Jack's office, the door was wide open.

"Jack?"

No lights were on. I glanced around the dim room.

"My god!"

The place was in chaos! Files were strewn everywhere! Chairs were overturned! I flipped on the light.

"Jack!"

I found him slumped on the floor in the corner. His head was bleeding. "Jack, can you hear me? Jack!"

He groaned, his eyelids fluttered and he slowly sat up. "Oh, my head. Those SOBs . . . they didn't give me a chance . . ."

"What happened?"

"I got jumped. A couple of goons were in here riffling through my files. I'm pretty sure one of them was our old friend Egbert. They must have heard me coming because they were hiding when I opened the door. Then *wham!*" He gingerly touched the lump swelling on his forehead.

"What did they want, Jack?"

The PI slowly rose from the floor. I helped him get to his feet. Once he was steady, he walked over to his secretary's desk.

"It's gone," he said with a disgusted

exhale. "I figured it would be. Everything was right here and they took it. The reports, the photos . . ."

"Nathan Burwell's file?"

"Yeah, baby. Even if I'd wanted to turn him into the feds or the state bar, I'd have no evidence to back my story. They took it all."

"So that's why you told me what you did the other day — not to bother looking for the file."

"Yeah." He patted the breast pocket of his suit jacket. "Mrs. Burwell's envelope's gone, too. The DA's hired goons took it all."

"All that money? Oh, Jack . . ."

"Looks like its back to the salt mines for me. But it's not a total wipe. I still got you as a secretary —"

"Excuse me? Don't you mean *partner?*"

"Partner, huh?" Jack shook his head. "I don't know . . ."

"After all we've been through, don't you think I've earned it?"

The PI's lips lifted ever so slightly. "I'll have to think about it."

"Fine. You just *call* me when you're done thinking about it —"

Jack caught my wrist before I could walk away. "Dames. Why are they so much trouble?"

"I'm no trouble!"

"Oh, yeah? Let's test that theory. C'mere . . ."

Jack jerked me close, into his arms. He kissed me and I kissed him right back. Then his lips were on my cheek, my jaw, my neck.

"Oh, Jack . . ." I sighed. "That feels like heaven . . ."

I closed my eyes, wanting the feeling to go on forever —

Ring-ring! Ring-ring!
Ring-ring! Ring-ring!

I opened my eyes. Sunlight was blasting through my window pane, morning had come without notice, and I was alone in bed. Jack's body was gone. His arms were no longer around me. His kisses had faded on the last wisp of dream.

Ring-ring! Ring-ring!
Ring-ring! Ring-ring!
Ring-ring! —

I sat up and slapped off my plastic alarm clock with enough force to crack the case.

CHAPTER 17
QUIBBLING
OVER CLUES

I sell gasoline, I make a small profit. With that, I buy groceries. The grocer makes a profit. We call it earning a living. You may have heard of that somewhere.

— Out of the Past, 1947

Bud Napp slammed his ball peen hammer on the table. "Motion carried," proclaimed the hardware store owner. "I'll draft a letter of protest to the mayor today, and deliver it in person first thing Monday morning."

He set the hammer down and lifted his paper cup of coffee. Bud paused, the cup halfway to his lips. "I'll inform 'his honor' that every member of this organization refuses to pay these unfair fines — and I can't wait to see the look on that mealy-mouthed politician's face."

Getting every last one of the Quibblers — aka, the Quindicott Business Owners Association — to attend a meeting at eight-thirty on a Sunday morning might have seemed insane a week ago. But a second round of two-hundred-dollar littering tickets written to every business on Cranberry Street automatically rendered everyone fit for a straightjacket.

The previous evening's Film Festival party on the Commons had left a pile of trash on the city streets, and the mayor decided to levy punishing fines on all of the business owners to cover the cost of clean-up.

As soon as Bud found the ticket plastered to his hardware store's front door, he made a few phone calls. He discovered, after dragging the police chief out of bed, that Ciders had been leaned on by the mayor, who was threatened with political punishment by none other than Councilwoman Marjorie Binder-Smith — and her wealthy Larchmont Avenue backers. So Bud had called this emergency meeting.

"Enough is enough," said Gerry Kovacks, owner of Cellular Planet. Like everyone else, Gerry had arrived at his business this morning and found the littering ticket taped to his door. "It isn't fair. We pay taxes already. Too damn many taxes, too!"

"You go get them good, Bud Napp," cried Mr. Koh, owner of the local grocery store. Then he ripped his ticket up and scattered the confetti-sized pieces across my hardwood floor.

"We've got to fight," Danny Boggs declared. "No way I can afford four hundred bucks worth of fines in a single weekend."

Seymour, who was sitting between Sadie and me, jumped to his feet. "I found a ticket on my ice-cream truck this morning. I don't control what those little bastards do with the ice cream wrappers after I sell them! This is fascism — and I know governmental persecution when I see it! I'm a federal employee!"

"What we need is a rebellion," Milner Logan cried. He punctuated his call with a militant power fist in the air. "Power to the self-employed business owners!"

Although Milner looked the part of an aging radical, the long straight ponytail that flowed down his broad back wasn't part of a political statement. He was one-quarter-blood Narragansett Native American and had worn his hair that way since childhood.

Milner and his wife, Linda Cooper-Logan, should have been at their bakery now, with Sunday being their busiest morning. But they were both so furious about the tickets, they'd entrusted their business to a pair of part-time workers to make their voices heard.

Linda ran an agitated hand through her short, spiky Annie Lennox eighties hair. "I can't believe it's come to this!"

"Well it has," said Glenn Hastings of Hastings Pharmacy. "And it's all because of one woman. Marjorie Binder-Smith!"

You'd have thought we were in the Movie Town Theater, watching a Boris and Natasha cartoon, the way everyone in the Community Events room booed the municipal-zoning witch. When the curses and catcalls faded, Aunt Sadie spoke up.

"Why don't you tell them your news, Bud?"

"News?" Fiona Finch asked, sitting up straighter. "What news?"

Sadie grinned. "Bud has *big* news!"

Standing on the raised platform, Bud nodded and rested the palms of his hands on the table.

"I don't know about the rest of you, but I've had it with this town's prohibitive business taxes, stifling regulations, and outdated zoning codes. I think it's time *somebody* stepped up and took the system on — starting with the municipal zoning witch herself. That's why I'm running for Marjorie Binder-Smith's seat on the city council this fall!"

The Quibblers greeted the news with loud

applause and shouts of support.

"It won't be easy," Bud warned, "since the councilwoman has had the backing of the town's wealthiest residents for years. They're fat, happy property owners who don't want our Cranberry Street business district to expand. But times are changing in Quindicott. We haven't seen better days in decades, and it's because of us! Our hard work! They thumb their nose at capitalists, but we don't have old money accruing oodles of interest in stocks and bonds and Caribbean bank accounts. We have to *work* for our living! And I promise you that I'll protect our interests and give my best if you see me through to victory!"

Everyone applauded and shouted their support; some even rushed up to Bud to shake his hand.

"Wow," Seymour said, sitting beside me. "I've never heard Bud talk like that before."

Sadie smiled and nodded. "He said he got inspired watching speech-makers on the History Channel."

"The History Channel?" Seymour frowned. "Then you'd better keep him away from the German documentaries."

"What do you mean?"

"I mean if you see Bud watching a little guy with a small, dark mustache giving angry speeches to throngs of blond people, *change* the *channel*."

His announcement over, Bud sat down.

Most of the group, now much more optimistic, headed out the door, hurrying to church or back to their businesses. As the room cleared, Bud raised his ball peen hammer.

"Okay. Guess there's no other business this morning, so I'll officially close this meet —"

"Not so fast!" Fiona cried. "I want to know how Penelope's investigation is going. And I think I have some information that may help."

Halfway out of their seats, Milner and Linda paused.

"There's an investigation?" Linda asked. Blue eyes wide, she plopped back down, dragging Milner with her. "Tell us more."

"Yeah, I'm kind of curious myself," said Bud. "So I cede the floor to Penelope McClure." He banged his hammer, and I noticed Brainert shifting uncomfortably in his chair.

I stood and brought everyone up to speed about the audio speaker falling in the theater and the tragic "accidental" death of Dr. Lilly in my store. I told them about the burglary of Dr. Lilly's lighthouse bungalow, seeing Dr. Rubino hurrying into the woods, then seeing him later with Harmony Middleton. Then I told them that I believed someone was trying to kill Hedda Geist-Middleton, too — and that Pierce Armstrong was tangled up with her past as well as Dr. Lilly's new book.

"Whew!" Linda cried. "That's a brainfull!"

"Don't worry, we can puzzle this out if we just apply a little logic," Milner insisted. "Anyway, it's more interesting at the moment than mixing another batch of pastry dough. I've been working like a dog and I can use a break."

Fiona Finch had already read Dr. Lilly's just-published book cover to cover, so she took the floor next. Today she wore a kelly-green pantsuit and a blue-and-yellow parrot pin.

"Well," she began, "I want to start by saying that *Murdered in Plain Sight* is a fascinating book. My only complaint is that the author waits until the final chapters to reveal her intriguing theory —"

"This isn't a reading group, Fiona," Seymour griped. "Don't waste our time with your literary opinions. Just cut to the chase!"

"Stuff it, mailman. I'm the one who read the book!"

Fiona then cleared her throat and proceeded to tell everyone the story of Hedda Geist's rise from nothing to minor stardom, and the events surrounding the death of studio chief Irving Vreen.

"Dr. Lilly believes Hedda Geist was involved in a conspiracy to eliminate Irving Vreen, and I think she makes a solid case for murder," Fiona concluded.

"She most certainly does not!" Brainert responded. "There's simply no proof at all, only innuendo. Why, I could not even discern a motive, and what's a crime without a motive?"

That's my problem with all this, too, Jack murmured.

As the ghost's deep voice rumbled through my still-sleepy mind, I automatically smiled. "Jack," I silently whispered. "Good morning."

Morning, baby. Enjoy yourself last night?

"What do you think?"

I think you know what I think.

"Have you been listening to all this?"

Yeah, sweetheart. And if I had a head, it would be aching by now. I'd rather be watching your backside in your bedroom.

"Jack . . . don't start, you're going to make me blush. Then what would I tell the Quibblers?"

That you got bored with their yammering and started daydreaming about a detective who's hot in the zipper for you. What else?

"Jack!"

"I'm telling you, Fiona," Brainert argued, as my cheeks reddened. "There's no motive —"

"You didn't discern a motive because you obviously skimmed the text." Fiona waved her copy of Lilly's book under Brainert's nose. Dozens of multicolored Post-its fluttered like tiny UN flags.

"Dr. Lilly claims to have read memos from Jack Warner, the head of Warner Studios, begging Irving Vreen to release Hedda from her contract so she could work for him. Warner told Vreen that he wanted to bring Hedda out west, to Hollywood, and give her starring roles in big-budget movies opposite the likes of Humphrey Bogart, Robert Mitchum, and Edward G. Robinson. Can you imagine a young woman in her twenties getting such an amazing offer?!"

"Where did you read that?" Brainert demanded.

Fiona thumbed a pink Post-it and flung the book open. "Here, on page 224."

Brainert snatched the book out of the woman's hand and scanned the page for a moment. "There are no footnotes here!"

Brainert exclaimed. "If Dr. Lilly really read such memos, then she should have quoted them, given them a proper citation in the back matter, provided photocopies in the appendix, cited an archive source!"

"How about the quote on page 233? It's highlighted in yellow," Fiona shot back.

Brainert flipped pages, read the passage aloud. " 'Benny Seelig, the studio manager and property master at Gotham Features, once heard Irving Vreen boast that "Jack Warner wanted Hedda so badly he tried to buy my entire studio." In an interview in 1966, Mr. Seelig claims Vreen had to cut Mr. Warner off with a sharply worded letter that ended with the line "I *own* Hedda. Don't ask again." ' "

I froze in my chair. "My god, Jack, Did you hear —"

Brother, did I ever. And if that wasn't a motive for Hedda Geist to punch Irving Vreen's ticket, I'll eat my fedora.

"Even the conspiracy makes sense now."

I follow, baby. If Jack Warner wanted Hedda that badly for his big Hollywood studio, then she could have promised Pierce Armstrong and Wilma Brody contracts with Warner, too. That would have been motive enough for them to help her.

"So, you see," Fiona continued to explain,

"Hedda must have murdered Vreen to get free of his binding contracts. But she was young and naïve — if not downright stupid. According to Dr. Lilly's book, when the news of Vreen's death hit the papers, the scandal ruined Hedda. All sorts of unsavory details were splashed across the headlines during Pierce Armstrong's trial. It came out that Hedda was having an affair with Vreen, a married man with a young daughter. No one would touch her for leading roles after the tabloids got done with her, not even Warner Studios. She went to the West Coast anyway, and when she found herself without a career, she used her sex appeal to land a wealthy TV executive as a husband."

"Did the newspapers ever accuse Hedda of planning a cold-blooded murder?" Brainert asked.

"Not according to Dr. Lilly's research. That accusation was never made at the time — not even by Pierce Armstrong, who, even through his own trial, continued to maintain that Vreen's death was a tragic accident."

"There! You see!" Brainert cried. "Don't you think Armstrong would have told the truth during his trial? After all, he was on the hot seat. He had every reason to point the finger at Hedda for planning Vreen's murder."

I shook my head. "No, Brainert, don't you see? If Pierce Armstrong had done that, then they would have tried him for participating in a *premeditated* murder. He could have gotten the gas chamber for that back then. Instead, the judge gave him five years for manslaughter. The man probably kept his mouth shut to protect his own hide."

"So why is he talking now?" Brainert folded his arms.

Seymour piped up. "Probably because Dr. Lilly tracked him down and encouraged him to tell his side of the story. He's an old geezer now, at the end of his life. He probably figures he has nothing more to lose by setting the record straight for posterity. And don't forget he's an actor at heart. A final bow in the spotlight through a book telling his story would sound pretty sweet to a guy like that."

"Everything you're saying is just speculation!" Brainert threw up his hands. "Dr. Lilly's version of the truth relies on hearsay from a forty-year-old interview with a man named Benny. If an actual letter from Jack Warner exists, then where is it?"

I answered that one. "I'll bet that letter, and those memos, are part of what was stolen from Dr. Lilly's bungalow. More evidence could have been included in Dr.

Lilly's missing manuscript, too. After all, Maggie Kline told us that Pierce Armstrong gave the woman extensive interviews."

"But any allegations made in this book should have been proven in this book!" Brainert replied.

"Says you," Seymour cut in. "If you recall, the press showed up to see Dr. Lilly's talk. The doctor herself invited them, which meant she probably *did* have the evidence. She probably wanted to make news by showing the reporters the memos and letters first. Then she could have published all that stuff in her second book. That way, she could sell two books to the public: the first book about Hedda's life story and the second with Pierce Armstrong's version of how the murder went down."

"Only she conveniently died in an accident," Fiona said. "And then her bungalow was *robbed.* If there's nothing to this story, why all the mayhem?"

"Dr. Lilly's death could easily have been an accident," Brainert argued.

"And I guess her manuscript, tapes, and notes were accidentally stolen, too," Seymour said. "Face it, Brainiac, you're resisting reality because Hedda Giest-Middleton is your business partner."

Brainert arched an eyebrow. "Reality? I'll

give you reality, mailman. In my opinion, Dr. Lilly wrote a sensationalistic attempt to cash in on a very public tragedy. She only dished up enough dirt to hurt a gracious old woman — and hustle a few dollars for herself. I hate to say such things about a fellow academic, but I'm afraid everything I've said is true."

"Come on, Brainert," said Seymour. "Dr. Lilly wrote a lot of books. Why would she need money now?"

"No one gets rich writing academic film studies, Seymour. And I know for a fact Dr. Lilly was no wealthier than you or I. But if she published a sensational book about a Hollywood crime — well, that kind of trash *always* sells."

"It's true," Fiona said. "I'm sure Dr. Lilly would have gotten Hollywood interest with a book based on this story — an original cable-channel movie at the very least."

Brainert nodded. "How many books of fiction and fact have been based on the Black Dahlia murder, for instance?"

"Sure," Milner said, bobbing his head. "I loved Ellroy's *Black Dahlia*. That's a great Hollywood mystery."

"Yeah," Linda agreed. "And didn't Dominick Dunne write a novel about the Dahlia murder, too?"

"Wrong Dunne," said Brainert. "The novel you're talking about is *True Confessions.* It was written by John Gregory Dunne."

"Hey, I saw that movie!" Bud said. "De Niro and Robert Duvall played brothers, one a priest, the other a cop. It was okay, but no *Godfather* —"

"You see what I'm saying?" Brainert broke in. "Dr. Lilly stood to earn hundreds of thousands of dollars — perhaps millions."

"Which doesn't make her wrong," Fiona insisted.

"I agree with Fiona," I said.

I let my comment end there, because I didn't want to insult Brainert. He might have been an expert on all things literary, but Fiona was the expert where true crime was involved.

Still, Brainert sensed my snub. Stung, he tossed Lilly's book on the seat next to him, then folded his arms. "Okay, fine. I'll play along. Let's pretend Hedda *did* commit this heinous crime sixty years ago. Who would want her dead now? And why would that person try to destroy evidence of the original crime at the same time? Seems like the killer is working at cross-purposes."

"Maybe we're approaching this from the wrong angle," Seymour suggested. "What if

Hedda herself was the one who unlocked the trap door in order to kill Pierce Armstrong? He's the only other person I can think of who knows the truth about Vreen's death, besides the late Dr. Lilly, who's already on a slab in the morgue."

Brainert vehemently shook his head. "I saw Hedda enter the theater, and I watched her the whole time she was there. She didn't have a chance to go under the stage and tamper with a door."

"Which would be pretty tough to do for an old woman," Bud agreed.

"Why?" Seymour demanded.

"Because she'd have to climb a high ladder, then wrestle two dead bolts open." Bud shook his head. "I doubt she could do it."

"Okay, okay," Seymour said. "Then what about Harmony? She's spry enough to manage a ladder. Maybe she's helping Granny off her enemies."

"It's possible." I nodded, telling them about the black onyx earring I found under the stage and Harmony's showing up at the party sans any earrings. "She could be helping her grandmother — and Randall Rubino could be helping them both."

Bud blinked. "Dr. Rubino? The new medical examiner guy?"

"Yes. Rubino is friendly with both Hedda

and Harmony, and I saw him near Dr. Lilly's bungalow shortly after it was burglarized. He claimed he was fishing near the Charity Point Lighthouse. But he could have run down to the beach when he heard the maid come to the bungalow's door — and since the steps up the cliff are the only way to get off that beach, he would have been trapped there until the police left."

Bud shook his head. "What would be his motive to risk everything?"

"A big payoff maybe," I said. "Eddie Franzetti told me his divorce wiped him out. And one more thing: He claimed he was fishing, but I didn't see him with a fishing pole, only a backpack. So what was he really doing there? And why did he lie about fishing?"

Bud shrugged. "I sell collapsible fishing poles in my shop that are small enough to fit in a backpack — they only cost a hundred bucks."

A C-note?! For a fishing pole! Jack yelped in my head. *In my day, a twig and some twine did the trick.*

"Maybe a crazy fan is helping Hedda," Milner suggested. "There are a lot of people who'd do anything for a beautiful film star."

Linda gave him a sidelong glance. "Is that

why you're always dragging me to Angelina Jolie movies?"

"Don't even go there." Milner rolled his eyes. "You're the one who has a thing for George Clooney."

"Wait a minute!" I said. "Barry Yello was taking photos of people as they arrived at the block party. If we look at them, maybe we can determine who was wearing an earring that matched the one I found. Hedda had her hair down, so I don't even know if she was wearing earrings. But Harmony may have been wearing one earring before I got to her. If I saw a photo —"

"It's a good idea to look at Harmony," Fiona said. "But I think you're off track in thinking she's in league with Hedda. I still think Hedda Geist is the *target*. One accident is coincidence. Two accidents is something else . . . something that smells a lot like attempted murder."

Everyone was silent for a moment. Then Seymour cleared his throat. "I hate to say it, but the only guy with a really strong motive to off Hedda is the Fisherman Detective himself: Pierce Armstrong. His leading-man career was ruined by Vreen's death, and on top of that he went to prison."

Brainert turned to Seymour. "My god, man, it must have hurt you to say that, seeing as Armstrong is your personal hero and all."

"At least I can look at the evidence *objectively* — something you academic types are incapable of doing. You guys always have an agenda."

"We do not! And I don't appreciate you lumping all academics into one muddy pile."

"*Muddy pile* is the perfect metaphor, Parker. 'Cause you know what they say PhD stands for . . ."

After a few more minutes of "spirited" discussion, it was generally agreed that Pierce Armstrong had the most powerful motive to kill Hedda. His motive to kill Dr. Lilly, however, wasn't as clear, but Brainert once again suggested that her death really could have been an accident.

"You forget the burglary of Dr. Lilly's room, which occurred within an hour of her death," Fiona noted. "Again, it's too much of a coincidence. Find the thief, and you'll find your killer!"

The buzzer rang. I glanced at Sadie. "A delivery on Sunday?"

She shrugged and ran to answer the door, then returned to the Community Events room with a special-delivery envelope in her hand. "It's here!" she cried.

Seymour blinked. "What's here?"

"Pen asked me to hunt up a book on the history of Gotham Features," she replied as she pulled a battered hardcover from the package. "This book was published in the early 1950s, after Gotham went belly-up. I had it sent overnight from a used book dealer in Ann Arbor, Michigan. That and the Sunday delivery cost more than the book itself, so I hope it helps!"

Sadie tried to pass the book to Fiona, but the innkeeper threw up her hands. "Sorry, I don't have time to read a book today," she said. "The big film festival dinner is being held tonight at Chez Finch. I've got too much to do!"

"That's the costume thing," Milner said, grinning. "I'm coming as Sam Spade."

"Costume?" Bud groaned. "It that really necessary?"

"I expect *everyone* to arrive dressed as their favorite film noir character," Fiona sniffed, her chin high. "It's required."

"Another fascist," Seymour griped.

"I heard that," Fiona snapped.

"Prove to me that you're not a storm trooper. Sell me those nautical paintings in the lighthouse."

"Forget it, mailman!"

Bud groaned again, still pondering the

dinner. "Maybe I'll come as Tarzan. Can't think of an easier — or cheaper — costume."

Aunt Sadie laughed. "Bud Napp in a leaf-covered Speedo?" She winked playfully at her beau. "Now that would be a sight I'd like to see."

"Except it won't fit with the theme," Fiona pointed out.

"It will if I throw a trench coat over it." said Bud with a wink of his own for Sadie.

"Careful, Bud," Seymour said with a snort. "In this town, they'll arrest you for dressing like a flasher."

Sadie tucked the book under her arm. "I'll read this myself for clues, Penelope, and jot down anything curious I notice in the text."

I smiled. "Thanks. And try to keep a running list of names you come across. If Pierce Armstrong is our murderer, it's likely he has an accomplice. I'll bring Brainert the list you make. He can cross-check it with the guest list and subscribers who bought tickets for the festival. Who knows, we might get lucky and find another person here at the festival who was associated with Gotham Features."

"My money's definitely on Pierce Armstrong as the guilty party," Milner said.

"Well, if he is guilty," said Seymour,

"Pierce either has an accomplice, like Pen said, or he's faking his condition and doesn't really need that wheelchair."

"Maybe it's about time we question the Fisherman Detective," I said. "Throw a few accusations his way and see if he'll bite."

Ouch, baby. And you thought my jokes were bad?

CHAPTER 18
DARK DISCOVERY IN
THE NOIR MUSEUM

Dead men make bad witnesses.
— *The Street with No Name,* 1948

"Speed up, Pen. I want this coffee to be nice and hot when we get to Dr. Pepper's crib."

Brainert, Seymour, and I were piled into my Saturn, its battery recharged, thanks to Seymour's ice-cream truck. And though our mission was urgent, Seymour insisted we stop at the Cooper Family Bakery for coffee and doughnuts.

Milner's lighter-than-air specialties were devoured by all three of us inside of two minutes. We'd all downed small, hot coffees, too. But then Seymour insisted on getting another, extra-large Mocha Java to go. Now he was in my backseat, cradling a full cup of steaming joe between his knees.

"You'll never finish that overdose of caffeine before we get to Wendell's house," Brainert complained.

"That's the point, Brainiac," Seymour replied. "I'm not going to drink it, I'm going to *spill* it."

"Spill it!" Brainert cried. "Spill it where?"

Seymour arched an eyebrow. "On Pierce Armstrong. I'm going to pretend to drink it, and then kind of 'accidentally' dump it on his legs. If Armstrong jumps out of that wheelchair, spry as an athlete, we'll know he's faking his condition!"

Brainert blinked once then squeezed his eyes shut. "My god. You *are* an idiot."

"Why? What do *you* think will happen, genius?"

"I think the old man will scream as the scalding liquid burns his flesh. Then we'll call an ambulance, and you'll be arrested at the hospital for assault."

Seymour squinted. "You're just jealous I thought of it first."

Brainert massaged his temples. "Armstrong's not a paraplegic, you dunderhead! Wendell told me he suffers from advanced arthritis, caused by all the injuries he suffered during his career as a stunt man."

"Oh," Seymour said. His shoulders slumped.

I pulled up to the curb. "We're here. Don't spill that coffee as you get out."

At the front door, Brainert buzzed several

times, but no one answered. He knocked and tested the knob. The door was unlocked. We exchanged surprised glances.

"Wait," I said. "Take a look around. Did someone try to break in?"

Seymour stepped up and examined the wooden door, then the doorjamb and screen door. He shook his head. "No damage. The door was unlocked, that's all. Maybe somebody's home . . . in the cellar or attic or something and can't hear the buzzer."

Brainert pushed the door open and stepped inside. "Dean Pepper? Wendell?" His voice rang hollow in the yellow foyer. The framed one-sheet of *Taxi Driver* loomed over us. De Niro's Travis Bickle was giving me the creeps. Seymour must have noticed.

"Gee," he joked, elbowing me, "I hope that witchy ex-wife of the dean's didn't murder his prune-flavored ass."

Brainert glared. "That's not funny, Seymour."

"Who's being funny? Virginia Pepper is one scary tomato."

"I was referring to your jibe at Wendell's name — Dr. Pepper being a prune-flavored soft drink." He looked away. "Your remarks about Virginia's violent tendencies are another matter entirely."

"You mean they're justified."

"Maybe." Brainert called out again, louder this time. "Wendell! Are you there, man?"

Seymour pushed past him impatiently and started looking around.

Brainert frowned. "Seymour, stop, we really shouldn't be here . . ."

"The door was open. Either someone is at home and didn't hear us at the door, or the house has been burglarized. In that case, it's our civic duty to investigate. And since I'm a federal employee —"

"You're a postman, Tarnish, not an FBI agent! It's our civic duty to call the police if we think something is wrong." Brainert fumbled inside his beige sports coat and pulled out his cell phone.

"You call. I'm checking things out."

Seymour kept walking. I followed. Nothing in the front of the house appeared disturbed — yet I felt the hackles rising on the back of my neck. Something wasn't right.

"Jack?" I silently whispered.

I'm here, doll. I got your back.

Seymour moved to the staircase and called upstairs. I cautiously entered the living room, afraid of what I might find. I spied a pair of men's shoes beside the couch and a glass of water on the coffee table, but the room was empty.

I heard Seymour calling as he climbed the stairs to the second floor, "Mr. Armstrong? Are you up here?"

As Brainert followed Seymour, I moved to the back of the house, hoping to find someone in the kitchen.

I arrived at the dining room first. The only sound here was the persistent bubbling of the fish tank. Morning sun streamed through the window, illuminating tiny dust motes in the air. They floated in front of the framed one-sheet of the James Bond *Thunderball* movie.

My gaze moved to the mahogany sideboard, and I realized that something wasn't right. A metal display stand was sitting there, empty. The prop it held was missing. Where was the heavy speargun from *Thunderball?* The one Seymour had admired?

"Virginia Pepper," I whispered.

Dean Pepper's ex-wife had threatened to take things from the house, sell them on eBay to get the money that Wendell had promised her. Yet it seemed odd that it was the only thing missing.

I noticed the Sunday edition of the *Providence Journal* spread out on the table's polished surface. A full cup of coffee sat beside it. Next to the cup, a half-empty tumbler of orange juice was stained by what appeared to be a large splash of ketchup.

A moment later, I realized the stain wasn't ketchup at all. When I stepped around the table, I saw a wheelchair overturned on the parquet floor. Pierce Armstrong was sprawled beside it, blood oozing from his battered skull. He didn't appear to be breathing.

Beside the body, smeared with thick, red blood was the speargun prop. It wasn't missing; it was the murder weapon!

"Brainert! Seymour!" Hands shaking, I frantically scanned the room.

Easy, sweetheart. Take it easy. The killer's long gone by now. Don't touch anything and back away.

Hearing Jack's voice helped me calm down and focus. I followed the ghost's advice and backed up until I bumped into another body. That's when I screamed.

"Pen, it's me!" Seymour cried, grabbing my shoulders. "What's wrong?"

Brainert appeared at my side.

"It's Pierce Armstrong. He's in there," I said, pointing.

Brainert stepped forward and his gaunt face went pale. He used his cell phone to call the Quindicott Police. After he notified them of the crime, we walked to the front door to wait for the authorities to arrive. A car pulled up the second we got there, but it wasn't Chief Ciders's men in blue. Dr. Wendell Pepper had arrived home.

"Parker!" called the dean, climbing out of his Lexus. "What brings you here?"

When Brainert failed to reply, Dr. Pepper hastily crossed the lawn.

"It's Pierce Armstrong," Brainert said softly. "He's dead."

The dean blinked. "What? What happened? Did he fall . . . a heart attack?" He glanced around. "Where's the ambulance?"

Brainert locked eyes with the man. "It was murder, Wendell. We came to see you and found the door unlocked and Pierce Armstrong lying on the floor, dead. The man was bludgeoned to death with the speargun prop from your dining room."

Dr. Pepper's eyes widened in horror. His square jaw went slack. He looked like he was about to go into cardiac arrest himself.

"When was the last time you saw Armstrong alive?" Brainert asked.

Pepper glanced at his Rolex. "This morning. Not much more than an hour ago. Maggie cooked Armstrong breakfast, then packed up her things."

"She's leaving?" I asked, surprised. "Already? With this weekend's biggest dinner party tonight?"

Brainert and I exchanged suspicious glances. Why was Maggie Kline bolting so quickly? Up to now, she'd been happily staying as a guest in this very house.

"She's not leaving Quindicott," Wendell replied, clearing things up. "Maggie was on a waiting list at the Finch Inn, and a room opened up. She got the call this morning."

That still seemed suspicious to me. "Maggie was staying with you. Why move to the inn?"

"Because of the big dinner at Chez Finch tonight," Wendell said. "Maggie wanted to check into the inn so she could stay as late as she wanted after dinner and wouldn't have to travel all the way back here to sleep. To be honest, I planned to join her. The rooms are very romantic, you know. And those dinners are always heavy drinking affairs, lots of toasts, people talking into the wee hours."

Brainert nodded. "So when you left, Pierce was fine?"

Wendell nodded vehemently. "I spoke with him, gave him the paper. Maggie even checked on him while I put her luggage in the car. I can readily assure you that Pierce Armstrong was very much alive an hour ago."

We heard sirens. Three squad cars raced

down Larchmont, bubble lights flashing.

"Sheesh," Seymour muttered. "Eighteen freakin' minutes for Ciders's boys to get here. Thank goodness it wasn't a *real* emergency."

Chief Ciders had come with his nephew, Bull McCoy. They went into the house and came back out again.

"So what do you think, Chief?" Seymour called. "Another 'accident'? What's your theory this time? Did ol' Armstrong get up from his wheelchair and bash himself in the head with the speargun?"

I heard Jack laughing in my head.

"Shhhhh!"

Seymour turned to me. "It's okay, Pen. He has it coming."

The chief narrowed his eyes on Seymour, and then he began to grill us. This time, when I mentioned the word murder, no one gave me any grief.

Finally, the police went back into the house and took Wendell Pepper with them. Alone on the front porch, Seymour, Brainert, and I didn't take long to agree on the identity of the killer.

"Hedda Geist-Middleton," Seymour declared. "She's the only person we know who had a motive to kill both Dr. Lilly and Pierce Armstrong."

"I don't want to believe it, but I fear Seymour is correct," Brainert said, frowning.

"I think so, too," I said. "While it's possible Virginia Pepper came to rob the house, I can't see an angry ex-wife being furious enough to bash in the head of an old man, even if he did catch her red-handed during some half-baked burglary. And besides, Virginia had no logical motive to kill Dr. Lilly or send an audio speaker careening to the Movie Town stage."

I jerked my head in the direction of Chief Ciders, who was standing in the foyer. "Our problem is convincing the law around here that Hedda killed a man in cold blood sixty years ago — with accomplices — and she appears to be staging a repeat performance."

"Well, don't look at me to convince Ciders of anything," Seymour said. "He thinks I'm a troublemaker — for *some* reason."

I glanced at Brainert, but he shook his head. "It's one thing to believe in Hedda's guilt. It's quite another thing to rat out your business partner. If word ever got around that I'd accused Hedda, and it *wasn't* true, well . . ."

"Okay, then I'll do it," I declared. "Frankly, I think by now Chief Ciders would be disappointed if I didn't point out at least one suspect to him."

The chief caught me watching him through the screen door. He tucked his thumbs into his gun belt and sauntered out to the porch. I noticed Brainert and Seymour fading into the scenery as Ciders approached.

"You wanted to talk to me, Mrs. McClure?" said the big man, almost politely.

"Actually, Chief, I do."

I told Ciders about everything I'd learned over the past two days: the history between Hedda and Pierce Armstrong; the details of Dr. Lilly's newly published book that finally exposed the aging diva as a murderer. Ciders listened. He even nodded a few times. But I could tell from his veiled expression that he wasn't biting.

"Hedda is eighty years old, Mrs. McClure," he finally replied. "She may be vital for her age, but I doubt she'd have the strength to kill Dr. Lilly or Pierce Armstrong. Those crimes were done by somebody younger, somebody who has at least a bit of physical strength."

Ciders paused, frowning. "Besides, Dr. Lilly's death was investigated and already ruled an accident by Dr. Rubino —"

"Rubino!" My temper flared, and I just couldn't curb my tongue. "You can't be dense enough to believe Rubino's conclusion? Not after this! And don't you think it's a little bit curious that Randall Rubino is Hedda Geist's personal physician? And what about Hedda's granddaughter, Harmony? She could very well have been helping her grandmother carry out these crimes."

"All right, that's enough!" Ciders' beady eyes narrowed. "Accusing Hedda is one thing, impugning our new medical examiner is another. Time to go, Mrs. McClure. I've called in the state for this one. Their crime scene unit will be here any minute, and you and your friends are in the way."

"But Chief, don't you think the state investigators will want to speak with me? I discovered the body, and —"

"I have your statement already, Mrs. McClure, and I'll discuss your theories with them myself. If we find any physical evidence that Hedda Geist-Middleton, or Dr. Rubino, or Harmony Middleton, was on these premises, I'll revisit your allegations. Until then . . . have a good day."

"But —"

"That's polite for *hit the road.* Now!"

CHAPTER 19
BOMBSHELL

I like troubled times. They keep the police occupied.

— *Singapore,* 1947

By the time I drove us all back to the bookstore, Aunt Sadie had just finished hosting another film festival author signing: Barry Yello and his trade paperback *Bad Barry: My Love Affair with B, C, and D Movies.* He was gone by now, but the aisles were still crowded with high-energy customers. They were aggressively browsing, asking questions, and buying, buying, buying (thank goodness).

I was also thankful that Mina Griffith was here again today, along with our newest hire, Bonnie Franzetti.

Eddie's little sister had jumped at the chance to work somewhere other than her family's pizza place, and she'd shown up at our store within an hour of Sadie's call this morning.

I felt guilty asking Sadie if she'd had a chance to look through the book about Gotham Studios, but I mentioned it anyway.

"Heavens no, I haven't had a moment," she told me as she rang up another customer's purchase. "But things should settle down in an hour or so, when the festival's matinee begins."

"Well, I'm here to help," I assured her, taking over behind the check-out counter. "You haven't had lunch. And neither have Mina and Bonnie. Do you want to go first or shall we spell the girls?"

"Let's have the girls go one at a time," Sadie said. "When they're done, I'll take my break."

I nodded and turned to the register, started checking out customers. Sadie went to release Mina from the selling floor. That's when Seymour tapped me on the shoulder.

"You want me to stick around, Pen?"

"No." I held my palm up to the next customer on line and motioned Seymour to lean closer. "What I want you to do is stake out the Finch Inn," I whispered. "Keep an eye on Hedda, and call me if the woman or her granddaughter does anything out of the ordinary. And don't needle Fiona; she might throw you out."

"Aye, aye, Skipper. But what are you going to do?" he asked before heading off.

"For now, I'm going to stay and help Sadie," I said, turning back to the checkout line. And while that was true, I also wanted some time at the store to think things through.

I'd told Chief Ciders that Hedda was a murderer. She'd killed Irving Vreen sixty years ago. And she'd had the strongest motive to kill Pierce Armstrong and Dr. Lilly. But there were two pieces of the puzzle that still didn't fit, and I knew it.

So do I, Jack said in my head.

With a sigh, I had to admit: "If Hedda was behind the killings this weekend, then who set the trapdoor trap for her yesterday? I don't buy the theory that it was meant for Pierce Armstrong. Armstrong and Wendell Pepper both moved across that stage without falling through it. And why would Hedda have joined Dr. Lilly on stage Friday night if she knew it was about to rain audio equipment?" I shook my head. "I don't know, Jack. It doesn't make sense."

Then keep digging, baby. 'Cause if the pieces don't fit, the puzzle ain't solved.

An hour later, Mina was back from her break. I put her on the register and spelled

Bonnie for her lunch. Then I spoke with Sadie about the inventory.

"Our Film Noir Festival display is looking pretty anemic. Do we have anything in the back that we can bring out?"

"Not much. We've sold just about every last one of Hedda Geist's coffeetable book, which is excellent news because we really stocked up on that one. Maggie Kline's novels are sold out, too. I'm pretty sure we still have a dozen of her female sleuth encyclopedias in the back, though."

"Great, I'll go find them and put them on the display table."

"Oh! Take a look around back there for any more copies of Barry Yello's books. He had a fantastic turnout for his signing, and we sold through everything we brought up front. But people are still asking for it."

"Okay, I'll see if we have any straggler copies back there."

I moved through the archway that connected the two storefronts, cut through the now-empty Community Events space, and made my way back to our stock room.

We had a library-style cart on wheels for moving books back and forth, and I filled it with what I could find — Maggie Kline's *Encyclopedia of Women Sleuths;* more copies of Barry Yello's *Bad Barry: My Love Affair with B, C, and D Movies;* even Dr. Lilly's backlist film studies.

I considered the boxes of Irene Lilly's newly published book, *Murdered in Plain Sight,* but I decided against putting it out. Things were bad and getting worse. I didn't want to tempt fate.

Instead, I scrounged some more of the backlist titles that we'd featured on our table this weekend. Most film noir fans were pretty savvy about source material. But some of the younger festival attendees were surprised to learn that their favorite noir films were based on novels — which is why I grabbed copies of *Double Indemnity* and *The Postman Always Rings Twice* by James M. Cain, *The Big Sleep* and *Lady in the Lake* by Raymond Chandler, and *The Maltese Falcon* by Dashiell Hammett.

As I packed up the cart, one of the books fell off. I picked up Barry Yello's trade paperback and placed it back on the stack. Now, as I pushed the cart along, Barry's round baby face was smiling up at me from the big color photo on his back cover. I noticed he was wearing one of his ubiquitous Hawaiian shirts. His long blond hair was caught in his signature ponytail. And then I noticed one more thing — an *earring.*

Barry had a pierced ear. I'd forgotten about that.

On Friday night, when he'd introduced Dr. Lilly, Barry had worn a single gold loop through his earlobe. In this author photo, however, he was wearing a simple post: a circle of black onyx in a silver setting.

The Comfy Time Motel wasn't in the town of Quindicott. It was a short drive away on the highway and I remembered Barry mentioning to me on Saturday morning that he was staying there.

After pulling my Saturn into the crowded parking lot, I hurried into the motel's glass-enclosed lobby. "Hello," I said to the young clerk watching TV behind the counter. "Can you tell me if a Mr. Barry Yello is registered here, and where I can find him?"

"Sure," the guy replied. He tapped a computer screen with his index finger. "Mr. Yello is in Room 216."

I thanked him and went back outside, climbed the stairs, and followed the balcony until I found the right room. The door was wide open, and I peeked inside.

A plump woman was sitting in front of a flat computer screen, intently tapping the keyboard. The room was well-lived-in, littered with bags and papers. Fast food wrappers were piled up on the desk, the table, and spread out on the bed.

"Excuse me," I called.

The woman swung around in her chair and tugged small iPod earbuds out of her head. "Sorry!" she said brightly. "I couldn't hear you!"

"I'm looking for Barry Yello?"

"He's not here right now, but he'll be back soon. You can wait if you want." She gestured to a nearby chair.

"Thanks." I moved a stack of magazines off the chair and sat. "I'm Penelope Thornton-McClure, by the way, I co-own Buy the Book on Cranberry Street, and —"

"Wow!" she said, her smile genuine. "That's such a cool place. I checked it out on the first day we came. But I haven't had a chance to go back — stuck here, you know? Updating the site and posting Barry's blogs."

I detected a Chicago accent in the way she flattened some of her vowels. The woman rose and adjusted her loose dress. It was a cute retro style with big colorful 1960's-esque polka dots.

"I'm Amy," she said, offering me her hand. "Amy Reichel. I'm Barry's Webmaster. Maybe I can help you. Why are you looking for him exactly?"

I hesitated, but Jack spurred me on. *She's a source, baby. Pump her. Find out what she knows about your mark.*

I paused, deciding on a line of questioning. I guessed her age at around thirty. She wore her black hair in a short cut, had a tattoo of what looked like an anime character on her upper arm, and a nose ring in her left nostril. She was heavy-set and wore no makeup. She didn't need to. She looked cute and fresh with porcelain skin, high cheekbones, wide blue eyes, and full lips.

"I didn't know FylmGeek.com had a Webmaster," I began, trying to sound casual and friendly. "I thought Barry did all that stuff himself."

Amy sat down again, threw her head back, and laughed. "That's funny. Barry can't even type, except with two fingers."

"You're kidding," I said, shocked that the star of an internationally popular Internet site wasn't a computer whiz himself.

Amy shook her head. "He's a great guy, and really sweet, but he doesn't know his ass from an open-source software program!"

"I guess you've known Barry a long time, huh?"

"Like forever. I met him right after he dropped out of college, back when he worked for Pulse Studio."

"A studio? So Barry actually worked in a Hollywood film studio?"

"If you can call it that. It was low-rent, you know? They made a lot of direct-to-DVD movies, that sort of thing. Barry's done a lot of things, but what he's always, always, *always* wanted to do was make movies. And it's finally going to happen for him, too. He's got one of his scripts at Paramount — and they told him they're actually going to make it. They're putting it into production. It's amazing, isn't it?"

I gave her a weak smile. "Amazing . . . so is that what he did at the other studio? Did he write screenplays? Do you think he ever worked with some older actors and actresses?"

I was fishing again, trying to find a link between Barry and Hedda — or even Pierce Armstrong. But Amy shot that down.

"Oh, no," she said. "He didn't do anything like that. He was just a grip at first, and then he built sets. He used to come home covered with paint."

Clearly, Amy and Barry had been a lot closer than employer and employee. "I guess that was a dead end for his career then? Or did Barry meet people there who helped him?"

"Oh, people helped him." Amy nodded.

"Barry learned a lot from the special effects people. In like, a year, he became the studio's main pyrotechnics guy. It paid pretty well, too, gave him enough money to launch the Web site. Now he makes his living on that. People know his name now, so he can sell books, too. He's got another one coming out this fall. You should make sure to stock up on it at your store. I'm sure he'd come back here for another sign-ing —"

"I'm sorry, Amy, back up a second. You said something about pyrotechnics?"

Amy's head bobbed. "Special effects. Fires. Squibs. Barry did it all."

"Squids?"

"Squibs," Amy corrected. "Little explosive bags filled with fake blood. A tiny controlled explosive detonates them to create bullet holes."

"Controlled explosives?" I repeated. "Barry knows about *explosives?*"

"Oh, you bet!" Amy grinned. "You haven't celebrated Independence Day until you've been to one of Barry's Fourth of July par-ties!"

My mind was racing now. Bud had told me that the falling speaker that had almost killed Dr. Lilly must have been triggered by a small explosion!

Bingo, baby. You found your crooked Boy Scout.

I glanced around the room, trying to think of what else to ask. I noticed Amy's laptop, and I saw Barry Yello's image peeking out from behind a sprinkling of program icons. He was laughing, eyes crinkled, blond hair was pulled back in a tight ponytail. His head was tilted, so he was almost in profile, and once again I spied that black onyx earring on a silver post.

The earring, baby! You should ask Betty Boop here about the —

"Right!" I reached into my purse and showed the earring to Amy.

"Oh my god," she cried. "Where did you find it? Barry came home last night and told me he'd lost it at the block party. I was so sad. I bought that for him in Mexico, back when we were going to get . . ."

Amy's voice trailed off. "Can I have it?" she said.

I shook my head. "I'll give it to Barry myself — just as soon as I find him."

"Well, like I said, he'll be here soon. He's at the Movie Town Theater now. He didn't want to miss *Double Indemnity.*"

I blinked. "Did you say *Double Indemnity*?"

"Yeah."

I cleared my throat. "Amy, I'm confused.

Barry told me that he was going to the showing of *Double Indemnity* on Saturday morning. He said that was the film's one and only showing this weekend."

"No," said Amy firmly. "It's playing right now. *Right now* is the one and only showing. I should know. I post the schedule every day on his Web site."

He lied, baby, Jack whispered in my head. *He didn't want to get tied down to signing books for you. So he came up with a fast excuse. The question is, why? What was he doing Saturday morning if he wasn't watching Barbara Stanwyck play Fred MacMurray like a cheap violin?*

"Oh, my god, Jack . . . didn't Seymour say he thought the door to the lighthouse bungalow was blown open with a small explosive?"

Yeah, doll. He did.

"Barry *must* have been the one! He blew his way into Dr. Lilly's bungalow. He stole her tapes, laptop, and manuscript!"

My thoughts exactly. Which means you better blow out of here fast, doll.

"Thank you," I said to Amy, quickly rising to my feet. "You've been a real help."

"A help? With what?" Amy asked. "I don't understand . . ."

I hurried out into the motel parking lot,

379

my mind still spinning.

"Barry has to be the culprit, Jack. All of the pieces of the puzzle are there. All except one."

Same problem I had with the Vreen case. A motive.

"What did Barry Yello have to gain from all of this mayhem?"

A payoff, doll. Yello's working for somebody. All you have to do is find out who.

"And how am I going to do that?"

Go to the source. You've got to find Barry and brace him.

"Brace him!"

Yeah, put the squeeze on him, like I did with Egbert.

"I can't put the squeeze on a guy like Barry. He's big. He's tall. He's young. What do I do, beat him up with strong language?"

You can put the fear of the law into him, baby, that's what you can do. Just call that cop friend of yours, Freddie —

"You mean Eddie . . . Officer Franzetti?"

Sure, You've got the goods, and the badge can provide the muscle. Between you and the cop, Yello should give up the ghost . . . and I'm not talking about yours truly.

CHAPTER 20
MELLOW YELLO

He's one of the smartest men I know. He's in the movie business.

— *Clash by Night,* 1952

I used my cell to call Eddie. He was on duty and patrolling Cranberry. I asked him to meet me in front of the Movie Town Theater. About fifteen minutes later, I double-parked beside his squad car.

Eddie yanked off his reflecting sunglasses and greeted me with a nod. I looked around. Bull McCoy, Eddie's partner, was nowhere to be seen.

"Bull's working the big homicide investigation up on Larchmont," Eddie said with a frown. "I'm on my own today."

"Well, if my theory pans out, I may have solved that crime *and* the burglary over at Fiona's place — maybe even the death of Dr. Lilly in my store on Friday morning. And as far as I'm concerned, if you help me, they're all yours."

Eddie didn't even blink. "What do you want me to do?"

It took me five minutes to fill him in. Two minutes after that, we stepped into the back of the darkened movie theater as the final scenes of *Double Indemnity* played out.

On the screen, the insurance claims investigator, played by Edward G. Robinson, stood over a bleeding Walter Neff, played by Fred MacMurray.

"Walter, you're all washed up," Robinson said, his expression wavering between pity and a scowl.

Inside the theater, I scanned the crowd, row by row. I thought I could spot Barry Yello's blond ponytail, even in the dark. But that proved to be more difficult than I'd imagined.

"Give me four hours to get where I'm going," MacMurray pleaded, draping a trench coat over his gushing gunshot wound. "I'm going across the border."

"You haven't got a chance," Robinson warned. "You'll never make the border."

"Just watch me," MacMurray rasped, stumbling to the door.

"You'll never even make the elevator," Robinson intoned as a grim epitaph.

That's when I finally saw the back of

Barry's head. He was sitting in the second row, on an aisle seat. The seat next to him was empty. On the big screen, the film ended with MacMurray collapsing dead at the insurance office's front door. Then the house lights came up, and people began to file out of the theater.

Barry didn't get up. For some reason, he remained in his chair.

"Come on," I said to Eddie.

Together we pushed against the flow of people as we moved toward the front of the theater. When we reached Barry, I decided he must have fallen asleep. His fleshy chin rested on his chest. A cup of soda was held limply in his meaty hand. A half-eaten bag of popcorn sat on his wide lap.

I stood over him, called his name. Then I touched the man's big shoulder. The soda cup dropped from his hand, exploded at my feet. My shoes and legs were instantly drenched, yet I remained rooted to the spot, watching in horror as Barry's large body slumped forward. His head bounced off the back of the seat in front of him. Popcorn tumbled to the floor like yellow rain.

Eddie gently pushed by me, pressed his fingers against Barry's carotid artery. "He's dead."

Using his police radio, he called for an

ambulance and backup. Only a few people remained in the auditorium, watching us curiously. But Eddie and I knew there was a mob of people waiting in the lobby to come in for the next showing.

"Pen, wait here, and don't let anyone get near him. I've got to secure the auditorium," Eddie took two steps up the aisle, and then he stopped to tell me again. "Stay *here,* Pen. I mean it. Chief Ciders is going to want to hear your story, and you're going to have to answer a lot of questions."

I nodded dumbly, staring at the back of Barry's head. I remained that way for what seemed like a long time, until I was finally shaken from my numbed paralysis by Jack's voice bellowing in my head.

Hey, Penelope! What the hell are you doing? Wake up! Get to work!

"Work? What do you mean, Jack? What do you want me to do?"

First, look for cause of death. Search him for bullet holes, a knife wound — any sign of violence. Find out what exactly killed this lug.

I shook my head clear and took a deep breath. I didn't want to disturb a crime scene. On the other hand, with people dropping like flies, I knew somebody had to solve this case. At least Jack was here. He was an ex-cop, not just a dead private dick. He

384

wouldn't steer me wrong — I hoped.

Have a little faith, baby.

"Okay, okay . . ."

I took tentative steps forward, approaching the corpse until popcorn crunched under my shoes. Barry had worn another Hawaiian shirt today; this one was yellow and green, and it was clear there were no holes, not even any bloodstains.

"He wasn't stabbed or shot," I told Jack. "Not that I can see."

You're missing something. Keep looking.

"For what, Jack?! There's a soda here and a bunch of spilled buttered popcorn. Maybe clogged arteries killed him!"

Maybe you're onto something.

"What?"

Something he ate or drank, doll. Maybe he was poisoned.

"Poisoned!" I crouched low, and stared into Barry's dead face. His eyes were half-open, the pupils dilated. There were flecks of foam around his lips.

"Oh, my god. I think he *was* poisoned."

I looked down at my wet shoes and slacks.

"And I think I have the stuff all over me."

Check the seat next to him. If someone gave the poor stiff the joy juice that killed him, it's possible the killer sat down next to Ponytail Man, just to make sure he drank it, and maybe to make sure he stayed upright in his seat until the show was over.

There was nothing left behind on the seat beside Barry. But as soon as I got close, I smelled something — the cloying scent of orange blossoms.

I'd only smelled that fragrance once before . . . in my bookshop, during an author signing. "It's Vouloir!" I realized. "Hedda Geist-Middleton's signature scent!"

Nice nose, baby.

"Thanks. But Jack . . ." I shook my head. "It seems so obvious. Did Hedda really come here and poison Barry to shut him up? Or . . . do you think maybe Harmony could have borrowed her grandmother's perfume?"

Good question, doll, because that's a good setup, too. Borrowing Granny's perfume to frame the old dame. That way, if Harmony is involved, the clue will throw the cops off her scent . . . literally.

I pulled out my cell phone and tried to call Seymour. Unfortunately, I couldn't get a signal right away, so I had to pace around the theater. Finally I found a spot where I got a decent signal, but when I called I got Seymour's voice mail.

"Call me as soon as you get this message," I told him. "I need to know if you located

Hedda, and I need to know her exact movements over the past hour. It's urgent!"

I closed my phone and it beeped. I had received a message myself, probably while I was out of range.

"It's Brainert." His tone sounded urgent. "I'm here with Sadie at the store and guess what? She found something in that out-of-print book about Gotham Features. Something that's going to blow this thing wide open. Don't bother to call. Get back here as soon as possible. It's a matter of life and death."

I closed the phone and looked around. The auditorium was empty now, except for me and Barry Yello's corpse. But from the lobby, I could hear Eddie shooting orders to the crowd. Far away, I heard sirens.

I raced all the way to the front of the theater and climbed the stairs to the stage. I hurried down the backstage staircase to the basement, and ran to the steel fire door, which led to the alley. Before I pushed it open, I switched off the alarm system, just like Bud had showed me the previous night.

A minute later, I exited the alley. On Cranberry Street, lights flashed and sirens wailed. I took off in the opposite direction, toward Buy the Book, my wet shoes squishing with every step.

I started to gripe about how gross the squishing felt when Jack cut me off.

If I were you, doll, I'd count my lucky stars.

"Why's that?"

'Cause I worked plenty of crime scenes in my day, and when it comes to walking around fresh corpses, there's a lot worse things to step in than soda pop.

CHAPTER 21
DYING FOR DINNER

JOHN: You're a bitter little lady.
EVELYN: It's a bitter little world.
— *Hollow Triumph,* 1948

"I'm back," I called, pushing through Buy the Book's front door.

The shop was still busy. Aunt Sadie was back behind the counter, ringing up sales. Brainert had been waiting for me in one of our overstuffed chairs. He leaped to his feet the second he spotted me.

"Where have you been?" he demanded.

"I went looking for Barry Yello at the Comfy Time Motel. You won't *believe* what I found."

Aunt Sadie turned the cash register over to Mina. Then she tucked the Gotham Features hardback under her arm, along with a few other books, and led Brainert and me back to the shop's storeroom, where we could speak in private.

As soon as the door closed, I told them what I learned about Barry Yello, ending with the grisly scene at the Movie Town Theater, and the scent of Hedda's rare orange blossom perfume Vouloir.

My aunt couldn't believe that the Fylm-Geek.com guru had been murdered. "We heard the sirens," she said, "but we didn't know what was going on. He was poisoned, you say?"

"I think the killer laced Barry's soda, which ended up spilling all over me."

Sadie glanced at my saturated slacks. "Bag them when you change your clothes. The forensics people will want them."

"So you saw everything?" Brainert asked.

"Well, I didn't see the poisoning, if that's what you mean. But I found Yello's body. Unfortunately, I disobeyed Eddie Franzetti's command to stay put. I took off before the police could grill me. Any minute, I expect Chief Ciders to come stomping into our store looking for my statement, so talk fast."

Sadie opened her book on the history of Gotham Features Studio. Just like Fiona, she'd attached Post-its to several pages. She flipped the pages to one of them.

"In the last chapter, we found this passage about Irving Vreen," Sadie said. She took the glasses that dangled around her neck — today's chain was faux-pearl — and balanced them on the tip of her nose.

" 'Within three years after Vreen's death, his wife passed away,' " she read aloud. "The studio, already close to bankruptcy, went into receivership and its assets were sold off. With the family fortune gone, Vreen's daughter, Margaret, twelve at the time, was adopted by a family friend, Sydney Kline, a production chief at Paramount Studios."

"Irving Vreen's daughter was named *Margaret* . . . as in Maggie?" I said. "And she was adopted by a man named Kline?"

"That's right," Brainert replied. "And look here . . ."

He snatched a paperback from Sadie's pile. It was one of Maggie Kline's mystery novels.

"I thought we'd sold out of those," I said.

"This is my personal copy," Aunt Sadie replied.

Brainert opened the book to the About the Author page. "Look here," he said, tapping it. "Maggie's biography says she's the adopted daughter of Sydney Kline, an executive at Paramount Studios." His eyes met mine. "Maggie Kline must be Margaret Vreen."

"Oh my god," I said. "Any chance it's just a wild coincidence? Is she even the right age?"

Brainert nodded. "I've already done the math — Maggie comes off as a youthful spirit, but she just turned sixty-nine. Wendell confirmed it for me. Her age is exactly right. She would have been twelve in 1951, when her mother died and she had to be adopted out to a family friend."

"If Maggie Kline is Vreen's daughter, then she has every reason to want to pick up where Dr. Lilly left off," I said. "Once she reads Dr. Lilly's book, she may even want to see Hedda prosecuted for her father's murder."

Sadie nodded. "If Hedda knows who Maggie really is, then she must know the woman is a terrible threat, and Maggie's life may very well be in danger."

Brainert nodded grimly. "We have to warn Maggie before the festival dinner tonight." He glanced at his watch. "Speaking of which, I have to go home and change. I'm expected to co-host this event so I have to arrive early."

I remembered my own damp slacks and soggy shoes. "I'll meet you at Chez Finch. Hopefully Seymour's there already, and he can keep things under control until we arrive."

Brainert left and Aunt Sadie went to the front of the store to close up for the day. My cell phone rang and I answered.

"You called?" Seymour said.

"Where are you!" I cried.

"In the lobby of the Finch Inn, waiting for Hedda to come down to the big dinner. She went upstairs thirty-five minutes ago and hasn't budged since."

"Where was Hedda before that?"

"Our diva told Fiona she was going on a long walk, but Fiona didn't know where. I followed the trails around the pond but saw no sign of her. Finally I gave up and came back to the inn. That's when Hedda returned."

I pondered the time line and realized Hedda's "walk" provided more than enough time for her to poison Barry Yello and stroll back to the inn, with no one the wiser.

"Where's Harmony?" I asked.

"Missing in action, so far. No eye candy for me today."

"Well, don't take your eyes off Hedda until I get there!" I commanded. "I'm convinced she's a murderer, and I don't think she's done killing yet."

"Whoa, hold on. Give me some kind of heads-up. Who do you *think* Hedda is going to kill next?"

"No thinking about this one. I'm sure Hedda's next victim is Maggie Kline."

I changed as fast as I could, tearing off my saturated clothes and stuffing them into a plastic bag. I washed my legs and feet off in the tub, grabbed an old, black cocktail dress from my closet and zippered it on, then slipped on patent leather slingbacks and grabbed my evening clutch.

Just as I was about to race out of the apartment, I turned around, ran back to my bedroom, and reached into my leather shoulder bag. I quickly transferred Jack's old buffalo nickel to my black purse.

"Okay, Jack," I whispered. "Come on!"

Good girl. I can't watch your back if you don't take me with you!

Minutes later, I was swerving my Saturn into Chez Finch's crowded parking lot. By now the sun had set and the restaurant was radiant in the deepening twilight. Light streamed through its romantic French doors and arched windows, reflecting off the water and giving the entire scene a golden glow. Laughing couples in 1940's costumes were already crowding the entrance, with more jovial guests crossing the parking lot.

I'd just climbed out of my Saturn when I

spied Maggie Kline rolling across the lot, behind the wheel of Dean Pepper's Lexus. She probably thought I was crazy, the way I waved her down.

"Stop, Maggie! Please stop!"

"Whoa, Mrs. McClure, what's up?" she called through the open window.

"I have to speak with you, it's urgent," I said. "It's about Hedda Geist-Middleton."

Maggie frowned. She jerked her head toward the empty passenger seat beside her. "Get in."

I climbed into the car. Maggie was dressed casually in jeans, a pressed white cotton shirt, and scarlet high-top sneakers. She circled around the lot until she found a spot well away from the other cars, near the path that led to the lighthouse. I saw the parade of solar lights marching up the trail into the darkening woods.

Maggie cut the engine, released her seatbelt, and faced me. "Okay, Mrs. McClure, I'm all ears. What's this about?"

"Hedda is going to try to kill you tonight," I blurted out. Then I slowed down and told Maggie everything I'd discovered so far, ending with a personal revelation.

"I know Maggie Kline is not the name you were born with. I remember you said people in Hollywood change their names all the time. You did, too, didn't you? Only not for a casting call. You changed your name when your father and then your mother died, and you were adopted. Your real name is Margaret Vreen, isn't it?"

In the uncertain light, I could see the pained surprise on her face. People often liked to bury their pasts, and I hated to invade her privacy, but this was life or death.

"You're right," Maggie said nodding slowly. "My father was Irving Vreen. The past was difficult for me, and I've done my best over the years to leave it behind me. It hasn't been easy. Every day of my life, I've lived with what happened — not just to my father, but to my mother, and to me. But listen, Penelope, just because Hedda was involved in my father's death, it doesn't mean she wants to kill me, too."

"No, Maggie, don't you see? Hedda's already killed Pierce Armstrong, the last witness to your father's murder. She killed the woman who wrote about it, too. Dr. Lilly was on the verge of making the Vreen murder big headline news again, maybe even the next big retro Hollywood crime story. With Pierce Armstrong's interviews I'm sure she could have done it, too. Obviously, Hedda didn't want that to happen. She murdered your father in cold blood sixty years ago. She let Pierce take the fall for her while she blackmailed a district attorney and exploited his statutory rape of an underage girl. Then she got off scott free!"

I took a breath. Maggie was still staring at me. She looked a little shocked that I knew so much, that I knew the whole story.

"Hedda Geist may have been a blonde beauty in her day," I added, "but the truth of her life is bitterly ugly, and if the details hit today's news cycles, it would ruin any standing she'd worked to gain for herself and her children. You're the only one left, Maggie. Don't you see that? Once you're gone, there's no one left to threaten Hedda Geist anymore."

Maggie's eyes glazed over; she seemed to be processing my flood of words. I couldn't blame her. It was a lot to take in.

"Okay," she finally said, "but even if everything you say is true, I think I should make an appearance at the dinner. Hedda can't murder me in plain sight, Penelope. Can she?"

"I suppose you're right," I said. "If we act naturally, we may be able to trap Hedda."

"I'm glad you told me all this," Maggie said as she reached for a huge tote bag in the backseat. She pulled it up front and set it down between us. Then she glanced up and appeared to see something out the window on my side of the car.

"Is that her now?" Maggie asked. "Is that Hedda over there on that path?"

I turned, giving Maggie my back so I could peer through my passenger-door window. I could see the dimly lit trail to the Charity Point Lighthouse. But I couldn't make out anyone on it.

Next to me, I heard Maggie open the zipper on the tote bag. Almost immediately, I smelled something familiar — orange blossoms? The cloying, familiar scent was so strong it quickly filled the car's interior.

I frowned, still squinting into the dark for any sign of Hedda. But my mind was quickly wondering — "What's Maggie Vreen Kline doing with Vouloir, the signature perfume worn by Hedda Geist-Middleton? The same scent I detected near Barry Yello's corpse?"

Look out, doll! Jack bellowed in my head.

I whirled around to see Maggie with a heavy metal flashlight in her hand. She'd pulled it out of her tote and was raising it to brain me!

Move, baby! Now!

Freezing cold air blew in my face. The shock of Jack's icy blast made me rear back away from Maggie at the last possible moment. I slammed against the car's passenger window, and the heavy swinging flashlight missed my head by inches, connecting hard with my thigh instead.

"Ahhh!"

Pain shot through my leg. Maggie quickly swung again, but this time I was ready. I put my left arm up to deflect the blow from my head, and she clipped my elbow this time. Stinging tears sprang to my eyes. But I was still conscious. And alive.

"Thanks, Jack."

Don't thank me yet, baby. Fight!

Maggie raised her arm again, ready to strike.

Grab her wrist, doll. Keep her from swinging. Then clock her yourself!

I lunged for her wrist, gripped it with my left hand, then swung at her jaw with my balled-up right fist, just like Jack advised. It was a clumsy attack. My hand missed Maggie, flailed backward, and bounced off the steering wheel. I yelled in pain —

Swing again, babe! Don't stop till she does!

I did. I swung again. This time I struck flesh — hard. Maggie grunted and her head snapped back. She slumped forward, her torso hanging over the steering wheel. I shook her, but her movements were like a rag doll's. The woman was out cold.

My thigh was bruised, my hand was throbbing, and my elbow was stinging something awful. I cradled my wounded joint until the agony faded to a dull but persistent ache.

In the struggle, Maggie's tote bag had spilled across the front seat. I saw an airline ticket among the debris. I picked it up and read the itinerary; then I glanced in the backseat and saw a small suitcase on the floor.

"Maggie never intended to go to the dinner tonight," I realized. "She booked a flight out of Providence, departing in two hours."

Back to Arizona? Jack asked.

"No. This ticket's for an international flight to Costa Rica!"

With Maggie's flashlight, I searched through the stuff that had spilled out of the tote. I spied a small glass vial. It looked medicinal but I couldn't read the prescription label — it was written in Spanish. And the vial was empty.

Did this contain the poison Maggie had used on Barry? I wondered. I was about to give up the search when I found a second, identical vial — also marked with a prescription label. It, too, was empty.

"Wait a second. If the first one contained the poison to kill Barry, then where did the

400

poison in the second vial go?"

Looks to me like she used it, doll.

"Oh, god." I closed my eyes. Hedda had been a killer once, but she wasn't the killer now. "Maggie must be trying to poison Hedda!"

You better warn her.

I jumped out of the car and raced across the lot. I entered the restaurant at a run and pushed past a crowd of people waiting to be seated. As I burst into the dining room, I saw a commotion at the center table.

I heard a woman's frantic call. "Grandmother's fainted!" I recognized the voice immediately. It belonged to Harmony Middleton.

"Hedda's collapsed, please give her room," Dr. Rubino commanded.

People backed away, but I pushed forward until I saw Hedda on the floor, her face white, a tiny bit of foam flecking her glossy red lips. I noticed a bottle of Napa Valley Sauvignon Blanc on the table.

"Where did this wine come from?" I demanded.

Harmony blinked. Then she stared at me as if I were crazy to ask such a question at a time like this. "It's Grandma's favorite," she replied. "It was delivered special to our table, sent by an anonymous secret admirer, according to the card."

"Did anyone drink from it?" I demanded.

"Just Grandma," Harmony said.

Rubino nodded. "I opened the wine and poured a glass for her. Hedda was enjoying it when she fainted."

"Don't drink that wine!" I warned. "It's poisoned!"

"Oh, my god, Mrs. McClure," Dr. Rubino said in horror. "If that's true, you just saved our lives."

"But what about Hedda?" I asked. "Is she going to be okay?"

Rubino frowned, shook his head. "The ambulance is on the way. We won't know until we get her to a hospital."

"You've got to save her, Doctor," Harmony cried out and began to sob into her hands.

I crouched down beside Dr. Rubino. He was cradling his patient's head in his arms. She looked old now and frail, a shadow of her former self.

Just then, the woman gasped and coughed. She opened her famous catlike eyes. Their vibrant emerald color was washed out now, the whites stained with tiny trails of blood.

I wasn't sure if she could hear me. But I thought, for a lot of reasons, that she should know the truth.

"Ms. Geist," I said, "you've been poisoned by the daughter of Irving Vreen."

Understanding darkened the femme fatale's face. Her lips moved but no sound came out. Then the former actress gasped once more, and her fading eyes closed for the last time.

Maggie was arrested in the parking lot. I led Officer Eddie Franzetti to the woman while she was still unconscious. My elbow still hurt like a son of a gun, but I was happy Eddie would get the collar. Bull McCoy might be the chief's nephew, but even nepotism couldn't trump a cop who brought in a multiple murderer.

"So what do you think, Jack?" I quietly asked the ghost as Eddie radioed headquarters.

Well, I don't know. Things got a little hinky there for a minute, but I guess you did all right.

"Just all right?!"

Don't push it, partner. You jumped to the wrong conclusion about Maggie at the end there. And if I hadn't been watching your back, you might have ended up with a cracked skull. Next time, bring the copper with you.

"Hey! Wait a minute! I heard that! You actually called me *partner*."

Yeah, baby, I guess this time you earned it.

"You *guess?* Wouldn't you say having a woman around who can clock a murderer is a tad more valuable than one who'll fetch you packs of Luckies?"

Well, that depends on how long it's been since I had my last drag.

Twenty minutes later, the Finch Inn looked like the triage zone of a disaster area. Local cops, state police, ambulances, a forensic unit . . . I lost count in the glare of the flashing emergency lights.

"It's justice, what I did!" Maggie Vreen Kline yelled at the top of her lungs as she struggled against Eddie Franzetti's handcuffs.

Oh, lookee. The broad's come to.

"Yeah, Jack, and I'd say she's royally ticked that she won't be getting any frequent flyer miles for that Costa Rican getaway."

I was looming in the background at the moment, amid a half-dozen curious members of our local QPD. A big state cop named Detective-Lieutenant Roger Marsh was there, too.

Maggie's unhinged outrage appeared to calm when she realized so many people were hanging on her every word. She'd already been read her Miranda rights, but then a reporter on the fringes of the gather-

404

ing called out, "Why'd you do it?" And Maggie suddenly seemed to understand that there was an audience here, one that wanted to hear every detail of her story. That's when the screenwriter in her apparently kicked in.

"Pierce Armstrong was the easy one," she announced, her eyes looking glazed and bright in the eerie red glow of the emergency beacons. "I beat him to death with that stupid prop. I wanted him to die a violent death, just like my dad."

Chief Ciders stepped up to Maggie, clearly wanting to keep her talking. "And what about Hedda?" he asked quietly. "You didn't kill her, too, did you?"

"Of course! Hedda had to be poisoned. Just like my mother, who drank herself to death, because of what happened to Dad. That's why Hedda deserved to die the same way as Mom: poisoned by her favorite wine . . ."

Ciders made a show of scratching his head. "That's all well and good, Ms. Kline, but you're not going to claim you poisoned Barry Yello, too, are you?"

"Maggie leaned back against the patrol car, a shadow crossing her face. "Yello was a no-talent loser." she said dismissively. "He agreed to do me a few favors this weekend in exchange for persuading my contacts at

Paramount to produce his low-budget horror movie."

"And how did you gain access to the theater?" Ciders asked.

"Easy." Maggie shrugged. "I had Wendell Pepper eating out of my hand — getting a set of keys to the theater from him was a cakewalk."

"Was Dean Pepper aware of your plans, Ms. Kline?" Ciders asked carefully. "Did he help you?"

"Wendell Pepper? God no. I just slept with the man a few times to get him where I wanted him. He was too gullible to suspect a thing. Barry was the one who knew what I was up to. He helped me rig that speaker to blow, just as a little 'thrill prank' — that's what I told him when I set the timer. But the whole thing got screwed up!" Maggie struggled against her cuffed wrists a moment, and then let her arms fall limply behind her back again.

"How did it get screwed up?" Ciders asked. "I don't understand."

Maggie rolled her eyes. "It was *supposed* to kill Irene Lilly! It didn't, so I had to take care of that myself the next morning." Maggie shook her head. "After that, I sent Barry to get me the woman's research — he stupidly assumed she died in an accident, so he didn't think it was a big deal to take her research. But after I made him open a trapdoor under the stage, he started getting antsy. Even with my bribe of getting his movie produced, big brave Barry started getting nervous, asking me too many questions. He wanted out. So I *put* him out — *permanently.*"

Maggie laughed. "Barry Yello is no loss to the world, believe me."

"What about Dr. Lilly then?" Ciders asked. "What did she do to deserve death?"

"Irene Lilly started it all. Don't you know that?" Maggie's face contorted in the shadows, her expression turning into something ugly. "Lilly called me up one day. Tells me, 'I know who you are!' She had the whole story down, she just wanted some actors to fill out her little play. Wanted us all here in one town, in one place, so she could stand in the spotlight. Well, when I found out Hedda and Pierce were going to be *honored* at this festival . . . that did it."

"That made you decide to kill them?" Ciders pressed.

Behind her bright red glasses, Maggie's eyes narrowed. "How would *you* feel? To hear that your father's murderers were invited to some festival to be *celebrated?* To hear the people responsible for your mother's misery, the ones who drove her to drink herself to death, were being honored. *Applauded?!* Oh, no. No, no, *no!*"

Maggie vehemently shook her head; her bouncy curls fell into her eyes. She hurled them back with a violent head toss. "I started making my plans as soon as Dr. Lilly contacted me. Only I was the one who would be using Irene Lilly, not the other way around. She didn't care about my father. She was set on resurrecting the scandal for her own recognition and profit. But, you see . . . she *knew* who I was, and that's why she had to be first. Before anyone else went, *she* had to go. And she did. All it took was one little push off a ladder."

Ciders noticed me then, standing among his officers. He met my eyes, nodded his head. It was the closest thing to official recognition I'd ever get. But, frankly, for this little town, it was good enough for me. Anyway, I had to hand it to the chief: For all his faults and bluster, he certainly knew how to keep a perp talking!

"And what about those innocent people at Hedda's table?" Ciders added tightly, his contained outrage starting to leak through. "They could've drunk that poisoned wine and died tonight, too."

Maggie frowned, looked away. "Collateral

damage," she muttered. "Crap happens."

Ciders cursed. He'd finally heard enough. "Take her away."

Two giant state police officers in gray uniforms and Smokey the Bear hats opened the door of the patrol car and guided Maggie inside. Then Detective-Lieutenant Marsh stepped up to Ciders.

"Who made this collar?" his voice boomed. "I have a few questions."

"It was my senior officer, Eddie Franzetti," Ciders said. "Eddie! Front and center!"

I wasn't worried about Eddie knowing the case. I'd briefed him well before anyone arrived. He was a smart guy. Always was. My brother, Pete, had loved him like a brother, too.

"Yes, sir?" said Eddie, standing tall, legs braced in front of the brawny state detective. "You have questions?"

"Dozens, son," replied the detective-lieutenant. "But at the moment I just want to say: Good work!" Marsh shook Eddie's hand. "You ever think about coming over to the state police, you let me know. Investigations can use a good man like you."

"Oh, yeah? Well, so can the town of Quindicott," said Chief Ciders, breaking the two men up. "Eddie's on track for a big promotion."

Eddie's eyes widened. "I am?"

"Doggone right!" Ciders insisted, slapping Eddie on the back. "You're a valuable member of the department, Eddie. I'm not about to lose you . . ."

As the lawmen continued to polish their laurels, I yawned and noticed my aunt Sadie hurrying up to me. She was looking quite smart in a forties-style wool suit and matching hat, white gloves on her hands, red gloss on her lips. Bringing up the rear was Bud Napp. My jaw dropped at the sight of him.

All that talk of dressing like Tarzan was obviously a joke; I'd never seen the man more stylishly attired. A charcoal-colored double-breasted suit hugged his tall, lanky form. He was clean-shaven (for once), and his usual ball cap with the frayed brim was replaced with a sharply boxed fedora. He wore a pearl silk tie with a diamond stick pin and a handkerchief to match.

"Penelope!" Aunt Sadie cried. "Are you all right? We heard what you did!"

"Who, me?" I said with a shrug. "I just bumped my elbow while I was waving to Eddie for help."

Bud folded his arms. "That's a load of crap, Pen. I know it was you who did the dirty work. You were on this case from the very beginning."

I smiled and lowered my voice. "Let's just keep that between friends, okay?"

I gestured to Eddie, who was getting patted on the back by the state officers and his fellow cops, including a petulant-looking Bull McCoy. That alone gave me satisfaction.

"So," I said, turning back to my aunt and her beau, "who are you two dressed as? You both look great."

"I'm Kay Bentley," Aunt Sadie said. "The brash and beautiful reporter from *Sleepers West.*"

"And I'm Detective Mike Shayne, Irish-American private eye, who can't keep his eyes off the brash and beautiful reporter — same movie."

I laughed for a second, and then I wanted to cry. "The dinner's totally ruined, isn't it?"

Sadie and Bud shook their heads. "Not at all. Fiona's serving now. Brainert's announced the dinner will be a tribute to Dr. Lilly, Barry Yello, Hedda Geist, and Pierce Armstrong. Don't forget, dear, this is a crowd of film noir fans. Everything that happened this weekend pretty much reinforced their view of this bitter little world."

EPILOGUE

Didn't I tell you all females are the same with their faces washed?
— *Dead Reckoning,* 1947

Hey, Penny with the copper hair . . .

"Jack! Where've you been? I haven't heard from you in days."

I needed a rest, baby.

"You're kidding? Are you telling me the excitement in this little cornpone town was actually too much for Wild Jack, King of the Asphalt Jungle?"

Something like that.

A full week had passed since the film festival murders, and the town was finally getting back to normal. Brainert's theater had moved on to showcasing European New Wave cinema, Sadie was out on a date with Bud at the Seafood Shack, and I was extremely happy to be sitting at home on the living room couch, finally looking after my son in person.

Spencer was getting so big now, growing up so fast. I knew there wouldn't be many more years where we could just play Scrabble, eat Franzetti's take-out pizza, and watch Jack Shield episodes on the Intrigue Channel until bedtime.

So I've got some questions for you, partner. Jack's deep voice rumbled through my head.

"Partner . . ." I smiled. "I do love the sound of that word."

I know you do.

"Okay, shoot — not with an actual gun or anything."

If you start with the bad jokes, I'm leaving.

"Wow, Jack. Who knew Borscht Bell one-liners could be a form of exorcism."

Listen, smartypanties, my question is about that academic broad, Dr. Lilly.

"Go for it."

Did the police ever recover the stolen items from her bungalow?

"You're taking about her laptop, manuscript, and tapes? The ones Barry swiped for Maggie Kline the morning she signed books at our store?"

Yeah, baby. That's what I'm talking about.

"Well, according to Eddie, the police found all of that stolen stuff in Maggie's luggage. And after they combed through it all, they found exactly what I thought they would — lots and lots of source material, the stuff Brainert said was missing from Dr. Lilly's first book. There were copies of Jack Warner's memos and Irving Vreen's written answers, too."

Where the hell did Lilly even get that stuff after all these years?

"Apparently some old studio executive died and left a storeroom of books, files, film clips, and movie memorabilia to relatives. They sold the stuff in lots on eBay. Dr. Lilly was doing research on another subject entirely — the casting process of film noir stars — but when she stumbled upon these old memos and letters about Hedda Geist, she started digging into that story and realized she'd uncovered a fresh angle on a sixty-year-old scandal."

Hmmmm . . . then our dead Lilly turned out to be some detective, huh?

"No doubt. Among her things, there was a paper trail showing how she tracked down Pierce Armstrong and contacted Hedda Geist. She had even obtained a copy of Margaret Vreen's birth certificate as well as her adoption papers, and other proofs of her true identity."

But Lilly never came out with the truth about Maggie. Why?

"I asked Eddie that, too. He said there was something on Dr. Lilly's laptop that was pretty incriminating. Maggie Kline had sent the woman an e-mail promising to give Lilly an exclusive interview during Quindicott's Film Noir Weekend — but with one stipulation. Dr. Lilly had to keep Maggie's true identity in the strictest confidence and only reveal it at the time of her *second* book's publication."

Very clever. The Kline broad knew Dr. Lilly would never get the chance to publish her second book.

"Right. Maggie was already planning to kill the woman and make it look like she'd died in an accident. Then Maggie could go on to exact her revenge on Hedda and Pierce, killing them without anyone suspecting she had a motive."

Jack whistled. *That was quite the little murder plot.*

"Well, it was concocted by a screenwriter. And guess what? After Maggie was arrested, I went back and took a harder look at her books. I even looked up summaries of her old screen and teleplays on the Internet, too. And lo and behold, most of the woman's stories were revenge fantasies." I shook my head. "Maggie Vreen Kline never got over what happened to her father and her family and herself."

But you said it yourself, baby, the key word wasn't *revenge.* It was *fantasy. If Dr. Lilly hadn't decided to dredge up the past again and rub Maggie Kline's nose in it, the Kline broad probably would have let the past fade away, just like Hedda and Pierce's careers.*

"I think you're right about that . . . I mean, she never actively tracked Hedda and Pierce down to harm them. Maggie said it herself the night she was arrested: She just couldn't take her father's murderers being honored, being celebrated." I took a breath, considering Maggie's story.

"It's so sad when I think of what she must have gone through as a little girl . . . knowing her father died a horrible death, watching the unfolding scandal in the papers, the shame her mother must have felt — even to the point of drinking herself to death. I can only imagine Maggie's own pain, finding herself alone in the world at such a young age, being adopted by a family on another coast. Her feelings of anger and vengefulness toward Hedda and Pierce must have been off the charts for a long time . . . and, I guess, after all these years, Maggie finally did get her revenge on them."

But don't forget, doll, she took innocent people out with them. She became as cold-

blooded a murderer as Hedda.

"And she almost got away with it, too . . ."

If it weren't for you. baby.

I smiled. "And you, too, Jack. Partners, remember?"

Jack grunted, which I took for full agreement.

"Anyway," I said, "it looks like your cold case is closed, too."

Yeah, and Hedda's granddaughter, Harmony, turned out to be an innocent after all.

"I don't know if I'd use that word. The girl's already started partying, I hear. She's moving to New York City next month. She's due to inherit a lot of Hedda's money — of course, there's one big stipulation."

Let me guess. She has to ride Hedda's horse two hours a day.

"Close. To keep her share of the inheritance, she's got to devote a large block of it to creating a Hedda Geist Museum, filled with costumes and scripts that the old actress kept preserved in plastic from her days as a femme fatale."

You know, doll, that doesn't really surprise me.

"Me, either."

Once a diva, always a diva.

Just then, another episode of Jack Shield started up on the television. Spencer and I watched for a while. Every few minutes I'd hear Jack gripe about how silly the show was or ask, *Do you know how often a real gumshoe would do that? Never.*

Finally, the show ended, and Spencer went off to bed. I kissed my boy goodnight and headed to my own room. Jack had gone quiet by now, so I clicked off the light and settled under the covers. Then, just as I closed my eyes and started drifting off, I heard the ghost's familiar deep voice again, rumbling through my mind —

Hey, baby?

"Yeah?"

Remember when I kissed you? Back in '48? In my ransacked office?

"Yeah." My eyes were still closed. I smiled. "I remember, Jack."

Remember what you were thinking?

"I was thinking that it felt like heaven."

Just wanted you to know . . . it felt like that for me, too. Heaven, I mean.

There was a long silence after that, so long that I thought Jack had gone away, until I heard the faintest whisper.

I'll see you in your dreams, baby . . .

Then the ghost's presence receded once more, into the fieldstone walls that had become his tomb.

ABOUT THE AUTHOR

Alice Kimberly is the pen name for a multi-published author who regularly collaborates with her writer husband. In addition to the Haunted Bookshop Mysteries, she and her husband also write the bestselling Coffeehouse Mysteries under the pen name Cleo Coyle. To learn more about Alice Kimberly, the Haunted Bookshop Mysteries, or the Coffeehouse Mysteries, visit the author's virtual coffeehouse at . . .
www.CoffeehouseMystery.com

We hope you have enjoyed this Large Print book. Other Thorndike, Wheeler, and Chivers Press Large Print books are available at your library or directly from the publishers.

For information about current and upcoming titles, please call or write, without obligation, to:

Publisher
Thorndike Press
295 Kennedy Memorial Drive
Waterville, ME 04901
Tel. (800) 223-1244

or visit our Web site at:

http://gale.cengage.com/thorndike

OR

Chivers Large Print
published by BBC Audiobooks Ltd
St James House, The Square
Lower Bristol Road
Bath BA2 3SB
England
Tel. +44(0) 800 136919
email: bbcaudiobooks@bbc.co.uk
www.bbcaudiobooks.co.uk

All our Large Print titles are designed for easy reading, and all our books are made to last.